LILLY, GOING WEST

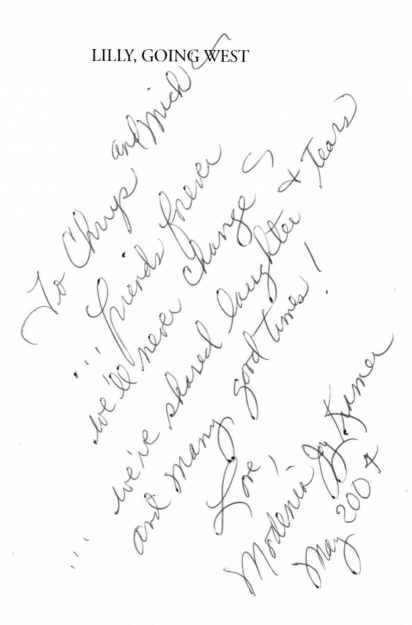

LILLY, GOING WEST

Modenia Joy Kramer

Red Anvil Press

Cover by Sid Kramer

RED ANVIL PRESS
1393 Old Homestead Drive, Second floor
Oakland, Oregon 97462—9506.
TEL/FAX: 541.459.6043
www.elderberrypress.com

Red Anvil books are available from your favorite bookstore, amazon.com, or from our 24 hour order line: 1.800.431.1579

Library of Congress Control Number: 2003116488
Publisher's Catalog—in—Publication Data
Lilly Going West: A Young Woman's Journey/Modenia Joy Kramer
ISBN 1-930859-94-5
1. American West—Fiction.
2. Coming-of-age—Fiction.
3. Women—Fiction.
4. Family—Fiction.
5. Western—Fiction.
I. Title

This book was written, printed and bound in the United States of America.

Dedicated to

Annabel

…without her encouragement this would
not have been written.

THANK YOU

Those who are listed below helped me with my vision and were willing to read through my story. To these people I am indebted and truly grateful. Thanks to each of you for your special gift to me.

Sharon Heath
John Kramer
Sid Kramer
Mick & Holley Gene Leffler
Ina Woods
Carl Wulfsberg

One

Torn Apart

We were just outside Carson City, Nevada when the desert flash flood came tearing down the dry river-bed. One minute the air was clear, dry and hot. The next thing I knew the sky turned black as night, and there was a crack of thunder and all hell broke loose. The wagon train was caught in a downpour. There was a terrible roar as the water came crashing down on us. The desert became a wide river with only desert plants that became markers to let us know where the ground was. Without benefit of direction we found ourselves thrashing around in water over our heads. The horses swam at first and then Jim, my friend, saw he had to unhitch the team and let them get out of there as best they could and under their own power. He fought the water and rain and somehow managed to unhitch the horses. Since I was driving I sat in the wagon helplessly watching as the other folks, their wagons, household goods, and animals were swept away. I could hear the screams of the people and the animals as they were hurled past us.

Our wagon twirled around and around and skimmed along the raging river. Waves eight feet tall whipped down the gullies. Ma was sitting on the wagon seat beside me when we were hit by one of the roaring waves. She was thrown out of the wagon, and I was thrown backwards down on the floor and to the rear of it. Before I was knocked back I could see Ma outside the wagon and right before my eyes I watched her drown. I screamed because I knew I could do nothing to save her. In her eyes I could see she wasn't going to fight for her life. She simply let the water carry her away. I tried to jump in after her, but at that time I was thrown backwards and knocked senseless. The last thing I remember seeing was Jim and Big Black, his dog, rolling and tumbling out of control, along with trees, muddy water and other debris.

Two

How It All Started

As I lay there in the wagon half asleep I kept trying to wake myself from the horrible nightmare, but I could not. I really believed it was just a dream, and I would soon wake up. This had not really happened. I kept mistaking it for a storm that occurred not long ago in my early childhood - this is where the dream seemed to begin.

It was late at night and I was snug in my bed in the loft of our home. Ma and Pa were asleep downstairs and life seemed very simple that year as I approached my ninth birthday.

I was born Lilly Benton in the year of our Lord eighteen hundred and sixty-five, the daughter of Earl and Grace Benton of Philadelphia. Our farm was in a green valley near the river on the outskirts of the city. Nothing ever seemed to change very much except that it had been raining hard for many days. The earth was soaked and Pa had been talking about the crops being ruined. He told Ma that a crop failure now would mean we would have to pack up and leave all we had. A plan was forming in his mind, I guess, because he said he had always dreamt of going West and maybe now was the right time.

That night as I lay there listening to the rain hitting the roof, I realized the storm was getting worse. The night sky was alive with lightning and crashing of thunder as it rolled over our heads. I was frightened, but I told myself it was only a storm - we had gone through other storms and I was not a baby. In fact I was a strong, healthy girl.

I finally drifted off to sleep, but it was only a short time later that I was awakened by the urgent calls of my parents. We had to get out of the house and head for higher ground. I dressed quickly in my cotton underwear, long soft wool pants, boots, a warm coat and knit cap. As I came down from the loft I was shocked to see water inside our house. The swollen river had overflowed its banks. Pa picked me up in his strong arms and lifted me off the stairs and carried me outside to a sloping hill where the water had not reached.

We fled to higher ground, and Pa pitched a tent from which we watched and waited. The house itself was engulfed as the water slowly rose to almost waist deep. Family treasures swirled in the turmoil of black water. I saw our family Bible being absorbed by the river and watched it disappear into the depths. Enough was enough!

Within days it was plain to see that the crops were ruined as well as most of the buildings surrounding our house. Our cow was missing along with all the chickens, and my pet pig. Pa and Ma were forced to admit we could not stay any longer. There was nothing left to call our own, so it was time to move on. After the crop failure and the flood, which destroyed our home, Pa just up and joined a group of other folks who, like him, had dreamt of going West. They waited until things were more settled on the frontier. As a child I had little say in the matter. However I had read some books and heard about the Wild West! It was a place where dreams came true, and since I had dreams of my own I was eager to get started. The thought of traveling on a wagon train to me was exciting.

As my mind continued to review the past I remembered what our teacher at school had taught us. It was about the Homestead Act of 1862 that provided anyone over twenty-one, who was the head of a family, the right to obtain title to 160 acres of public land if he lived on the land for five years and improved it. Well, that was my Pa. He was certainly over twenty-one, and it was his hope to find some public land in California. A lot depended on how far we could travel on the money Ma and Pa had saved and how settled the area was in California when we arrived. We were full of hope, and anxious to start over, in a new part of the country. We were in agreement so our motto, "California here we come," filled us with anticipation.

Pa had an adventuresome spirit and wanted to see some of the country, but he was not as healthy as some men were, so he had doubts about living on the trail. He believed in himself, his family, and that his skill as a furniture-maker and woodcarver would provide for us wherever we settled for a short time. He had always preferred to work with wood rather than with the soil. Though he was a weak man, he claimed that in his youth he was so tough he could whip a bear. I always doubted it, but if he said so it was probably true.

His muscles were still strong and he moved with agility. But he had a stubborn cough that appeared now and then, mostly in the winter when the wind blew.

Ma was worried about him, though she never said a word.

She was content to do as he wished, an obedient wife who served her family and home. She was a church-going woman and taught me from the Holy Book. Night after night I listened as she read to us by candlelight, her beautiful voice gliding over the words as easily as a sunbeam skimmed over frozen ice. It made the darkness seem almost pleasant. It was at her knee that I learned my letters and much of my morals. The school I attended was far away, and because there wasn't a steady teacher I'm afraid that part of my learning suffered.

Everyday of my life was spent with Ma, except when I was off at school, so by the time I was eight I knew how to run a house better than most girls did at my age. As I remember those years were pleasant; a time full of social gatherings, quilting bees, canning days, and long walks. Sunday we were always going to church and play parties. The play parties were the most fun! Since my parents didn't hold with dancing we never attended a dance. But at the play parties we played games with lots of skipping, and turning. I loved the music and moved like a dancer whenever I heard it. I think I was born with natural rhythm. When there was a dance in town sometimes Pa would drive our buggy near by and just sit outside and listen to it. My feet never stopped tapping and I often imagined myself twirling and dancing with some handsome gentlemen. And about the time I was really enjoying myself, in my daydream, Pa would say it was all right to listen as long as we were not inside taking part. His words always brought me right back to reality, and I felt guilty because of my wanting to be part of the party.

Monday was spent doing the wash and that was a lot of fun for me. We all worked together. It was Pa's job to get the fire started under the large black kettle in the back yard. Washing was not easy, but it had to be done on Monday according to Ma. She said, "Cleanliness is next to Godliness." When the water was boiling hot she would add the homemade lye soap, and with a long pole she would dip the clothes in the kettle and stir them around in the mixture. After the clothes had boiled for some time she would lift them out and place them in a big tub filled with cold well water. It was my job to push them around and up and down, which I did with a vengeance. Next, Ma would wring them out and hand them to me to hang on the line or on the bushes growing nearby.

Since Monday was wash day, Tuesday was naturally ironing day. We used heavy irons of different sizes. They were heated on the big black wood-burning kitchen stove. Starch was made for Pa's Sunday-go-to-meeting shirt with a little cornstarch mixed with water. It took all day to iron for the three of us. It was one of my favorite jobs because I was kept home from school and I didn't have to do any other chores.

I learned to cook by standing at Ma's elbow. She said a woman's place was in the home and I'd best be learning all I could about it. I never doubted her word. I admired my Ma and wanted to be like her. She taught me how to sew, properly clean a house, and maintain a kitchen garden.

But now we had to leave all that, taking very little with us, just a few clothes and Pa's tools. He had saved enough money to buy what supplies we needed for the trip. He hoped to make more with his skill as a furniture maker, since every small settlement was growing in the country. Surely there was money to be made across the West. It was a compulsion with him. I think I had the fever too. I was as determined as Pa to see California, where people were rich and dreams came true. We knew the trip ahead would be a struggle, however we were willing, as so many others were, to try it.

We purchased the Conestoga wagon in Philadelphia and joined a wagon train. When we made our way though the Cumberland Gap, we drove our team through the beautiful forest and snow-capped peaks of the Appalachians. Along the way we enjoyed the sweet scent of laurel and beautiful rhododendron which covered the ground. At places the gap was very narrow with steep-sided cliffs reaching about 500 feet in height. It was a sight to see.

At night, sitting around the campfire, we heard stories about Daniel Boone and how he blazed the Wilderness Road through the Cumberland Gap and led settlers westward. We also heard how the Union army invaded Tennessee in 1862 and 1863 using the same trail we were traveling. Many folks had gone this way before us so it was just a matter of contacting the right people, getting the right supplies, and being told what to do. And, I might add, learning how to follow orders from the trail boss.

Some folks were afraid of Indian raids and talked bravely about fighting them to the ground and protecting what was theirs. I secretly wanted to see one of these wild Indians, and if fighting was to take place I was sure we would whip them with ease. When I asked Ma about fighting Indians she told me not to worry, because there were very few wagon trains attacked these days. Well, that didn't matter, I still longed to get in the wagon and play like we were under attack with the men riding along our wagon shooting and yelling. I imagined Pa driving the horses as fast as lightning with Ma shooting and me loading for her. Of course, this never happened.

When we got to Independence on the Missouri River, Pa bought a fresh team of horses to take us through miles of wilderness ahead. He looked over the wagons that were for sale and decided our Conestoga wagon with its large, heavy, broad-wheels would be the best transportation we could have for our westward adventure. It was the best built wagon he could own. Pa knew good work when he saw it.

The long trip through the Gap was exciting, but hard. And

thinking back now I realize how very meaningful it was for me. The weather cooperated and was beautiful most of the time. We had few dangerous accidents on the trip, and I suppose the worst complaint was the long hours of walking or riding in the wagons, which were never meant to be comfortable. However, forested trails lay before us, beckoning us to follow, and follow we did. Wild birds chatted at our passing and small animals scurried away from us.

Since Pa was not a well man, because of his cough, he found life hard on the trail. The physical labor soon began to tell on him. By the time we reached the salt flats in Utah he needed a rest. We had to leave the wagon train.

So far the trip had cost more than we planned. Ma was not able to earn any money for us, because Pa was too proud to let her do anything outside our home, be it a tent or a wagon. And yet if a man did not have any money he and his family could starve - there was little charity around in those days. It was the belief of the times that "charity begins at home." So Pa was forced to take on a job, any job! All that was available to him was work in the salt mines, no matter what the pay or conditions, at least until he saved enough money for us to continue to California.

In the salt mine Pa worked far beneath the surface of the ground. There were sunken shafts with pulley drops where the men went down into the mines. Large buckets were used to transport the salt to the surface. It was backbreaking labor, so Pa grew increasingly sick and pale, but he never missed a day of work. If he did none of us would eat, and he was too proud to ask for help.

One day his chest was hurting, so he sat down to rest and began sculpting a small religious statue from a chunk of salt lying near by. His sculpting so moved the men that they encouraged him to keep carving long after he should have stopped.

Finding his work both fascinating and beautiful the men came up with a proposition. In one unused portion of the salt mine there was a cave about the size of a small room, and since most of the men in the mine were drifters they had no place to worship. Most had a belief in God, but their choice of worship was different from the folks in Utah. They asked my Pa to join them in turning the cave into a chapel. Pa was pleased to be asked to do such a special job, but he was concerned as to just how he would be able to feed his family if he did not do his share of the digging. The men said they had discussed the situation and had decided that each would contribute some work time to him if he would only create this place of worship for them. They would jointly pick up his workload so he could keep on getting regular pay from the company. They had also gotten Darcy, their foreman, to turn a blind eye to what was going on. If the company ever found out about it, no one mentioned it to Pa.

It took about two years before the small cave was transformed into a beautiful chapel with a sculpted altar, the front carved with a beautiful religious scene showing angels hovering gracefully over the holy Family. It was truly a work of art. The details of each sculpted figure amazed the men. When the chapel was lit with candlelight it took on an unearthly quality, full of sparkling, jeweled light. It was a true place of worship.

Ma and I were escorted down in one of the large buckets one evening when the mine was not operating. I was afraid to get into the big bucket for fear it would plunge to the bottom and we would be killed, but I didn't tell Ma. She was so happy to be able to see the chapel that I kept my fears to myself.

I will never forget the feelings I had at the time. I am sure no cathedral in the world could equal the beauty of that little chapel. All that was missing was a priest.

When Pa saw us coming he stood back and watched our

reaction. He knew the chapel was charming and the carving of a true artist. Seeing it for the first time caused us both to be totally silent. There were no words to express our feelings. Ma just moved closer to the altar, knelt and prayed. So I followed her example and Pa never said a word.

The months of close confinement had taken a toll on Pa. His deep cough was worse now, strong enough to crack his ribs. When he finally went to see the company doctor, he was told that the constant breathing of salt was not good for his lungs. He had developed a disease common to salt miners and the only cure was a change of climate. Once more we were obliged to go West.

During the time we were in Utah Pa and Ma had saved enough money to buy the supplies we needed to continue to California. This time the travel was worse on Ma and me because Pa could do even less on the trail. We met up with a wagon train headed West and soon found ourselves in company with a lot of folks, who were also headed across the salt flats and beyond. There was one family we got acquainted with that became like our own kin. We would have never survived had it not been for their son, Jim. He was a strong young man of about seventeen and eager to help in every way he could. Ma said he was sweet on me, but I was too young for such foolishness so she discouraged any closeness between us.

Though most of the land we crossed was flat country, there were deep ravines and gullies often crossing our trail. One time we came upon a deep wash that cut our path. It was very steep on our side, but had a more gradual slope on the other side. It was decided to take the wagons, one by one, down the steep side using a block and tackle. I had seen this contraption work when Pa stored hay in the loft of our barn, but this was much bigger than the one we had. It proved to be an eventful day. The wagon master told us to lighten our wagons. Well, that was easy for us since we carried precious little in our big wagon, but for other folks it was a problem. Many of them had furniture, household goods and even organs. Some carried plants and trees they had watched over since leaving their homes in the East. Those who had less goods offered to help divide the loads so very little had to be left behind.

When the wagons were ready and the men set, the first wagon was lowered into the wash as well as the oxen and horses. It was such fun for us children watching all the commotion. Since the land on the other side was sloping the animals were hitched to the wagons as soon as they were lowered. Then they made their way slowly up the hill on the other side. All went well until the last one which happened to be Jim's parent's wagon.

Now Jim's Ma was sick with a fever and his Pa would not leave her side. He was one stubborn old man. When he refused to leave her there was a big argument between him and the wagon master. However, finally the wagon master gave in and the old couple stayed inside while it was being lowered. This was not what the wagon master wanted, but the work proceeded. As the wagon made its descent something went wrong. I don't know what because I couldn't see what was happening, but all of a sudden we heard a loud snap and then the wagon was rolling over and over tumbling down into the wash. The men yelled and the women screamed, but there was nothing anyone could do. By the time the men reached Jim's parents they were both dead. His Pa lay under a wagon wheel and his Ma was thrown several feet from the wagon. While all of this was happening Jim was away hunting game for the evening meal. He was unaware of the danger to his folks.

When Jim returned all work was stopped and a hasty funeral was provided. No one wanted to touch the body of Jim's Ma so my Ma and Pa tended to the dead. Ma wouldn't let me any where near the bodies for fear I might get the fever too. And that was fine with me. I stood around patting Jim's shoulder and trying to remember some words of comfort I had heard folks say after a funeral. Nothing I said seemed to help.

Later, Jim lamented that he had not been with them. He said he would never have let both of his parents ride in the wagon, sick or well, during the time it was being lowered over the edge. I don't think he ever forgave the wagon master for his error in judgment in allowing both parents to be in the wagon together. It was a heartbreaking time for all of us.

I overheard some folks wondering if it was not an accident, but deliberately staged since they were the last wagon and Jim's Ma was sick with a fever. Folks were scared to death of the fever because it could mean danger to all the people on the wagon train. Once a fever got started it could wipe out the whole group. If Jim ever thought it was not an accident he never mentioned it. If he had thought otherwise he would have sworn vengeance on all the men involved and spent a lifetime getting even with them. He was growing into a big man and would be hard to reckon with. He was as stubborn and determined as his Pa.

Very little was salvaged from Jim's wagon. All he possessed was the clothes on his back and his dog, Sam. I had my own name for Sam. I called him Big Black, and that big dog gave us all hope. He kept us going when life got rough. A real friendly animal, he was also a good watchdog. Anyone come prowling around Big Black was on his feet immediately. His deep growl alerted us more than once when trouble was threatening.

After the accident Jim became the son my Pa never had. He and Pa did everything together, with Jim watching over him like a hawk. They hunted wild game, walked and rode side by side day after day. They never seemed to run out of things to talk about. Pa was not a big talker until he met up with Jim. I guess he was more comfortable with Jim than most other folks.

After leaving the Great Salt Lake we joined up with another wagon train headed to Nevada, a land of rugged snow-capped mountains, sandy deserts, and grassy valleys, so we were told. The new wagon master explained that we would make our way to the Humboldt River and follow it about three hundred miles, which meant we'd have water all the way. Once we reached the end of the river we would make our way south to the hot springs and then on into Carson City. This was not where Pa wanted to go but he decided once we were there, we could join another wagon train going farther west. Starting a new life in California was still his dream.

Pa never saw the state of Nevada. We had been on the trail for a short time when his cough became worse. We watched him grow weaker with each passing mile. Early one morning Ma woke up thinking Pa might be getting better since he hadn't coughed much during the night. That is when Ma found him dead, lying peacefully beside her. We buried him proper along the trial in one of the pine packing boxes. The women helped Ma wash, dress and wrap his lifeless body. I was scared to touch him so I stood by, once again, watching and crying. Jim and some of the other men helped lay Pa in his makeshift coffin. We stood around as the men dug Pa's grave and when the last shovel of dirt was tossed over his coffin we gathered together and sang a mournful song. It was a terrible day for Ma and me.

After Pa died Ma and I depended on Jim to help us with the wagon, horses, and putting meat on our table. He mourned the loss of his parents, but he like to have never gotten over the loss of Pa. It didn't seem right to him to lose the people he loved most. In time he talked less of what he had lost and more about what was going to happen when we reached California. Sitting around the campfire at night he bragged about all the gold he was going to find, just waiting for the taking. And how rich he was going to be when we got there. He really had gold fever, I do believe, or maybe he just dreamt a lot. More than anything, he said he wanted to own a big mansion.

Getting rich was not my concern. I just wanted to get Ma to California safe and sound. Since Pa's death she was so grief-stricken she couldn't make any decisions for herself, so it was up to Jim and me to take care of her. My hope was to reach the home of Ma's sister, Aunt Bertha, who lived in San Francisco. I believed if I could get Ma that far she would be happy and well again. The thought of traveling such a distance seemed impossible, but my mind was set and so was Jim's—this time we would not stop until we saw the Pacific Ocean ahead.

Of course one never knows what lies around the next bend of the trail, and none of us was expecting what was about to change our plans.

Three

Back to the Present

I came out of the daze of nostalgia and back to what had just happened, out there on the Humboldt, being washed along on a terrible, muddy tide. Where had it taken me? The moon was setting over some rolling hills to the West and to the East were dark sage flats. I was in Nevada, and I was alone. I wondered where the water had carried Ma, and if I would be able to find her. I prayed the sand had buried her poor fragile body in some peaceful place. I assumed Jim and Big Black were both gone too. My heart felt like it was breaking apart, but there was no time for tears. The question now was what should I do? Where should I go?

I was shaking from the cold and I was extremely tired. I wanted to close my eyes, drift some more, and maybe just go on and die. But I was too much of a fighter to give up. By now I realized I was hungry, I needed to eat, so I'd better get up and get moving. All around me were deep shadows, and I heard the scurry of small animals nearby as I crawled cautiously out of the wagon.

It had lodged itself on the side of an old riverbank, half of it high and dry while the other half was still submerged in the water left by the flood. After gathering what little of my belongings I could salvage, I moved away quietly - the long nights and days on the trail had taught me to be careful and trust no one. Not that there was anybody around to threaten me. As morning came I walked westward toward the hills, which rose into steeper mountains. I could see now that this was the range we had seen from the distance as we came down the Humboldt. After a while I picked up a trail, maybe even the one we had been following.

I'd been able to save one orange from the provisions, and I sucked on that as I trudged onward. By late afternoon I came to the outskirts of a town. It looked wild enough to be Carson City, which according to the wagon master had been a frontier post since 1858. As night came on, I hung around the town and watched silent as a cat.

A lot of men were brawling, shooting off their guns and yelling wildly. It looked to me like they had been hitting the bottle a little too much. I could see some of them playing cards in their tents by coal oil lamps and drinking strong corn liquor. I knew a girl my age would not be safe in such a place, but I was so hungry I went against my better judgement and stole up close to the back of the cook tent, looking to get some food from the cook. Oh, he saw me all right and grabbed me by my collar and jerked me around thinking I was a boy. I let out a muffled cry, my hat flew off my head, and my long hair came falling down my back. He was so surprised he nearly dropped his teeth. One minute he was trying to beat me up for stealing and the next he was standing there dumfounded. After a while he spoke to me in a gruff voice and told me to get out of there, because as he put it, "A tent city full of no-good cowpunchers is no place for a wee mite of a girl like you." He picked up my cap, smashed it down on my head, and told me to get moving. I quickly hid my hair under my cap and moved out into the darkness. He didn't even give me a piece of bread, but I figured he was too afraid. If I had been spotted by one of the men there was no telling what would have happened to me. As I recall, he was a big man and an Irishman at that.

Walking on under a moonlit sky, I came to a more settled part of town. There were a few houses, outhouses and barns here and there. Looking around I saw a house off by itself, sitting apart from every other place, with lamps glowing like a lonely sentinel in the night. By the light of the moon I could tell it was newly built, nicely painted and even had a fence around it. There were other houses just as new on the landscape, but they had very few lights showing in the windows. I decided to go closer, and when I got near enough to look in the windows I saw a big party going on. Hidden in the shadow of an old tree I watched men going in and out of the front door, standing on the porch taking a smoke. The young women inside were singing and dancing around, while a beautiful girl played the piano. It looked like the people who lived there were eating and drinking, and that reminded me of how hungry I was. I reasoned, surely these folks could use some help in the kitchen with that many guests to be served. Anyway, I just had to try to get something to eat.

All of a sudden I heard someone coming up fast behind me. Not being one to be taken easily, I whirled around to face whoever it was. Just as I did, to my great relief, I caught sight of Big Black. That dog was hunched over following my scent, and when he looked up and saw me, he came running. I grabbed his big old head, sat down and finally let myself cry with my face buried in his long matted fur. Big Black must have been tracking me all along and I didn't realize it. Where he had been and how long he had been following me was a mystery. Well, it didn't matter, for it was a great reunion we had. I held his head and looked into those deep brown eyes of his, and told him to be quiet. He sat obediently at my feet not making a sound while I figured out what to do next. I wondered about Jim, but he was nowhere in sight, so I thought he must really be dead.

Big Black and I were both extremely hungry and tired, so we made our way around the rambling two-story house to the kitchen. I told Big Black to sit and wait, which he did, a shadow in the night. As I approached the back door I heard an awful, wild fight in progress. The cook was carrying on something terrible and speaking in a language that sounded like Chinese. Pots and pans were flying around the room, and dishes were sailing through the air. There was a woman in the kitchen trying to talk to the cook, but not getting very far. I decided this was no place to be for the present, so I backtracked and sat down once again with Big Black on the back porch steps.

If I couldn't go near the kitchen, what was I to do? Looking around a bit we found our way to the smokehouse. Whoever had been there last had forgotten to lock the door, so I opened it slowly, walked in and found no one inside. I saw some smoked sausages hanging within easy reach. I had not planned on stealing food. I knew Ma would not approve. I had hoped to work for our meal, but not being able to enter the kitchen to ask for work, I simply felt I had to do something before Big Black and I starved to death. I pulled down one sausage and ate half of it and gave the other half to the big dog.

When our hunger had been satisfied I decided to try the kitchen once again. By this time it was empty. The door stood gaping wide open as we slipped in. There was only one oil lamp burning in a far corner of the room. The place was a mess—dishes had been thrown everywhere. There was food lying on the table and floor. Apparently whoever had been doing the cooking had left in a hurry. What had once been a white apron now lay smudged and dirty in a heap on the floor. A plan began to form in my mind. I went around softly picking up the place, but it was hard because there was so much to do. No one came near the kitchen; in fact the house was now almost too quiet. The sound of the piano had stopped and the laughter had died down. I supposed the party was over and the guests had left. And of course the people who lived there were in their beds by now. I could hear a few muffled voices, but they seemed to be far away. I decided everyone must be sleeping, or at least getting ready for bed because it was so late.

It was a surprise to me to see the amount of dishes and food left over from the party. Looking up I saw funny little brass bells hanging over the kitchen door with numbers over them, so I imagined this must be some kind of academy of young ladies, like those fancy boarding schools back East Ma told me about. I wasn't sure what those bells were for, so I just kept busy picking up all the broken glass shattered on the floor and wondering what kind of a place I had come to. It took several hours, using the warm water from the tank on the stove to wash all the dishes, glasses and pots and set them in their proper places.

When I finally got the kitchen presentable, I fed Big Black and me a proper meal and we crawled under the kitchen table to sleep. A little before dawn I woke with a start because the dog was nudging me to let him out. At first I wasn't sure where I was. Soon it came to me, all that had happened the day before, but there was no time for tears. I backed out from under the table, let Big Black out the back door, and decided I had better see the outside of the place in the light of day.

From the kitchen door I stepped out onto a deep porch that appeared to go around the house. Chairs and tables were scattered about it and I could imagine what a lovely spot it would be to have tea in the afternoon. Suspended on chains at one end of the porch was a swing moving slightly in the morning breeze. There were steps leading to the front door and a rail that was painted white. The house itself was tall, two stories high, painted gray with white trim. It seemed to be well maintained.

In front ran a road that curved away several feet from the house, but I turned in the opposite direction and followed a path around to the smokehouse and other outbuildings. On the west side of the house I found a sorry excuse of a garden which hadn't been cared for in some time. Weeds grew in patches among the vegetables. I decided if I stayed here for any length of time I would put the garden back in shape. But for now I went back to the kitchen.

Since the Chinese man had not appeared, I decided this academy was in need of a good cook so naturally I got busy. To begin I started a fire in the fireplace, at the end of the room near the long kitchen table, and also in the new black cooking stove to take the chill out of the air. Then I went outside to draw water from the well, which was covered by a round wooden structure. There was a long slender metal tube I lowered into the well. When the tube was brought back up I pulled on the handle and let the water cascade into the bucket. The water was cold and crystal clear. I carried the bucket of water inside and heated it, because I knew there would be a need for lots of hot water to get the place neat and clean like Ma taught me.

Soon Big Black was at the kitchen door scratching to get in. He looked like he had been running all over the place getting to know his new territory. His coat was a mess and his eyes were fixed on me telling me he was once again powerful hungry. I let him in and fed him. Like the obedient dog he was he soon curled up under the work table and was fast asleep. This was already his favorite place in the kitchen.

The next thing I did was to find the bread starter and get busy. I remembered Ma mixing her starter, and I knew in any kitchen a bread starter would be found. Ma began with a cup of cooked mashed potatoes, a quarter cup of sugar, two teaspoons of salt, and a cup of warm water. Then she poured the mixture in a quart glass jar, covered it with a clean cloth and left it in a warm place for two days until it fermented and bubbled up in the jar. When I located the starter I reminded myself to use only a cup of the starter. To keep it going and active I had to add a three-quarter cup of flour and three-quarter cup of water. This done I covered it and returned it to the safe (a wooden cabinet containing several shelves with closed doors). After mixing the dough I left it to rise. As I figured it, by the time it was ready to bake I would have most of the kitchen cleaned and the rest of the breakfast prepared.

Looking around I spotted an old coffee grinder and set to work. Grinding coffee was one of my favorite jobs when I was small. I found a large blue enamel coffeepot sitting on the back of the stove, so within a few minutes coffee aroma filled the big house. I decided the coffee would be strong enough to wake the dead, the bacon crisp and crunchy, the eggs fried to perfection and bread to tempt a saint or sinner alike. The house was soon filled with tempting and enticing odors.

The folks in the house were sleeping later than I had expected. I guess it was the aroma of the coffee that got their attention because those funny little bells began to ring. I noticed there were cords coming from different places on the ceiling, leading to the box, and these seemed to make the bells ring - first one and then another and after a while all of them were going at once. It nearly drove me crazy, so I climbed up on a chair and, with a big kitchen knife, cut the cords. I sure didn't want to be the cause of waking up this household, at least before breakfast was ready.

It wasn't long until I heard some very angry voices yelling for the cook to bring up the coffee. I went to the bottom of the stairs and listened, but couldn't believe my ears. I had never heard such language, especially from young women. Then I yelled back inviting the people in the house to come down for their coffee.

At the top of the stairs, a woman appeared out of the first door on the right and looked at me. She was dressed in a long red silk gown, her curly hair was the color of red flame and her face was made up like a circus queen.

Seeing a stranger the woman was a bit taken back. She said, "What in the hell are you doing in my house?" I told her I had made breakfast and put the coffeepot on. Then as briefly as possible I related my story. I was used to people rising up early and getting a fresh start on the day, so I added that her daughters or young ladies were sleeping rather late this morning, and should have been up long before now doing their chores. She looked at me as if I had lost my mind, and then she smiled and laughed and laughed. I believed that I had not said anything funny, and I told her so. She only laughed harder until tears ran down her rosy painted cheeks and her knees buckled under her. She was laughing so hard she was about to hit the floor. Watching her I moved up the stairs for fear she might fall down and injure herself. Once there, I could see the long hall and the various bedroom doors. Then composing herself, she called each girl by name, in a stern voice, and told them to get their "asses" downstairs as soon as possible for coffee and breakfast. I was shocked by the way she spoke.

Hearing this, one door after another opened as each girl came out of her room. All of them looked like they could use a strong cup of coffee, besides a lot more sleep, and if I was not mistaken I could even smell liquor on their breaths. I couldn't believe their appearance, half dressed, feathers still in their hair from the evening before, and their hair twisted this way and that. They looked like a bunch of stray cats. Their faces were even unwashed, with powder and paint still visible. I was embarrassed and almost ashamed for their mother or head mistress. The woman with the flaming hair just said, "Well girls, we have a newcomer among us, and she tells me she's cooked breakfast for us."

At this point, the girls began to grumble and all of them at once started to turn around and go back to their rooms, when the woman added, "No breakfast in bed this morning girls. After all, we have a guest and one who says she can cook. Shall we chance it?"

They glanced at each other and immediately picked up speed and moved down the stairs nearly knocking me over heading for the big dining room. When they got there they stopped dead in their tracks to see the table set with dishes and trays of freshly prepared food. It looked wonderful, even if I do say so myself.

Apparently, each girl had her own special place at the table. They each moved to their chair, but as they began to sit down I noticed they kept looking for something that was not presently on the table. I wondered what it could be? What had I forgotten? As I checked the table I knew nothing was missing - it was perfect. The food was indeed tempting, but no one ate it. It was as if they were unsure of what to do next. Then the woman with the flaming red hair made herself comfortable at the head of the table.

All at once it occurred to me what the problem was. They were waiting for the blessing to be said. I waited, but none spoke so I bowed my head. "Thank you, Lord, for this food which we are about to receive from Thy bounty. Amen."

When I finished my simple blessing there was a startled look of surprise on each young lady's face and you could have heard a pin drop it was so quiet. As it sank in what I had said, the place was alive with a stream of laughter. I was puzzled and a bit upset, because at Ma and Pa's table we always gave thanks before eating. It was the proper thing to do! The woman with the red hair didn't seem to notice the laughter, she just pulled her napkin into her lap, helped herself to the nearest dish, and began to eat with relish. When she looked up, and saw the girls watching her, she told them to go on and eat, which they did with equal enthusiasm.

After she had finished her coffee she looked carefully at me. "Tell me, dear, what is your name? I can see you are a girl, but pray tell me why are you dressed like that?"

Well, it was a long story and I hardly knew where to begin. "My name is Lilly and I came to Nevada on a wagon train, all the way from the East. My Pa died from salt-miners' disease in Utah, and my Ma was drowned in a flash flood. It took everybody off. There was nobody left but me and Big Black, my friend Jim's dog. I reckon Jim's dead, too, 'cause I saw him washed down a gully, so I guess Big Black is mine now." I stopped for a big breath, looked around and then continued.

"Anyway, last night when I came upon your place I could see you and the girls were having a party, and I didn't want to disturb you, so I went to the back door, wishing I could do some work in exchange for food. You see Big Black and I were awful hungry. But then I heard your cook having a terrible fight with somebody, so Big Black and I just sat down on the stairs at first, and then when the voices got louder and louder we left. I found the smokehouse was unlocked, so we helped ourselves to a sausage. I didn't plan to steal it, and I will pay you back honest. I promise."

The lady interrupted me by a wave of her hand. "Lilly dear, you don't have to pay me. I always like to help a girl in need."

Then she looked around the table and smiled, as if she had her own private secret. "You're welcome to stay here as long as you like." Glancing at each girl, she added, "I'm afraid we've forgotten our manners. Lilly, you see we are not accustomed to speaking to the Lord around here or getting a decent meal for that matter. I'll trust that you will accept our thanks for such a lovely breakfast."

As she said that, I felt she was somehow making fun of me and I blushed with embarrassment. Then she added, "What the girls are looking for is the wine. We are always served wine with our meals, along with the coffee."

"But Miss, uh..."

"Longdom dear, Ruby Longdom."

I was polite as always and said, "That's a right nice name, Miss Longdom."

"Ruby, dear, Ruby." She corrected me. "As you may have guessed, our cook quit on us last night and we sure could use another one. Guess that Chinaman thought he was over-worked or something. I went to speak to him about our dinner being late, and he went into a rage. I couldn't understand a word he was saying." Then looking at the girls she added, "Besides he couldn't cook worth a damn — I mean, a bit. We haven't ever eaten like this, have we girls? Can we get you to stay?"

Just as I was about to answer, one of the girls smiled at me, and said her name was Peaches. Then added, "God, this is good food, but if I keep eatin' like this I'll be as big as a barn." And it must have been true because she was plump as a cherry and didn't look like she had ever missed a meal. She had a beautiful round face, bright pink cheeks, full painted red lips, black curly hair which hung halfway down her back and dark brown eyes that sparkled with mischief when she talked. She wore a beautiful hand-quilted robe that was made with a lot of attention to the small details around the collar and cuffs. Even though it hung loosely around her shoulders, exposing a part of her breast, I admired the robe greatly. There was a lot of elaborate needlework on the garment.

As I stood watching them eat, Miss Longdom invited me to sit down at the table, and then she asked me more questions which I was happy to answer. She explained about the wine, saying some folks didn't think it proper, but since she was French it was as natural to have wine with our meals as it was to drink water and probably a whole lot safer.

"Besides, Lilly," she added, "it is sort of a custom."

"Custom or not, Miss Longdom, it just wouldn't be proper to serve wine in the morning, and especially to young ladies." That brought another peal of laughter from all of the girls except one, and she was sitting rather to herself being quite indifferent to what was taking place. I watched her out of the corner of my eye wondering what she was thinking. She never as much as raised an eyebrow, but I was sure she didn't like me. I couldn't imagine why, because she didn't even know me.

Looking at me in a strange and unbelieving way, Miss Longdom said, "Tell me, Lilly dear, have you ever heard of a bordello - a parlor house or a house of ill-repute?"

I was startled and bewildered at her question. I looked at her in disbelief. "You mean a whorehouse?" I blurted out. "I thought this was some kind of school for young ladies. Isn't it?" Hearing what I had said the whole room erupted with laughter and some of the girls were almost rolling on the floor they were laughing so hard.

Miss Longdom, Ruby, didn't laugh. She just looked at me and smiled. "Yes, Lilly, that is what you have come to, as you call it - a whorehouse, a house of pleasure. Now dear, if you want to be one of my girls that would be fine with me, and we'll find a place for you, won't we girls?"

Just as I was about to answer her the quiet one stood up and said to Ruby, in a haughty voice, "May I be excused, Miss Longdom? I think I am going to throw up, but I'll be careful not to spoil my morning frock - while you get rid of this little saint."

Ruby spoke up then, giving the girl a displeased look, "Laurie, sit down! You've said your piece. Leave this to me."

Well, it seemed I had an enemy already, and that was the last thing I wanted. Each of the girls gazed at one another and then at me. It was plain to see they wanted me to stay and I did need a job. Cooking for them couldn't be all that bad as long as I didn't see what they were doing upstairs. To Ruby I said, "I don't want to be one of your girls, ma'am, but I have lots of experience doing housework and I am a good cook. All I need is a place to sleep - only not upstairs." Again there was a peal of laughter except from Laurie. She sat down and gave me a dirty look. Ruby glanced around the table, "Well, girls, let's vote on it. Raise your hand if you want Lilly to stay and be our cook and housekeeper."

They all immediately raised their hands except for Laurie. She stood up and looked me straight in the eyes and said, " If they want you around here that is their business, but you keep away from me! Do you understand me, you little saint?"

I was shocked by her manners and her language, so I quickly answered her, "Sure, Laurie, I wouldn't think of bothering you. You go right on your way and I'll stay clear." She sure had a burr under her bonnet and I couldn't figure out what was making her so angry. For such a pretty girl she had a nasty way about her. The look from her eyes was as hard as nails and as stubborn as a cow that wouldn't be milked.

As she started to leave the room she had to take a parting shot. "I warn you, Ruby, that girl will be nothing but trouble. Look at her, she's not even built like a girl!"

I tried to explain. "Ma made me dress like a boy on the wagon train, so no one would take advantage of me." But then I looked at where my breasts were supposed to be, and when I glanced around the table and saw how ample their breasts were, pushing up and out every which way, I had to agree with them - my baggy pants and floppy shirt were not too flattering. All the same, that was no reason for Laurie to make fun of me.

Before I thought, I spoke back to her. "I noticed you liked the breakfast all right. So you just stay out of my kitchen and I'll stay out of your bedroom."

Ruby almost choked she laughed so hard. "Steady there, girl, Laurie's harmless. She's just been here the longest. She likes to have her say." Leaning back in her chair she went on. "Lilly, you aren't old enough to be one of my girls anyhow, but we sure as hell need a cook and housekeeper around here. All right, honey, it's a deal. You can have the cook's room at the back of the house, plus free board and a little money to fix yourself up. Nobody will bother you back there in the kitchen. Just be sure you do your job," and with a chuckle she added, "we'll do ours."

"Yes, ma'am. I'll make you right happy you hired me. Now don't you worry about a thing. I'll have this place in good shape real soon." At the time I didn't know what I was saying.

The truth is, I had a tall order to keep my promise. These girls were not good housekeepers and were lacking in plain old common sense. In fact, they hardly ever turned a finger. All they did was entertain the men who came to visit, and I guess they had lots of experience doing that. Otherwise, it seemed to me that they were downright lazy.

When I mentioned it to Ruby she said, "I'm sure you are right, Lilly, but there are a few rules we have in this house that you should know about. I am the madam, I run a high-class place, and whatever I say is law. Each of my girls is checked once a month by the local doctor and given a certificate of clean health which she has to pay for and it is expensive. So far we have had no problems. We don't allow just any man to frequent our doors. Every girl is by appointment only, and she just takes care of what she can handle each night. Nobody is forced to work here. In fact, if a gentlemen wants to come here he has to have a letter of introduction signed by the mayor."

I could not believe my ears. The mayor of the city knew about this place, and he approved. I knew I was young and inexperienced in life, but this did not make any sense to me. I must have looked strange because the girls snickered and laughed even more. Ruby hushed them and continued, "I want you to know, Lilly, all the men coming here are gentlemen, and as ladies living in this house we have to abide by the local city rules. You see, my girls can only go into town on Monday mornings for two hours at a time. The rest of the days of the week they are hid away here like little mice. Anyway, I expect you to not disturb any of them when they are working, and to call me if you have any questions. Do you understand?"

No, I did not know how this house operated. However, I needed the job too badly to question, so I nodded my head and told her I did. Then it occurred to me that maybe Ruby could not go to town either, except on Mondays. Apparently she really needed someone to do the shopping and get supplies for the week. This was something I knew I could do. And that is how my life with Ruby and the girls began. Though I had been told what kind of house I was working in, it was hard to believe. Only later did I realize what I had gotten myself into.

Four

Ruby and Her Girls

*I*t's true, I knew about housework, but I'd never tackled thirteen rooms before. My job started off with all the kitchen duties, but after a while I found most of the work in the house rested on my shoulders. Since I liked things neat and tidy I tried to get the house in good working order as fast as possible. At first the girls did not like my cleaning and rearranging things, but soon they got used to it and even began to like the changes.

In the beginning I left the upstairs alone, but later that changed too. All the girls had pretty good natures and even gave me a hand once in a while, but not Laurie. She would not allow any of us to help her with her precious things. She had maintained her room all along and she did not need us snooping around, as she put it. Finally I was allowed to change her linen and keep her vase filled with wild flowers, but that was all.

The parlor was like none I have ever seen before or since. It was decorated rather wildly, with red drapes, red flocked wallpaper, fancy French furniture, large Persian rugs here and there, and one of those fancy chandeliers from Paris hanging from the ceiling in the middle of the room. There were a lot of gold-trimmed pictures of fancy ladies and there were many brass vases from India stuffed with wildflowers. It was quite an assortment of furnishings. Ruby showed me through the house and gave me instructions on the first day, but at the time I did not really hear her, because I was too busy making mental notes about what had to be done. The house needed a total cleaning and airing out. It smelled like stale cigars and stale perfume, even though it was the most expensive perfume money could buy.

Ruby loved the color red, as well as other bright colors and floral prints, so that is how she had decorated most of the house. I had no idea then that the color red was associated with houses like Ruby's. The only room that was rather plain and pleasant was the music room. It was here that Laurie had had her say. The room was decorated in shades of blue and white with a touch of rose. Laurie polished the furniture, as well as her beautiful piano. She informed me I was to do it her way or forget it. Well, I did it her way and it became my favorite place in the house. The music room was the most elegant of all.

The office was really an interviewing space, where a gentleman would meet with Ruby and make arrangements to meet the girl he wanted for the evening. It was costly to say the least, fifty dollars a client no matter how long he stayed. Out of that, Ruby took her half. She was not greedy, but the house had to be maintained, expensive wines and brandy purchased, as well as fine pieces of jewelry and perfumes, which she felt were needed. The girls did pay money for the rent of their rooms, their fancy clothes, and what drinks they bought themselves when they could not talk some fellow into buying one for them.

The viewing room was of interest. It was more masculine, with large pieces of furniture, a solid oak wood desk and chair to match, an ornate coat rack and a big leather couch. It was where the men were allowed to smoke, but not anywhere else in the house. That is why I saw them going in and out, the first night I was there. Ruby discouraged smoking because it made the place smell bad. She wanted the men to feel the feminine atmosphere when they walked in the door. Ruby liked her smoke about as much as any man, but she discouraged the girls from doing it because she wanted each girl to smell sweet and pretty. Why else did she buy the expensive perfumes? It was good for business, as she always said. I suspect that more than one of them smoked, but I never could prove it. Ruby liked her girls and maybe even loved them, but it was still a business, so the house was run like a business.

Next to the kitchen, separated by swinging doors, was a large dining room with an oblong table, which sat in the middle of the floor. On one side was a tall buffet cabinet its drawers filled with linen from Ireland, china from England and silverware from some place back East. Large silver candleholders stood on each end of the table. It was all very elegant. I was impressed. But the kitchen was my first concern.

When Ruby walked into the kitchen that first morning she was shocked to find it so neat and clean. She immediately spotted Big Black and he spotted her. She knelt down and spoke in a strange sweet sounding voice, and he came running to her. It was like love at first sight. He turned and looked at me as though he felt guilty. He turned slowly and came over to me, nudged me and then moved back to Ruby. She was delighted and said, "Well, hell, Lilly! Didn't know your dog here was so friendly. He is quite an animal and I do like fine animals. This big fellow reminds me of when I was a kid in France. I had a dog just like him once. Now don't look so surprised, after all, I wasn't hatched full grown! I did have a childhood."

Yes, I believed her. I thought, *I bet you were a pretty child and you still could be pretty if you'd let your hair be natural and not wear all that greasepaint on your face.* However I knew it didn't matter what I thought as long as I kept my mouth shut and did my job, so I began my duties.

It was like living in a different world. I spent my first day trying to find something to wear. Since the last cook had been a Chinaman there was nothing left that I could use. Ruby suggested that one of the girls share some of her clothes with me. Of course, it was good-hearted Peaches who offered. Her gowns were several sizes too big for me, but she managed to take a stitch here and there, and soon I found I had three dresses I could wear, all suitable to my station.

It wasn't long before the girls became acquainted with Big Black. At first they were a bit afraid of such a big dog, but Ruby recognized how a dog his size could be an asset to the house, so he was allowed to stay, and soon she and Big Black were as close as thieves. After a while all the girls in the house enjoyed the dog's antics. He was a great retriever. I began to look at him as my helper. When any of the girls left a shoe, dressing gown or shawl anywhere other than in her bedroom, Big Black would carry the article to her. In the future it was almost a game with the girls. They would leave something lying around just to see if it would be returned to them. In the beginning, their doors were shut tight in the early mornings, and Big Black just deposited their various articles in front of their door. However, they soon learned to leave their doors slightly opened and found they were awakened each morning by the soft nuzzle of Big Black carrying something that belonged to them.

As time passed we settled into a routine. The girls handled their business and I handled mine. Laurie, Emma, Charlotte called Jesse, Irene called Maggie, Peaches and Myrna - as I began to know them I found that they had come from widely different backgrounds. For one reason or another each had been drawn to Ruby. She had a kind heart and a need to mother these young women. She had a hard time not gathering all the unfortunate girls she saw to her "family." If she could not hire the young lady she would arrange for her to be employed in another town. Most parlor houses were in contact with each other because of a "professor", a piano-player who traveled the circuit of houses and entertained in the evenings for little pay and free drinks. He kept up with all the changes and he knew where various girls were located. Most women moved frequently, because each house liked to present new faces for their clients.

In Ruby's house this was not always true. She often tried to hire a professor but Laurie ran them off. She didn't like anyone touching her precious piano. Ruby's girls were more like a family of sisters - none wanted to leave. Besides, most had their clients who frequented the house regularly. Why leave when you have a good thing going?

In her youth, Ruby had been a beauty and had earned some of her money the same way, lying on her back! She was still attractive, according to the men who came to her bed. To me she appeared strange. Her skin was real pale and I was sure had never seen the light of day. Her hair was the color you get from using a tin of henna on light-colored hair, making it almost orange with red highlights. Her lips were painted a bright crimson and her cheeks were equally rosy.

Getting to know her better, I found she had been born to rich French parents who had come to America to start a new life. I could understand that very well. She had been separated from them when she was just a child. Both parents came down with pneumonia and died, leaving her alone in a strange country before she had even learned the language. Since little work was available to a girl of eleven, she chose the only thing she could do at the time. She became an entertainer in a saloon in Silverton, Colorado. Mature for her age, with the ability to dance and sing, she brought the men in with her French ballads. The barkeeper was a nice enough man, but he saw her only as a way to make money. When she began she entertained for a place to eat and sleep, but before long she was introduced to the world of "upstairs and down the back hall." It was not the life she would have chosen, but the saloon keeper made it clear to her—do as he said or he would kick her out on the street! Since she had no other talents she felt this was all she could do. So she decided to save what money she could hide, and when she was eighteen, apply to the court for the release of her parents' money which they had brought to America. After this she hoped to start her own fancy parlor house. It wasn't the greatest profession in the world, but as she thought on it, there were a lot of other young girls that got caught up in this kind of life just due to circumstances. Her dream was to take care of girls like herself and provide a decent house for them to live in.

And that is how she and Laurie first met. Laurie was also a singer for the same saloon keeper. She doubled the bar's customers, keeping things lively with the rinky-dink tunes she played on the piano. They were not to her taste, though. She loved "real" music, as she called it. Many times she had shared with Ruby her wish that she could find a better place to live and play the piano. However, she consoled herself with the knowledge that she had once known a better day, and secretly felt she was superior to most of the bar patrons.

Night after night, after the last customer had staggered out of the saloon, she sat and played the piano until early morning hours - selections she had learned as a child. It was then she became truly beautiful, dreaming of a life that was no more, a life she could never recover. Thoughts of leaving the saloon often came to her as she played, but she could never figure out how. So her sad music filled the ugly barroom and for a while in the dim light, she relaxed and sipped her sherry.

The barkeep, Sam McGee, listened, and he too dreamed, weeping at the young girl's sad songs. The girls upstairs often were drawn down, after their clients had left, to spend the remainder of the night listening to Laurie play her piano.

On summer nights in Silverton the guests at the hotel down the street fell asleep to Laurie's music. According to Ruby, she was never asked to stop playing. It almost became a nightly ritual for the town's folk to come outside, sit in their chairs and enjoy the music. Her voice was one of the purest and sweetest they had ever heard, and it could move the meanest person to tears. Her voice was like magic.

To the shock of Ruby, it was old Sam who tried to get Laurie to better herself. He suggested she quit the saloon business and sign up with a troupe of entertainers. He wanted to marry her, but Laurie would have nothing to do with that proposal. She was not interested in him or any other man.

The opera houses across the country were doing a big business, and Sam believed she had talent enough. Why, he figured, she could even appear at Maguire's Opera House in San Francisco if she wanted to. Sam said he had been there once, and that place had first-rate entertainment like minstrel shows, novelty acts, and even singers. He had been there in 1859 when the Opera House had been refurbished. That is when opera was first introduced to San Francisco. Famous stars came from all over the world according to Sam. He said, at the time, San

Francisco was considered the theater capital of the West. He didn't think much of opera, but he was sure Laurie could make it. He just couldn't convince her.

When Ruby realized Laurie wasn't ready to take off anywhere, she began to see how the two of them might help each other. By now Ruby had her inheritance and planned to leave Silverton, Colorado to go to Nevada, maybe even to Virginia City. She finally chose Carson City because it was more than "a one-horse town." It was a perfect place, still a bit wild, but somewhat civilized, a good place to establish a parlor house which would attract other young women who had no place to go.

Laurie liked the idea. She had always known Ruby had some sort of plan to leave the saloon, but wasn't sure what it was. So on one of those summer nights after the saloon closed, while Laurie played, Ruby told her of her plans. She had already written the Carson City Sheriff and asked for a permit to open up a house. Of course, the Sheriff had replied with a resounding, "Yes!" He was eager to have an organized house with healthy high-class working girls - it would get the freelance prostitutes off the streets. However, he explained, there would be some restrictions so the good folks of Carson City would be appeased. Ruby had never met a restriction she couldn't get around. To get away from the saloon, she was ready to accept anything, so she and Laurie took off for Nevada.

Through her lawyer friend, Ruby arranged for a house to be built to her specifications. Since she would not be allowed to appear to own the place, it was in her lawyer's name, but in truth it was all hers. She and Laurie were elated to have a place to call home! They spent the next few months decorating the house, most of it done to Ruby's taste. But Laurie was adamant about the music room, where her precious piano would be placed. She would decorate it her way. She made it clear that no one was to touch her piano - ever, not even Ruby.

By the time they were ready to open for business, other young women had heard of their parlor house - each with a different story, which I will tell in due time. Soon a nice group of men were frequenting the place. Some just wanted a haven where they could relax and play cards, drink a brandy and smoke a good cigar in the company of beautiful ladies. They gathered in the music room where Laurie's piano wove its spell. It wasn't until more girls arrived that Ruby really began the upstairs part of the business, and Ruby's Parlor House became known to men as a home away from home.

At that time, so I was told, many married men never saw their wives fully unclothed. It was that Queen Victoria thing. I guess women were not supposed to enjoy worldly pleasures. What I couldn't understand is why? Ma said what happened between a man and a woman was sacred. Whatever that meant, I did not have the slightest idea, but if Ma said so it was true!

Well, I guess I had better get back to my first months with Ruby and her girls. We finally settled into a routine of sorts. Each girl slept late except for Laurie, and I often wondered if she ever slept at all. I knew she had men visit her room, but it didn't matter. She would rise early and sit on the front porch, or take long walks while most of the town's people were still sleeping. She never spoke to me and always avoided the kitchen until the rest of the household got up. It was an empty place during the day so I moved quietly through the downstairs cleaning and straightening with Big Black's help. Our first meal was at midday. Not as hardy as the first morning meal I cooked, but it was still breakfast. Most of the girls loved to be spoiled and wanted their breakfast in bed. I didn't mind, but Ruby began to insist that everyone eat together at both meals. She maintained it was a good time to discuss business, and it gave her a chance to look each girl over, from head to toe.

During these hours in the dining room Ruby instructed the girls in proper etiquette. Since Laurie had been raised in the East and attended proper schools she was encouraged to teach each girl to read and write. Sometimes she would read the classics and set them off to dreaming. Once in a while, Ruby got a bit of conscience and had me come in to teach from the Holy Book. This I did with great exuberance and only after careful study. I had to be cautious and not upset the girls too much. When their studies were over, they would go into the parlor, relax, visit or play a game of cards. It was then, in the early afternoon, that I cleaned the upstairs rooms. Around four o'clock they would retire to their rooms for a brief rest and remain there until the evening meal. Ruby believed a hardy supper was good for the girls. She didn't like them working on an empty stomach, and it kept them from drinking so much. When the gentlemen callers came in the evening, each girl was well fed and ready to entertain in the music room or upstairs.

Ruby didn't believe, as other madams did, in piling her girls in an open wagon and carting them around town to show them off. She said they were decent human beings and not pieces of meat to be picked over. She believed her parlor house business was built on a good reputation.

The news got out about my cooking, and many of the gentlemen callers began asking permission to arrive in time for our late evening meal. It seemed I served a better supper than they could get in town. And soon I noticed the men began sitting in the parlor longer having a smoke (which was frowned on but allowed), or going into the music room to listen to Laurie play and sing. The girls also began sitting around later and later, enjoying the company of each other and the men callers. It was almost like a family get-together. There was plenty of food for munching and lots of lemonade to quench a body's thirst. Though the crystal decanters sat filled with excellent brandy, very rarely did the gentlemen consume an unreasonable amount of any beverage. The most expensive imported wines were served for the evening meal, so very little hard whiskey was consumed even though it was available too.

Everyone gathered in the music room night after night. Near the piano sat Big Black sporting his shiny black coat with that identifying white left paw. He looked like he really enjoyed the piano playing and singing. At times he even joined in with a rolling growl or howl, to the amusement of us all. He truly was one fine animal.

Of course, our center of attraction was always Laurie. I learned she had been married back East before she teamed up with Ruby. She was quite a musician and had studied in the best schools. However, she was hopelessly in love with her young husband, so when he suggested they go West, she agreed. He had visions, as many still had, of getting rich. But before they reached California, he became ill and died of a fever. Young and inexperienced, he had gambled away all of the money his parents had given them for their wedding present. So Laurie was left destitute due to no fault of her own.

The only link Laurie had with the past was her beautiful upright piano, which she had insisted her husband bring in the wagon. Somehow it had survived the long journey from the East. It was a pretty piece of hand-carved woodwork, with cupids on each corner and vines with leaves winding around the front top panel. That same piano now sat in Ruby's music room giving the place a look of elegance. It was treasured by all of us.

I really had a liking for Laurie and her piano, and I sure was sorry we had gotten off to a bad start. She continued to totally ignore me, and I stayed out of her way as much as possible. But somehow I was always running into her, or getting caught in her room, cleaning or changing her linen when she didn't want me there. One evening after supper, she had been given some flowers from a rather handsome young gentleman and had asked me to put them in some water in a vase in her room. I had forgotten to do it before they ate, so I ran up the back stairs, to the far end of the upper hall where Laurie's room was and entered. I hurriedly put the vase of flowers on her bedside table, but just as I did, I heard Laurie and a man returning to her room. Why, they had not even had time to eat and here they were, coming down the hall talking softly to each other.

I was scared to death to be caught at this time of day in Laurie's room, so I dashed into her wardrobe closet and quickly closed the door, leaving a small crack so I could breath. I realized my mistake, but it was too late. I just hoped she would not want anything out of the closet or would see the door was slightly ajar. I had noticed she had put her lounging gown neatly over her dressing room screen, so I was fairly sure she would not be opening the closet, at least for awhile. This was my introduction, in a peculiar way, to the activities taking place in the upstairs rooms of the house.

At first, as I listened, it was real quiet in the room and then I heard their voices - Laurie's, sweet and gentle, so low I couldn't understand a word she was saying. Then I heard the man make a comment about taking his pants off and climbing into her bed. Well, I was a bit uncertain about what was going on, and then I became aware of the furniture being moved all around. Thump, thump, thump! And after they got through moving the furniture I heard a low moan from Laurie. The conversation went something like this, "Aw, come on, Laurie. Do it this way. It works better that way. Oh, God that feels good! Are you ready? Now?" Then there was a sound, something like a groan, coming from Laurie and almost a shout from the man, and then the room got strangely quiet. I couldn't see a thing in that dark wardrobe closet but I sure imagined a lot. I was still a mite puzzled why they had moved the furniture though. After all, if Laurie had wanted her room rearranged I could have done that the next day. That handsome gentleman didn't have to help her.

I knew Laurie would never forgive me if she thought I had been snooping around, spying on her, so I settled down into a ball on the floor of the wardrobe. I hoped they would leave or even fall asleep. I felt like a squashed potato sitting curled up in the bottom. Sure enough the room was soon quiet so I slowly opened the wardrobe, peeked out and saw quite a sight. It was at twilight so there was just enough light to see the bed. There was that man, as handsome and lean as he could be, lying on the bed next to Laurie. His body skin was dark compared to her snow-white skin. Both were as naked as jaybirds and in a way, pretty as a picture. I'd never seen a grown man naked before, but I found it rather amusing. His manhood was all shriveled up, but the look on his face was of pure contentment. I decided I had better high-tail it out of there before they woke up and saw me. After all, what Laurie didn't know wouldn't hurt her, or me for that matter.

After this episode it was quite clear to me that my place in the house was certainly not upstairs. Since I didn't have much of a figure and was kind of a plain girl, I guess it never occurred to Ruby that I had any idea of what went on upstairs. They never explained and I never asked.

In the evening when the meal was over and the kitchen cleaned, my time was my own. I sometimes ventured into the music room and listened to Laurie play the piano. I knew I was welcome, but I felt a bit uneasy because they were all dressed up in their finest undergarments. A chemise and bloomers or a fancy gown, depending on what their gentlemen caller preferred, while I was still wearing the dresses Peaches had made over for me, and most of them were everyday, very plain, no lace or ruffles.

I often went to bed early since my chores were many and the housework very physical. However, one night I remember in particular, I had joined the group in the music room. I was enjoying listening to Laurie playing the piano when there was an unexpected knock at the front door, a knock I did not recognize. I slipped out, closed the music room doors behind me, moved toward the front door and opened it. As I did my heart leaped up into my mouth, because standing there was the handsomest man I had ever seen. He was downright pretty, and young - I'd say he was about twenty to twenty-five years old. I took him to be rather rich too, because his suit was the latest cut, gray flannel pinstripe with matching soft suede leather boots. He wore a large gray cowboy hat with a black band around the crown. Seeing me, he quickly doffed the hat and put it under his arm. Why, he almost bowed to me as I opened the door - and me a housekeeper and cook. He said he had business with Ruby, the Madam of the house, and wished to see her immediately.

He stood there looking all dreamy and sweet, and I was trying to figure out what to do next when Ruby came slowly down the stairs. She had been keeping to her room in the evenings, but not when she heard his voice. I was so taken back I couldn't say a word, I just stood there like a silly schoolgirl gazing at him and gawking like a ninny. He was the only man I had ever looked at in a romantic way. It made me feel all giggly inside, from my toes to the top of my head. I just plain tingled at the sight of him, and at that moment I wished I could just lead him up those stairs and do whatever it was you do with a man. I knew if that man took hold of me I would faint dead away.

Then I looked up at Ruby and was astonished to see the

look in her eyes - as if she knew him. Turning to me, she said, "Lilly, aren't you going to show the young gentleman in?"

Well, I nearly fell over my feet trying to answer her. "Yes ma'am, of course. I mean - won't you come in? The girls are in the music room. I'll show you in there." However, Ruby had grabbed him around the shoulders and called him by name. "Joel, your mother does me a great honor sending you here. She wrote me of your engagement. Said that you are soon to be married. It is a wise mother who sends her son to me. When you leave here, my boy, you will be a man, I guarantee it!"

I didn't mean to say a word, but before I thought I blurted out, "Well, I don't think so. It just isn't proper!"

At this, Joel hugged Ruby and gave a small chuckle. He glanced at me and winked, and I nearly dropped my teeth, as well as his hat, which I had taken from him earlier. I couldn't believe my ears. There he was, about to be married, and he had come to Ruby's house. I wondered whom she would select for him, but she ushered him up the stairs to her own door. I watched crest-fallen and thought, if I had been one of her girls I'd have volunteered. I couldn't teach him about being a man, but I figured he sure could show me a thing or two about being a woman.

Still standing at the door I realized I was holding onto his hat and gawking after him long past the time I should have remained. I could hear the festivities warming up in the music room as the piano got louder. Soon the double doors would swing open and several couples would spill out arm in arm, advancing toward the stairs for an evening of "pleasure and delight," as Peaches called it. I knew it was time for me to retire to my bed, but my mind was so full of thoughts of Joel I didn't feel sleepy.

This Joel had accepted Ruby's invitation so willingly, but she was old enough to be his mother and should be ashamed.

I found myself really resenting her, having him to herself. I was also full of curiosity. Who was he and why would any mother send her son to Ruby?

Since it was too much for me to figure out I lovingly hung his hat on the wall tree with the other gents' hats. Dismayed and feeling lonely, I sauntered off to my bedroom. Big Black was there waiting for my return. I guess he had not been in the music room that evening. He greeted me with a soft nuzzle and then settled himself down near the small fireplace in my room. When I was ready for bed, in my flannel gown, I sat and braided my long hair, and slid between the cold sheets. My feet felt like two chunks of ice until Big Black climbed up at the bottom of the mattress and lay down on my feet.

Even as I enjoyed the warmth I couldn't go to sleep. I lay there, thinking of Joel and of Ruby and the other girls in their rooms with some man. I had strange feelings all through me. I kept feeling my breast, knowing I was developing into a woman, wondering why my body ached in various places and my mind was full of unsightly thoughts and pictures.

I remember the stories from the Song of Solomon in the Bible. Ma hadn't encouraged me to read that book, but I did and I liked it. Now some passages came back, "How beautiful are thy feet with shoes, O Prince's daughter! The joints of thy thighs are like jewels, the work of the hands of a cunning workman. Thy navel is like a round goblet, which wanteth not liquor; thy belly is like a heap of wheat set about with lilies. Thy two breasts are like two young roes that are twins." I forgot what came in between but I remembered, "This thy stature is like a palm tree, and thy breasts two clusters of grapes. I am my beloved's, and his desire is toward me." As I thought of my breasts, they were small, round and firm but certainly not like clusters of grapes.

I wasn't too sure what all that meant in the Bible, but it

seemed to be part of this powerful desire I had for that man, Joel. I guess I soon fell asleep with all those foolish thoughts swimming around in my head, because I dreamed, woke up and dreamed again. The first dream was all mixed up. I wasn't in my room anymore, but in a large bedchamber with fluffy pink curtains hanging on the windows and pretty pink-flowered wallpaper. It was quite fancy for a girl like me. There were wildflowers in vases on every table in the room giving off a sweet smell like perfume. It was a spring night and there was a slight breeze with the scent of lilac in the air. I saw the starlight shimmering through the open windows, and the moon was as bright as day, streaming its light over the night. Why, you could have read a newspaper by the light of that moon.

There I was just lying in a big four-poster canopy bed with silk curtains pulled aside. I could see the door and I knew someone was coming. I felt, at the same time, fear and excitement. In my dream I had purposely locked my door but I knew if the person coming up those stairs wanted to get into my bedroom a measly little lock would not stop him.

One minute it was quiet, with only an occasional hoot of a night owl to disturb the peace of the moment. Then the next thing I heard was heavy footsteps on the stairs. It was the sound of a man's determined walk - he knew where he was going and what he planned to do. I was sure it was the dashing impulsive Joel that I had met earlier. And I secretly knew I wanted him to catch me. He tried the door and muttered some very disapproving words. Then without further ado, he hit the door with a mighty kick of his boot, causing the lock to let go. I sat up in my bed, and pulled the covers high around my neck. The door flung open and slammed against the wall. I huddled down in the bed, but I did not scream.

It was Joel, all right, and he was indeed a handsome one. I wanted him to seek me out, but I had hoped it would be somewhat different. I wanted him to "come calling", courting me like I'd heard young men did with proper young ladies. Just about the time he started toward my bed I looked up and saw the preacher standing at the foot of my bed, and my mother kept calling me to come home. Hearing her call my name, I woke up wet with sweat and most confused.

I knew it was just a dream so I finally made myself relax, and once again let my ears get accustomed to the night sounds. By now it was getting late. As I lay there listening I heard the good night whispers of the men who were leaving the house. I must have fallen asleep because I dreamed again, but this time I heard a pleasant voice calling my name. I rose from my bed and found myself in the arms of Joel, my beloved. We were dancing to the music of an unseen orchestra as he held me closer and closer. His lips hungrily pressed on my lips as he drew me protectively to him. He cuddled me as a mother does her child. I felt his hand move over my face, slowly down my neck and then to my less than full bosom. To my surprise, a swelling occurred as I felt a warm sensation run through my body. I was alive! I was not just a skinny girl with long braided hair wearing a drab plain, cotton nightgown. I was a desirable woman dressed in a beautiful see-through chemise with lovely silk hose and garters. I was a real woman - and I even looked like one!

Joel held me in his tender embrace, gently lifting me off the floor while holding me in his strong arms. I lay against his panting chest. Where there had once been clothes, now there was only warm moist skin with curly hair that tickled my nose and sent shivers down my spine. The smell of him was over-powering. I was helplessly head over heels in love with this man.

He lifted me in his arms as if I were a feather and held me close to him like a prize he had just won. I thought, O, joy of joys, wonders of wonders, I would soon be his. He brought me closer to him and buried his face in my unbraided hair which now cascaded over my nude body as gracefully as whipped butter on hot bread.

The bed stood waiting, a feather mattress as soft as fluffy white clouds, with cool rose satin sheets and a mauve velvet coverlet made ready for the exciting event. There were fancy soft pillows arranged perfectly. The room was lit by candles, which gave off a soft glow. I was giddy with the perfume of the flowers and the sweet scent of honeysuckle growing just outside my window. My mind swam in a mist of joy and bewilderment. My heart raced as Joel gently laid me in the middle of the large four-poster bed. He was nude and sweat was glistening on his body as he moved toward me. He began to come down onto me from his position at the side of the bed. I half rose to meet his young, lean pulsating body. Our mouths sought out each other and we kissed over and over again. He then moved over my body with gentle kisses, and when I thought I could stand it no longer, my body rose to meet his as we fulfilled our desires. He rose and sank over me like restless ocean waves rolling in and out over the rippling sand. I felt the sensation of pain and excitement all at once. I felt the uncontrolled gushing of liquid fill my body as he exploded inside me. I cried with the knowledge that I was a woman at last. Tears fell on my pillow and sorrow consumed my mind. I wanted to wake up, but I didn't want the dream to end. I realized what had taken place and asked myself how this could have happened. I thought I loved him and I wanted to experience being a woman with him, but I didn't want it like this. Something was wrong, very wrong. I began to cry so hard that when I did wake up it was with Big Black licking my face trying to comfort me.

I pushed Big Black off my bed and jumped up in total shock

at what I had dreamed. For a moment, I forgot where I was because my dream was so real, so explicit that I believed it had actually occurred. I went to the window and gazed out onto a bleak winter's night. A chilling rain was beginning to fall on the window with cold indifference to my needs and anguish. I stood there staring out the window, shivering in my long homely cotton nightgown. Nothing I had ever experienced had prepared me for this feeling. I tried to think back to Ma and Pa. I wondered if they had had these feelings? Were these the urges that drew Ruby's girls to this house? Were they content to give their bodies so freely without love? I didn't understand any of it. I made up my mind right then and there I would settle for nothing less than the love of a man with a commitment of marriage.

I asked myself, had I not sat at my mother's knee and heard her read from the Book of Solomon? I thought of the love song written by him, and the descriptive words he used to express his love for a woman. He was said to have been a very wise man, yet he had many wives and many concubines. Was it right or wrong to have many partners? As I stood there pondering these things I became aware of my feet being cold again and the realization that I had no one to crawl into bed with. I was lonely - oh, so lonely! I wanted someone to love me and I wanted to return that love.

I lay in my bed musing about my dreams. I asked myself if it was wrong to live in a house like Ruby's. Thinking of the girls who lived in the house, I realized each one had many good attributes, and Ruby, with all her fancy ways and painted face, had a heart as big as all outdoors. Maybe it was better not to judge and just let life take its course. If I were to ever meet my true love I decided that too would happen in time. Finally, as I snuggled down into my feather mattress I became warm, and it was with a peaceful feeling that I returned to sleep.

Five

Change in Ruby's House

*I*t is hard to say just when it happened or what caused it, but there was indeed a steady change taking place in Ruby's house. You see, none of the girls were what you would call bad women. They were just trying to make a living, enough good food to eat, a nice private room to call their own, and a spacious house to move about in. They had pretty clothes of imported lace and velvet, not to mention all the interesting gentlemen callers who frequented the house. And sometimes, it was just plain fun! It was like living in a big house with a family of sisters, and none of them really had to turn a hand as long as I was there.

For me, getting into a routine was easy. I still rose early each morning because it was habit with me. Pa always said,

"Early to bed and early to rise makes a man, healthy, wealthy and wise." Healthy, yes! Wealthy - I doubt it. And wise, I didn't really know. Anyway, I went about my chores quietly each day, asking few questions, but wondering about a good deal of things.

For some time I had known that we needed to have more fresh vegetables and fruits in our diet. Only being able to get to the store on Mondays had made it hard to have what I considered proper meals for the house, even though the girls and gents seemed to enjoy my food. I decided if we were to get more fruits and vegetables we needed to grow them ourselves. So early one morning I started to work on that sorry plot of ground we called a garden. The Chinaman had tried to grow a few crops, but now it was a mess of weeds and dried up plants, and yet I believed it could be productive if cared for.

So before the sun rose one spring morning I put on my old long-sleeved dress, bonnet, and plain gloves and went to work. I began by pulling weeds and turning the soil, meanwhile making a plan for which vegetables to plant: Carrots, beans, beets, squash and lots of potatoes - both kinds red and white. If I had any doubts as to what would grow best, I knew the man at the local store would help me out.

Big Black was right beside me, running up and down the weed patches like an inspector checking on his worker. He would nuzzle me and then turn around and around trying to get my attention. I guess he thought that if I were out playing in the dirt anyway, I ought to be playing fetch with him.

While I was busy pulling weeds and getting blisters on my fingers I could feel that I was being watched. Looking up at the house, I was surprised to see two of the girls leaning out of their upstairs windows, Maggie and Jesse. I smiled and waved hello.

They laughed and yelled down to me, "Lilly, can we help?

Looks like fun, and we're tired of being inside all the time." I
could have fallen over dead. Those two wanted to come outside in the early morning hours? I figured they must be touched
in the head. I couldn't believe my ears, but if they wanted to
try, I was not about to stop them. I laughed inside, thinking of
them doing any kind of work, especially gardening. I knew
they had no idea how much strength it took to turn the soil
and pull those blasted weeds.

But I called back up to them, "Come on down, only first
put on a dress with long sleeves that will cover your arms and
legs. Be sure to wear a big hat and some old gloves." I was sure
Ruby wouldn't be pleased if they got sunburned. She wanted
their bodies as white as snow and smooth as satin. Beauty to
her was skin deep!

I had taught the girls to take off their face paint at night
and use my mother's recipe to keep their faces and hands soft.
I remember it well. It was a combination of 1/2 pint of cow's
milk, 1/2 oz. glycerin, 1/2 oz. bicarbonate of soda and 1/2 oz.
borax. I made it myself by warming the milk and slowly add-
ing the dry ingredients until they were dissolved. To store it, I
poured the mixture into small brown bottles and put them in
the icebox. Each girl had her own personal container. We all
agreed it was a refreshing concoction.

When I gave them permission to join me, their windows
slammed shut. Then I could hear their running feet and sup-
pressed giggles. They were making so much noise they were
going to wake up everyone in the house. They finally arrived
at my side dressed in costumes that had obviously just been
thrown together. Big fancy hats flopping up and down on their
heads, dresses made with lace inserts, and long white gloves,
which looked almost brand new. I almost laughed out loud,
but then thought better of it. I really doubted if either of them
had been up this early since they were kids, and at that mo-

ment they reminded me of children.

At first they played at their work, but after a while they got the hang of it and proved to be no slouches at digging and weeding. They lost all track of time, so I couldn't help worrying about their faces getting too much sun and Ruby being angry with me. I figured if Ma's recipe wasn't strong enough to soothe their faces, I could always use cold buttermilk packs which would do the trick.

The whole house was awakened with all the chatter going on outside. Every upstairs window opened except Laurie's and Ruby's, and before long each girl was leaning out her window watching and wanting to know what in the world we were doing up so early in the morning. As I said, by now most of them washed their faces before going to bed, so the faces we saw were bright and clean, and somewhat sleepy. They yawned and leaned on their windowsills. The girls watched us in complete fascination. They asked questions from time to time, but seemed to be content to just watch.

Big Black continued to run up and down the rows and even tried to help us dig until we sent him away. Finally, he found a good place to rest under the shade of a small tree. He sat watching all the commotion as if on guard duty. I believe if that dog could have talked he would have been telling us how to do it. He liked all of us being outside and took to following us wherever we went. Big Black had been a puppy when Ma, Pa, and I met up with Jim and his family on the trail. Now he was in his prime. It seemed like a long time ago, and when I remembered my plan to go to California, it made me sad. Well, some day maybe I would go there, but who knew when that would be? Finally, I made myself quit thinking of the past and went inside the house.

When I left the garden Maggie and Jesse were still hard at work. I tried to get them to stop, but they had just a few more weeds to pull and wanted to complete the job. Finally they did give up and came in. They were a sight to behold, with dirty faces, clothes spotted with gritty dirt and weeds hanging all over them. Their hats were tilted over to one side with their hair tangled down their backs, but their flushed pink cheeks were happy and their smiles were radiant. They were laughing and chattering like two magpies, oblivious of how they looked.

I had baked breakfast bread the day before, and the coffee-pot was boiling away, sending out a tantalizing aroma. One by one the other girls came downstairs, and then Ruby joined us. She was shocked to see the appearance of Jesse and Maggie. Their cheeks were rosy with excitement and their well-cared-for nails actually had dirt under them, even though they had worn their long white gloves.

Ruby immediately asked what all the noise had been out-side her window in the middle of the night, and why they were in such a frightful condition. I quickly spoke up and explained what had happened and why we were out in the garden. At first, the other girls didn't like what they saw any more than Ruby. But as Jesse and Maggie explained what they had been doing and told them it was fun to be outside and that it felt good to work in the sun, the other girls became more inter-ested and listened. After all, they were tired of being inside all the time too. Jesse and Maggie were as excited as two kids and were prepared to help me care for the garden and plant some fruit trees, if it was all right with Ruby.

She looked puzzled but also a bit pleased, even though she didn't say it at the time. She had always wanted each girl to find other interests, but she wasn't sure about them working like farmhands. Finally she consented, just as long as they were still able to entertain in the evenings.

Well, I did obtain the vegetable seeds and some healthy fruit trees, and when our first crop came in it was mostly due to the loving care of Jesse and Maggie. They were out there at the crack of dawn every day, cultivating and working. When bugs attacked the various plants they got upset, not knowing what to do. Then I remembered what Ma did in her garden. I bought a tin of tobacco snuff and sprinkled it on the plants to discourage the insects. Also, we learned from the owner of the store to plant marigold flowers here and there in the garden to help rid it of other pests. They planted a row or two of onions on the outside of the garden to keep wild deer from eating the vegetables.

Water had to be drawn and hauled from the well, and those two did it willingly. It had gotten to be a sociable activity. Often times I heard voices outside and saw the girls hanging over the fence talking to some of the town's people who had stopped to chat. They asked many questions about how we made things grow so well. In fact, as I had expected, we had more vegetables than we could use - which gave me an idea.

My thought was to take some of those extra crops to town and see if the storekeeper would buy them from us. The next time I was in the mercantile store, I stopped by and talked with the owner. Sure enough, he was delighted and said he would buy all we could spare. This gave me another idea, so I asked him if Jesse and Maggie could bring the vegetables to him since they were the gardeners. I reminded him that they would have to make their deliveries on Monday mornings only, in accordance with the town's ruling. He laughed and said he didn't care when they came. And that is how our Maggie, a pretty little blue-eyed blonde, made the acquaintance of Mr. Jedidiah Abrahms.

Jesse was too arrogant to deliver the vegetables to Mr. Abrahms, but Maggie welcomed the chance to get away from the house. Once in a while some of the girls went with her, but she was often left alone with the storekeeper. Mr. Abrahms was a lonely widower. Before his wife died in childbirth with their only child, she had helped him manage the business. Now he did all the work by himself - the child had also died. He vowed the pain was too much to bear, so he decided he would never marry again. Most folk understood and respected him for it. However, he was a lonely man, too young to be alone and yet too busy to concern himself with looking for a wife even if he had wanted one. He was a good-looking man, and an honorable one.

Well, it wasn't long until the inevitable happened. Mr. Jedidiah took to waiting each Monday morning outside his door, just to see Maggie coming down the road carrying her load of vegetables in a large wicker basket. She was a mighty pretty picture. As she passed by, she turned many heads. The men appreciated a pretty face and figure, and the women couldn't help liking her because she was so friendly. They admired Jedidiah because he was such a God-fearing man and good Christian. He had never frequented Ruby's house. But now that he had actually met one of the girls, he realized they were not bad women. He liked Maggie, and in fact he'd fallen in love with her - so he did what any respectable man would do. He started calling on her at the house and made it quite clear she was not to see anyone else. It was funny at first, but after a while we all began to sense they were quite serious about each other. He said he wanted to get to know Maggie better, and since she could not come to see him except on Mondays, he would come to the house for the evening meal. She was delighted and quickly agreed to not see any other man, a decision I think she found hard to keep.

Ruby agreed too, but told him he would be required to pay the regular fee for seeing Maggie. This he did, and even offered more money if it meant no man would be allowed into Maggie's room. Night after night he came to the evening meal, forsaking his own cooking, which he said wasn't very good anyway. Each evening they visited in the music room or the parlor and then he would say his good-byes and leave. You can imagine how that set with Maggie. She wasn't used to this type of treatment, and she missed her other gentlemen callers. She came to me and asked what a girl was supposed to do when she wanted a man to marry up with her? She was used to having physical contact with a man and she wanted this man real bad. So that is how I got involved.

What did I know? I was just a girl myself, but I remembered Ma talking about Pa courting her. She said he had come around looking like a scared rabbit and twice as skittish. He and my grandpa would sit on the porch and talk for hours, and she would watch and listen. This went on night after night until finally she lost her patience and told him not to bother coming over any more. Of course, she didn't mean it. It had been their constant talking that got on her nerves, because all they spoke about was the farm, and never about her or what she might want. She said she was sorry for her hasty words, but it was too late. Being a sensitive man, his feelings were hurt, and he stayed away. She cried and pined for him, but he wouldn't come back.

Then, she said, one day all the families of the community were invited to a barn raising, and as they left the party she accidentally ran into Earl, my Pa. When he saw her, he didn't know what to do. Ma said she was determined he wouldn't get away this time. Right then and there she threw herself into Pa's arms, acted like she had sprained her ankle and could hardly walk. When she tried to stand, she groaned in pain and promptly fainted. Well, Pa bought her act - hook, line and sinker. He was standing there, holding her, when her father, my grandpa, came along. He mistook what was going on, raised his shotgun and said, "Young man, you are a-fooling around with my daughter, and that sir, is a marrying business." Consequently, they were wedded a short time later. Ma said, "Sometimes a girl has to take things into her own hands."

I felt this was not the way Maggie should proceed. If she made some sort of open move, Jedidiah would run like greased lightening. So what to do next? He was a robust and healthy fellow, so waiting around didn't suit him either. He needed a woman as much as Maggie needed a man. Each morning he would come around the corner in his buggy with fancy-stepping horses on the way to his store. He would rein in and look up at Maggie's window, and shout good morning to her, unless she was out in the garden. Then he would tie up those animals, walk over, and chat across the fence. After a while he began stopping by for coffee with me, waiting for Maggie to come down for breakfast. That gal had been up early, working in the garden, and when Mr. Jedidiah started coming by she made sure she was inside fixing up before he got there. They shared their eggs and bacon many a morning sitting at the oval table in the kitchen, like two lovebirds cooing in the trees. It was fun for me to sneak a peek once in a while and hope someday I'd find a man to love me. But I was sure that day would never come.

Maggie didn't give up hope. She and Jedidiah kept on sitting close together in the kitchen or in the music room listening to Laurie sing and play her piano. It was on one of these evenings that we heard a whoop and a holler out of Ruby. Mr. Jedidiah Abrahms had asked Ruby for Maggie's hand in marriage and, of course, Maggie had said yes. Maggie was eager, but a little worried what people would say. Mr. Abrahms knew it might be bad for business, but he was so all-fired-up he didn't care. She was the girl of his dreams, and he was determined to have her for his wife no matter what the town's people might think. He flat didn't care!

The whole parlor house was in a tizzy. Peaches made Maggie's wedding dress, a pretty pale yellow floor-length gown with puff sleeves and real French lace overlaid on the bodice. Imported pearls were sewn in the center of each flower. The skirt was fitted in front with a lovely train in the back, which flowed out on the floor as she walked. It was an elegant sight to see.

The day of the wedding there was a lot of excitement in Ruby's house. Some of the girls were a little afraid to go to the church, to stand up for Maggie and Mr. Jedidiah Abrahms, but it all turned out fine. The sheriff gave special permission for all the girls and Ruby to be in town on Sunday. The preacher gave a nice little talk about loving, being loved, and also about forgiveness. I think the forgiveness part was mostly for the ears of the town's folk.

Mr. Jedidiah looked as proud as a peacock, and Maggie was a beautiful, smiling, blue-eyed bride. The girls and Ruby sat in the first pew looking like regular citizens now. I sat in the second pew and watched with great pleasure and some envy. I cried big wet tears and used my handkerchief until it was a limp rag.

None of us were too sure how the town's people would take to such a marriage, but we did not have to worry. Everyone in town respected and liked Mr. Jedidiah, so if he wanted to marry up with Maggie, a former working girl, it was his business. Maggie had endeared herself to several of the ladies in town because of her vegetable garden and her out-going ways. Her former men callers never opened their mouths, because if they had they would have had to deal with Mr. Jedidiah - and that was not a good prospect.

A big party was planned following the ceremony where there would be wild square dancing, lots of eating, and a little cold cider drinking. However, the men couldn't stand it, so they spiked the punch more than once and everyone had a rip-roaring time.

Since Mr. Jed owned the mercantile, there just wasn't time for a short trip after the wedding, so he promised Maggie he would take her someplace in the future. Maggie didn't care about a long trip or even a short one for that matter. She was just happy to be starting a new life.

She took to that respectability like a duck takes to water. Because she was so happy she fit right in with all of Mr. Jedidiah's customers, though she got a few sidelong glances from the women, at first. However, her proper manners and modest dress made everyone forget her past. And if a few busy-bodies still gossiped, somehow that didn't matter to Maggie. In her new dresses even her old customers seldom recognized her. She was what they called "a solid citizen."

The married couple became pillars of the church. Maggie confessed her sins, was forgiven, and began her marriage as a new person. We heard they did a lot of good work, like sharing their worldly goods with the poor and the ailing. Maggie always did have a way with sick folks, so it was only natural for her to nurse them. She and Myrna, another girl of Ruby's, were better nurses than any women I have ever known. They could have been in one of those fancy hospitals in some big city back East. Of course, when a real epidemic of the fever came along, we all went out to do what we could, except for Laurie. During the sickness Ruby was up early and was one of the last returning to the house in the evening. I guess this action endeared her to some folks too.

Well, when Maggie left Ruby's, it was Jesse who missed her the most. She was the biggest puzzlement to me. She was quiet, never said much to anyone and always seemed to be thinking on secret things. When I looked at her she sometimes had a far away look in her eyes. She continued to care for the garden with my help, but we didn't talk much, just content to be working together. The more time she spent with the plants, the less she cared about her gentlemen callers. Ruby wasn't too pleased, but respected Jesse's right to chose who and when she was willing to entertain. As I said, Ruby was more like a mother than a boss. But if Jesse had not done her part Ruby would have told her about it. Ruby may not have liked it, but she was tolerant of Jesse's excuses, as to why she would not be downstairs in the evenings.

Her Indian blood was very prominent, showing in high cheekbones, and coal-black hair which she wore in long braids during the day. At night she pinned it up and looked very exotic. Her deep-set blue eyes gave her a seductive look while her full lips were more than enticing. Her golden brown skin and long lean legs would have turned any man's head. Once I overheard one of her regular customers say, "Making love to Jesse is somehow different. She has the body of a native queen, and is as mysterious as a deep blue lagoon." She knew this and was very selective in her clientele. She would flirt with the newcomers and watch their response. The men thought they chose her, but it really was the other way around.

As time passed, Jesse and I became fairly good friends. She often shared with me how lucky Maggie had been and how she wished she could start a new life also. Then she would add, "But who would want a half-breed with blue eyes?"

Jesse's mother was a full-blooded Indian and her father was a white man. Her mother was ashamed of Jesse because even with all her Indian looks, dark hair, high cheek bones and firm straight mouth, she had those bright blue eyes. She was not considered part of the tribe because of her "white man's eyes."

Her father was a man she never knew or met. He was one of those visiting Englishmen who saw Jesse's mother, made love to her once and left the next day. Jesse never knew if it was in desire or rape that she had been conceived. Her mother never spoke of her father. It didn't matter much because being a half-breed was painful to her and her mother. I guess she never felt like she belonged anywhere because she was neither white nor Indian. She was not accepted by either race, although when it came to looks, Jesse had the best of both. She had always felt cheated in life, so when Ruby took her off the road and gave her a home, she was thankful. She looked on Ruby as the only true friend she ever had.

So you might say she was ready for plucking, ready to do the picking, when this Texas man came along. He boasted about his ranch, how you could sit on his front porch and every way you looked, as far as you could see, he owned it all. But how could he prove it? To me he seemed almost too eager to get a bride. I just plain didn't trust the man.

Of course I said nothing to Jesse about my doubts. She was right smart and had learned all I could teach her about cooking and taking care of a house. On slow nights she would come into the kitchen and have coffee with me. We'd talk about our past and what we would like to have happen in the future, while she did what we called "seat work" - beautiful bead stringing she had learned as a child in her mother's lodge. I'll never forget the beaded collar and bookmark she made for me. They were treasures I planned to keep forever. They're around here someplace. While she created pretty collars and bracelets, I did the mending.

If she ever married that Texan we at the house never knew but what the heck. One day she packed her trunk, said her good-byes and rode out of town sitting high and proud with Mr. Weber in his fancy buggy. She got her chance. I met up with her later in New Orleans, but that's another story.

Six

Attitudes and Outfits

Now Ruby was down to four girls and me. We really didn't need the money the girls earned in their trade because the garden brought in some, and Ruby was doing well with her investments. Two of the other girls had learned how to earn some cash in an exceptional way: Peaches and Emma were excellent dressmakers. I think I told you earlier about my first morning at Ruby's - how I saw the dressing gown Peaches was wearing. It was beautifully hand-made with special attention to a detailed design. She and Emma had always sewn all of the dresses for the girls, as well as for Ruby and me. I could mend my own clothes, but I was not schooled in design and fancy handwork until I learned from Peaches and Emma. Ma only taught me the basic skills in sewing. The knowledge I learned from those two would serve me well later on in my life.

In fact, it was my fault they got into the seamstress business. You see, I would always wear a special outfit when I went into town - something copied from the newest pictures shown in the most recent catalog or one of those picture cards from Paris, France. When the town's women saw the outfit, they were impressed. Mr. Jed and Maggie wanted to bring the latest fashions to Carson City. Therefore they always stocked their shelves with the finest items for ladies, such as piece goods, gabardine, cotton, and silk when they could get it. Accessories like ribbons, grosgrain and satin, lace, imported and domestic, bonnets of cotton and satin, shiny black and white straw, Sunday-go-to-meeting hats, parasols of every color and fabric, and shoes for all occasions filled half their store. Of course, it was probably Maggie who was most interested in clothes, but Mr. Jed was so proud of her he would have given Maggie anything she wanted if he could arrange to buy it.

At that time most women made their own clothes by hand or on the new treadle sewing machines. However, few women owned those and stitching by hand was time-consuming. Many of the women had their best gowns brought in by the wagon trains which were still coming West, or shipped by railroad from the East. So local dressmakers were in great demand if they were any good at all, and Peaches and Emma were the best.

When the women in town asked me about my clothes and wanted to know if I had purchased them or sown the dresses myself, I told them about Peaches and Emma. Knowing where the girls lived, the ladies were surprised and some even said they would like to have similar fashions, but they wouldn't dare be seen coming to Ruby's house, or leaving there. It just wasn't respectable for a church-going woman to call at such a notorious place. One woman, Mrs. Abernathy, was especially loud until I reminded her how Maggie had changed since she married Mr. Jed. She said that was different. Maggie was married now. But I told her I thought Peaches and Emma deserved a chance too. I also mentioned that the town's women needn't worry about their husbands getting upset, because most of the men in town had visited the house. If not for "pleasure and delight," then for my home cooking! Sometimes I thought these good women sent their husbands to Ruby's just to get them out of the house. Never mind about what happened there. At least, nine months later they weren't having another baby. And how the girls kept from getting pregnant I never knew until I was older.

After talking to Mrs. Abernathy, I shared the problem with Maggie and she came up with a solution. She put up a sign in the store window saying that once a week there would be a dressmaker in the store for fittings who would sew any type of garment a customer wanted. And so Peaches and Emma began their little dressmaking business. They were at the store early every Monday morning sitting, sewing and waiting for any woman customer to appear. When the news circulated, the ladies of Carson City came willingly to look over the catalog pictures, pick fabrics and choose the style of dress they wanted. Even some of the men requested shirts to be sewn by the girls. But they were turned down because Peaches and Emma didn't want any complications. What was so exciting about their sewing was that they could draw, cut and sew their own patterns. As a result, their business grew and soon they had a very large clientele of ladies - and not gentlemen!

Maggie and Mr. Jed finally went to the sheriff and explained what Peaches and Emma were doing in their store and asked for special permission for those two to come in town each morning, so they could fill the demands for their dresses. He agreed for mornings only to be spent in the store under the watchful eyes of Mr. Jed, like Peaches and Emma were some kind of criminals. They were having so much fun creating and sewing pretty things they were not interested in leaving the store anyway!

For Emma and Peaches it was a new way of life, early to bed and early to rise. There wasn't any more time for entertaining at night, which made some of their gentlemen callers mad, so Peaches and Emma moved out of Ruby's House. This turn of events was unusual for any parlor house girl, because most of them ended up in the bordellos, saloons or dead of a disease. But those two were determined to start off clean, so they complied with the town's restrictions - visiting the county doctor, and then the sheriff, who gave them a writ saying they were no longer involved in prostitution. Both were put on probation for one year.

Ruby helped all she could. Through her lawyer the girls were able to buy a little house on the other side of town, and really establish a dressmaking business. Once they experienced this new way of prospering they never again planned to sell their bodies for money. They enjoyed respectability and being in control of their own lives too much. However, like Maggie, they never forgot that Ruby's house had expenses. So each month they gave Ruby some money to pay off the mortgage and to help ease the household expenses. It was their way of saying "thank you."

Of course, they were still approached by gentlemen callers, but they put out the word: if you want to bed one of them, it was only with a wedding ring and a preacher. Eventually both girls did get married, for they were truly lovely mature women.

Peaches looked round all over, plump and warm. She would have made any man a good wife, and she just ached to become a mother. Peaches did not remember her parents at all, so she

was unsure of what kind of mother she would be. As I understand it, her parents died in a fire while she was still an infant.
At the time of the fire, Nellie, a friend of the family, had taken
Peaches for a stroll in her baby carriage. While they were gone
the fire broke out, and burned the wood structure to the
ground. Her parents died in the fire and nothing was saved.
Since there was no known relative, Nellie accepted the responsibility of Peaches' up-bringing. Nellie took Peaches to her home
place—a rather poor dirt farm where Peaches spent her young
years working very hard from sunup to sundown.

It was a tough life because Nellie turned out to be a very
cruel person. She treated Peaches like a slave in every respect.
Peaches often told us about when she got big enough she was
taken to Carson City and dumped. That was when she met up
with Ruby. Ruby was buying goods in the local mercantile
when she spotted Peaches sitting in a corner looking lost and
forlorn. She had walked right over to Peaches and asked her
what was bothering her. Peaches, between tears and sobs had
told her how Hubert and Nellie, the people who had raised
her, had abandoned her in town. Nellie was mad at Peaches at
the time. Peaches had grown into a beauty and Hubert had
been making advances toward her. Peaches didn't like what he
was doing or how he was touching her so she told Nellie. Of
course, Nellie said it was a lie and that she couldn't believe her
beloved husband had an eye for Peaches, and that he was above
touching her in any way. She said Peaches was just trying to
make trouble. And when Nellie confronted her husband he
denied all, that no-good son of a gun. Of course, the wife always wants to believe her husband.

It wasn't long after that when Nellie told Peaches she could
not remain with them anymore. Apparently the next time they
went into town for supplies they planned to leave Peaches in
town alone. Nellie told her she could stay in town and find her

own place to live. She even was so cruel as to suggest that the local house of prostitution would be a good place for her to start looking. She told Peaches she would make a really good whore, since she had so much experience with the local farm boys. This was not true, because up to that time Peaches had not slept with anyone except Hubert and he had forced her. This hurt her a lot and she became confused and really didn't know what to do or where to turn. She knew what Nellie meant, but it had not been her fault that Hubert had kissed her, touched her breasts, and raped her. She said she was afraid to not let Hubert do what he wanted because he always threatened to kill her if she didn't go along with his desires. The worse part was, after he had sex with her, he would blame her and tell her it was all her fault. She was just too young to fight back, and too afraid of loosing the only family she had ever known. And as far as the farm boys, she had not known any of them.

As Ruby got to the truth of the matter she knew Peaches would certainly end up in the wrong place. She figured the girl would mess up her life for sure if she followed the suggestion of Nellie. The house Nellie spoke of had a bad reputation and any young girl who found herself there would end up on the street sooner or later.

So Ruby encouraged Peaches to come with her and live in her house. It was rather funny. Here Ruby was offering Peaches a place to live which was a whorehouse too - but one she saw as a house for homeless girls and not for bad girls. She gently explained to Peaches her home was a bordello, but with the best clientele. Peaches would live in a lovely house, with her own bedroom, enough to eat and beautiful clothes to wear. Peaches liked Ruby instantly and decided she could trust her, besides she had no other place to go. She agreed to live with the other girls and do what she was equipped to do best - entertaining men and giving them what they desired. Ruby told her it was really her choice, but that once she made the choice to be one of the girls, she would be expected to do her job. She'd also be restricted as to where she could go and with whom.

The prospect of living in a clean, well-decorated house, having plenty of food to eat, and pretty clothes to wear was enough to entice any young girl, especially Peaches. She wanted so much to belong. To have a family of sorts was better than no family at all. Being restricted wasn't new to her. She had been treated like a slave all of her young life and anything seemed better to her than the treatment she had been use to. She had never been allowed to go anywhere, had never had a really new dress, and went hungry a good deal of the time. Working hard wasn't new to her either because she had done it from the time she was old enough to remember. She didn't know any other way of life. To be one of Ruby's girls represented a new chance, which was what she wanted most. She was bright and eager to learn and using her body didn't frighten her that much. Ruby's house was like a palace to her. There were much worse places to live.

But now that she realized her sewing ability was worth money, she dreamed of being independent and even maybe finding the right man and being some little person's mother.

She had a steady caller when she lived at Ruby's - a rather humorous man named Charley Wilkins. I believe he was once the postmaster in Carson City, but that was a long time ago so I don't quite remember. In any case, he was one good working man, and he was single - always maintained he was not the marrying kind. When Peaches wouldn't let him call on her in her new house, he was frustrated. He really loved the girl and decided if he couldn't have her any other way, he would have to become a family man.

Finally he made his move, went to Ruby, of all people, and asked for Peaches' hand in marriage. Well, Ruby was all for it, but told him he had better ask the lady herself. If Peaches agreed then it would be fine with her. Ruby said she never felt so respectable in all of her life. She realized that her life was changing too. She had been putting money away for years, and had been investing all she could spare in local properties. In fact, she had grown quite wealthy, and she had to admit she felt almost respectable giving away her girls in wedlock.

Peaches married Charley Wilkins in a little church, with organ music, a preacher, a ring, and all the proper sayings. She was a beautiful bride in the gown she had made with her own hands. The dress was a light peach satin trimmed with lovely peach-colored lace and small seed pearls sown in clusters in the center of each flower of the lace design. Peaches' hair had never looked prettier piled high on her head with small wild flowers tucked here and there. Her cheeks were pink with a healthy glow that would have made anyone jealous. She and Charley made a perfect couple. He was not much taller than Peaches, a rather short man with a trim figure. He was as slim as she was plump. Charley was always jolly, laughing and smiling. He loved telling funny stories and jokes. We were sure their home would be a fun, happy place full of laughter. They had made it quite clear that they both wanted to have children - so they wasted no time.

About two months later Peaches announced she was with child and she truly looked radiant. She never had a sick morning the whole nine months and she ate like a horse through the whole pregnancy. She gave birth to a little boy they named Jamie. He was a charmer. When he was about nine months old he started walking. I remember the first time he walked was when Peaches came visiting to show off her young son. Now, Big Black was still with us and as frisky as a pup. Being older hadn't slowed him down any and he was very patient with the little boy. Jamie learned to walk holding on to Big

Black's long black fur. It was funny to watch. The dog would lower his head and let Jamie pull himself up holding on to his fur. Then he'd move slowly around the room with Jamie hanging on for dear life. When Jamie was taking his nap on a pallet, that strong calm dog would stand over him like it was his duty to stand guard. He would always get as close to Jamie as possible.

Peaches flourished with motherhood and relished her time with Jamie and Charley. I don't think she had ever been any happier. Peaches went on sewing for other people as well as her own family. Her life was pleasant and rather routine.

Emma remained in the cottage dressmaking shop, and began sewing for wealthier people. She refused to sew the plain clothes that Peaches did. She preferred the fancy gowns and capes that the upper class wore in Carson City. Although Peaches had the ability to sew the fancy garments, and often helped Emma with special designs and embroidery work, she still knew the satisfaction of sewing for the less fortunate ladies. Emma was a natural businesswoman and charged a high price for her work. She was a dressmaker out of necessity only, and chose to make money with her abilities.

One day, a man from Sweetwater, Texas named Robert Conley, came to Emma and Peaches' dressmaking shop. He was in town on cattle business and had heard about their little shop, so he brought his mother in for a fitting. When he saw Emma he was struck with cupid's arrow. He couldn't keep his eyes off her, so he made all kinds of excuses to bring his mother back time and time again. His mother was an elderly lady and was worried about her son never finding a wife, so when she saw the interest he was showing Emma she was delighted. His mother shared with Peaches her hope that she would live long enough to see her only son married and then her first grandchild.

Finally, Robert came calling on his own once a week and then almost every night. It was a quick courtship, and an odd one, with Peaches as chaperone, sitting in her quaint little parlor. If Robert or his mother knew of Emma's past involvement, at Ruby's, neither ever said a word. I don't think it would have mattered much anyway. Robert was a type of man who, when he saw something he wanted, didn't wait around too long before he got his desire. He soon asked Emma to marry him because it was becoming a problem for him to spend so much time in Carson City. He raised horses in Sweetwater and wanted to get back to his spread.

Emma planned to leave the city and go with Robert to Sweetwater, but she was not too happy about leaving. Her small wedding took place at Ruby's in the music room, with Laurie playing the piano and Ruby and me standing up for her. Charley, looking like a proud peacock, gave her away. Peaches and Jamie were there, as well as Robert's mother. It was a sweet wedding with vases of wild flowers sitting around here and there lending their fragrance to the warm spring air. Emma wore a conservative, but fancy, dark blue silk dress with a lace jacket over the dress. It was plain, but like Emma, it was elegant - and, of course, the best that money could buy. She was too proud to make her own dress or have Peaches sew it for her, so she sent all the way to New York City for it. I'll be danged if she didn't almost look like she was in mourning.

No preacher for her either. A Justice of the Peace was brought in simply because Emma was too honest and practical to spend a lot of time getting married. But to join the ranks of respectability, she had consented to please Robert - and for his mother's sake. She would just as soon have lived with Robert rather than marry him, but that was not acceptable. So it was a rather quick ceremony with no frills or long speeches.

Now Emma didn't have anything against preachers but she

felt it wasn't in the best interest of a preacher to be in Ruby's house. People still talked about Ruby's like it was a wild and woolly place, but nothing was further from the truth. Sometimes I think the good folks were a bit proud of their "pleasure house," in a strange sort of way. They had seen Maggie, Jesse, Peaches and now Emma take up respectable lives, and I think they felt good about it even if they never let it be known. Robert's mother seemed to not realize who Ruby was and what kind of house she was in. It was almost like she had been there before and didn't care where she was, so long as her son was properly wed.

It was natural for Robert to move into the cottage dressmaking shop with Emma. Peaches and her family had moved to a new farm house that Charley had built just outside of town. Emma took over the little cottage and changed it to look more like a business and less homey which suited her taste.

Robert had a hard time adjusting to married life. When he suggested his mother come to live with them hoping Emma would learn from his mother, and maybe even settle down and have a child, Emma put her foot down. She made it clear she was not a nurse maid for some old lady, nor was she interested in having any brats to raise. Well, poor Mrs. Conley was heart sick because she was so lonely. I think she just grieved herself to death because a year later she passed away.

Robert had planned to take Emma back to his ranch out of Sweetwater, but Ruby knew Emma did not want to leave Carson City. She made Robert and Emma such a good deal they could not refuse - Emma was to take over Ruby's business accounts and Robert was to manage her recently acquired ranch outside of the city. Robert hired a man to take over his ranch in Texas. He brought some of his best stock up from Texas and ran them on Ruby's ranch. She gave him a free hand on running the place. In time he built a livery stable in town and established a good business.

Emma was greatly pleased that she did not have to leave Carson City. She thought the place was going to grow and wanted to be part of it. It was with the business of investments and property management that she helped Ruby. Ruby was a stockholder in one of the bigger mines that opened in North Carson. It was about three miles due north of Carson City, in the hills east of the hot springs. Early on it seemed to show promise of gold and silver, but according to some folks, it was never successful. Ruby never said much about it. She also owned several other pieces of property and needed Emma to manage them for her. She felt she had worked all of her life and now it was time to give someone else a chance - and she trusted Emma. Emma was as natural with figures as she was with a sewing needle, but she was quite different from Peaches. Where Peaches had wanted a good husband, a home of her own and babies— Emma wanted more, much more.

Emma loved working for Ruby and increasing her own bank account as well. You have to remember, this was a time when there were few women in business positions, but Emma had a way about her few men would challenge. She was always talking about the future of Carson City. Little did we know or realize the extent of her dreams.

When she was a child she had heard tales of kings, queens, and princesses, as well as the stories of King Arthur and his court. She was always wishing her prince would come when she was living in Ruby's house. Well, he did come, but Robert was not the prince she had envisioned in her dreams. He was not a strong-willed person when it came to his wife. He tried to give her everything she wanted. In truth, he spoiled her and she would have none of that. When Emma realized she had married a man she could control she lost respect for him and treated him with total disregard.

It wasn't long before she was tearing down the little house and drawing up plans to have a showplace built for all Carson City residents to gawk at. She wanted her place to be fancy, with electricity throughout the whole house just like the St. Charles Hotel. It would be every bit as elegant as the hotel which was located on the corner of Carson and Third Street, not far from Jed and Maggie's mercantile store. As I remember, that was where Jesse's Texan had stayed when he blew into town, and bragged about it being patronized by the most prestigious people in the world, meaning himself of course.

I guess the hotel food was all right, but as far as home cooking went, no place in Carson City was as good as mine at Ruby's. The meals at the hotel cost twenty-five cents each, and the lodging was twenty-five or fifty cents a night. Ruby, Laurie, and Myrna's clients paid handsomely, but of course they were getting a lot more too - if you know what I mean.

Seven

Understanding of Laurie

Only Laurie, Myrna and I were left in Ruby's house besides Ruby. We four rattled around from room to room and almost got lost. I still cleaned and cooked, but it wasn't the same. It just wasn't fun anymore. We missed the big evening parties and all the men going in and out. They still came by for the evening meal, but didn't always stay for any other activity. Most of them came just to eat, sit a spell in the music room listening to Laurie sing and play, and then went home. There was little romping around upstairs, although with Laurie it was business as usual. She still had her regulars. And Myrna, in her quiet way, went on about her business too. Ruby had only one gentlemen caller, a man she had been seeing for years.

By this time, Laurie allowed me to clean and move around

in her room freely. She no longer mistrusted me, but she continued to be a strange, withdrawn person. When she played and sang she always chose the saddest songs and the most woeful ballads I ever heard. It had always been this way, but now that most of the girls were gone her songs were even sadder. Big Black accompanied Laurie with muffled growls and mournful howls as she played and sang. He seemed to sense her moods. He sat next to the piano, and now and then Laurie would smile at him, reach down and pat him lovingly. I suspected her smile was a pasted-on smile, for I am sure she disliked her way of life very much. Four of the girls had their wish to leave Ruby's come true, but Laurie was still there. She never complained, but her unhappiness was quite evident.

I knew she would not like me meddling in her affairs, but I couldn't help myself. She had talent, and I believed she could have sung in any opera house anywhere in the world. I felt I had to help her get out of Ruby's house, so I came up with a plan. Every day I read the local newspaper, especially the society articles. There was this right smart newspaper reporter who lived back East and wrote about high society in New York City. He also wrote about the theater and performers of the day. He talked about Lillian Russell, an up-and-coming singer and actress. It was rumored she would appear at the Bijou Opera House in New York City in the future. I had read about her, with her voluptuous figure, high plumed hats, and flamboyant lifestyle. It was said wealthy men showered her with glittering diamonds. The newspaper articles reported that her lovely voice, peaches-and-cream complexion, and brilliant blue eyes were very attractive. Why they even said she could effortlessly reach high C, with her clear soprano voice. Well, Laurie could do that too, if she only would, but she seemed to want to hide her talent under a basket.

This reporter seemed to know everybody in the theater

and in the upper crust society of New York. If anyone could help Laurie get her start, I figured he would be the one. I asked our local editor how to get in touch with this fellow and he told me to write to his newspaper in New York. So I sat down and wrote him a letter telling all about our Laurie.

Within the year he showed up on our front doorstep. Of course, I had neglected to tell him where we lived because by this time it didn't seem important. When I opened the front door it was to a rather surprised and tired gentlemen. He introduced himself as Mr. William T. Clark. He said he had received my letter and was so tantalized by my glowing report about Laurie he had decided to come to Carson City and meet her for himself. I was shocked to see him, because somehow I didn't really believe he would actually ever come. I asked him in, introduced myself, and talking very quickly explained about the other girls and how some had become respectable citizens. He just grinned at me and chuckled. Then he said he would like to meet Laurie after he had been shown to his room and freshened up a bit. We had not been renting rooms out, but it seemed like a good idea at the time so I said, "Sure, right this way." I picked the least feminine room in the house and helped him get settled. On the way upstairs he commented on my letter and said if Laurie had the kind of singing voice I had described to him, it wouldn't matter what kind of a house she came from.

Well, I was in trouble again with Laurie because I had neglected to mention to her that I had written the letter. She had not been in the best of moods and I wasn't sure how I could tell her about Mr. Clark. She just might not want to leave Carson City or continue with her music career. I meant well, so I decided to tell Ruby and ask her to try to explain what I had done. After telling Ruby we had a special guest in the house, and he had rented a room, I proceeded to tell her about the letter. She just looked at me with amazement. She said she thought it was a good idea and wondered why she hadn't thought of it herself. That was a relief! She told me to go tell Laurie and Myrna we had a special guest in the house and he would be there for our evening meal. They were to dress in their finest gowns and not dilly-dally getting down stairs. I told them, but I didn't volunteer any more information.

If we had just had Mr. William T. Clark coming to dinner it would have been all right, but what made the whole evening awkward was that our regular guests were expected too. A new face at the table wasn't all that unusual, but one from back East brought a lot of attention. Men were eager to hear about what was happening back there and would be full of questions about business transactions.

As our guests filtered in, they sat a spell in the parlor and waited patiently for me to announce dinner. While they waited Laurie invited them to sing along with her and then she sang a special ballad. After she finished I called them to come and eat. Mr. Clark sat at the table between Ruby and Laurie. They were speaking softly and seemed to be planning something. Ruby told me to have Jenny, who had been hired to help me in the kitchen, serve the meal. Jenny was about twelve years old and big for her age. She was very capable and grateful for the chance to learn how to cook and serve a meal, as well as how to clean a kitchen properly. Then Ruby proceeded to tell me to join them at the table. Me sitting at the table, at dinnertime, was highly irregular. I truly felt uncomfortable, but I did as I was told. I sat down by Myrna feeling like a fish out of water. Jenny did an excellent job serving our meal, even pouring the wine, which was the best quality Ruby could buy. This was a special occasion.

I had cooked an extra special meal too. The menu was pot roast, which was smothered in onions, carrots, and potatoes from our garden. Baked yeast rolls and a pie crust peach cob-bler finished off the meal. I wanted to impress this handsome man so I was somewhat worried. I figured if I couldn't get Mr. William T. interested in Laurie's singing, maybe I could get him interested in my cooking, and then somehow in me! He was a real handsome fellow and I figured I was getting old enough to latch onto someone. He looked like a good catch. I was lonely, but my opportunities were few now that most of the girls were gone and we had limited visitors.

Well, I shouldn't have worried about Mr. William T. Clark. He loved my dinner and ate his fill. Ruby opened the conver-sation by asking Mr. Clark who he was and what he did for a living. Being quite a talker he jumped right in and kept the conversation lively throughout most of the dinner. The other gents asked him questions about every aspect of life on the East Coast. You would have thought they were getting ready to move back there the way they talked. Somehow we had to get the conversation off of business and on to the theater. Our guests were really not interested in New York society, but their wives would have been, so they listened. When the topic of the legitimate theatre was mentioned, of course burlesque came up. They wanted to hear about the latest female singers and dancers. Most of them were really only interested in a good meal, a quiet smoke in the music room, and an evening listen-ing to Laurie and Myrna sing.

After a while, Ruby and Myrna got around to the topic I had been expecting - of the theater and show business in gen-eral. Mr. Clark understood what we were getting to, so before we said anything else he looked at Laurie and said, "After hear-ing you sing earlier this evening I am convinced you have the talent I am looking for. Would you do me the honor of singing some of your favorite ballads following dinner?"

Laurie looked at him and then at Ruby. She turned to Myrna

and then to me. "All right, what's going on here? Is there anything you want to say to me? I've been watching all of you this evening and I can tell something is brewing. And the fact that you, Lilly, are in here and not in the kitchen, makes me suspicious. Now out with it. What is going on?"

Ruby laughed and looked at me. "Lilly, tell her what you did and why our special guest is here this evening." The jig was up, so I quickly explained what I had done. To my surprise, Laurie wasn't mad or even upset. In fact, she seemed a little shocked, but pleased.

When dinner was finished I joined them in the music room. Laurie went directly to the piano and she and Myrna sang a duet. Mr. Clark listened to them and it was plain to see he was enchanted. Then Laurie played and sang a song by herself. Not an everyday tune, but a piece of music she had learned in her childhood. I had never heard it before. She sounded like an angel, hitting the high notes with ease and complete control. Mr. Clark sat in stunned silence at first, then stood up and applauded. Laurie sat at the piano watching him and said not a word. He blurted out that Laurie was more talented than he had expected, and more beautiful than he had ever imagined she would be.

That ended my dream. I was out of luck looking to him for a gentleman caller, or for a husband for that matter. However, I really didn't care because I just wanted him to hear Laurie - and so it was. The rest of us might as well have been statues, because he only had eyes for Laurie the rest of the evening. He talked to Myrna, but was too captivated by Laurie to really see Myrna and realize that she also was talented. It wasn't long before Laurie and Mr. Clark's heads were together and he made her a proposal. It was not a proposal of marriage, but one of making a contract with her. She could be, as he said, the "toast of the East or West coasts or even the world!" He wanted to manage her singing career from that moment on. He would represent her and no other, and would leave his position as a reporter. He spoke of introducing her to audiences in New York, perhaps even at the Bijou Opera House. He believed her voice would bring audiences to their feet, wherever she chose to be, but he suggested they first go to San Francisco whereshe could perform before a large audience. Laurie was pleased with the prospect and happy to be leaving Ruby's house. She signed the contract.

Before she left Ruby's, Laurie called me to her room, as a friend. For the first time since I had showed up in Ruby's kitchen, Laurie wanted to talk to me. She began, "Lilly, I owe you an apology. I really never liked you, because I always hated your innocence. I was married once to a man who I thought loved me and I too was innocent. We were married back East and traveled out West with a wagon train, just like you. Along the way I found my husband, in bed with another woman many times, and I hated him for it. I wanted to get back at him any way I could. I will never forget, we stopped in one town because he had lost all of our money and, by now, his self-respect. Out of desperation, I became a dancehall girl. Then one thing led to another and before long I found myself in bed with other men. I wasn't proud about what I was doing, but after a while having intercourse with strangers became easy. At first I cried a lot, but soon I learned to put on a poker face and just imagine I was with my husband. He was a gambler, but not a very skilled one in the game. He often gambled in the saloon below while I was upstairs turning some cowboy inside out. He really didn't seem to care where I was, or what I was doing, as long as he got half of what I was paid. It was a very degrading situation, and I hated it."

Then she paused, looked at me and took a deep breath. "Finally, with a string of good luck, he won enough money, so we left for the West on another wagon train. He spent all his time betting or looking for a card game, while I took on the responsibility of driving the horses and all the other things expected of people going West. I chose not to let anyone know I had been a married prostitute. I was living a lie and in fear that some man would recognize me. Eventually my husband gambled away our horses and wagon, leaving nothing but the clothes on my back and the contents of our wagon, which was precious little, except for my piano. He probably would have gambled that away too, but I told him I would kill him if he touched my piano. He then proceeded to get sick before we reached Colorado and when we arrived in Silverton, he just up and died on me. I was alone with nothing but my piano and my clothes. The reason I would not let anyone touch my piano is that I had hidden several gold pieces inside it for just such a time. That was one reason I always was determined to pack it along. I didn't want to use the coins since they had been a gift from my mother and father on my wedding day.

I went to the wagon master, Ward Morgan, and cried. Being a fairly decent man, he decided to introduce me to Ruby, who at the time, was working in a saloon in Silverton. It was here that Ruby and I started working together. Then when we came to Carson City, I was her first girl and helped her start this house. I'm sorry I made it so hard on you from the first, but now I want to thank you for bringing Mr. William T. Clark here. I promise you'll be proud of me some day, Lilly."

After hearing Laurie's story I didn't know what to say, but it did explain a lot to me. I thanked her and accepted her apology.

Eight

Respectability

The next day Myrna, Ruby and I stood outside the big house and watched as Mr. William T. Clark put Laurie and her trunk in a carriage for the ride into town. Laurie was dressed in a plain but elegant brown walking suit. It came to her ankles so her smart high-top shoes showed, peeking out under her pleated swing-back skirt. The suit jacket had long, rounded, padded sleeves that puffed out toward the shoulder with a small curved collar and cuffs. Her blouse was cream colored with a high ruffled stand-up collar on which she had pinned a delicate gold cameo pin. Her small hat was brown with a quail feather sticking back on one side. The hat sat precisely in the middle of her head and dipped between those expressive eyebrows of hers. She was a handsomely dressed woman and every inch a lady. She wore just the right amount of face paint, which was next to nothing as suggested by Mr. Clark, for she was a natural beauty and needed little to make her more attractive.

I knew in my heart Laurie would be the toast of the country and maybe even the world. I have kept up with her all of these years. After she and Mr. Clark left us there would be a mention of her in the local newspaper now and then. She apparently was a great success wherever she sang. People raved about her beautiful voice and her exquisite figure. There was never any mention of her being at Ruby's, only of her childhood days in the East. I guess Mr. Clark saw to that. Eventually she did appear at the Bijou Opera House in New York. She also played in Europe, and I even heard she was in New Orleans once. My regret is that I never saw her again.

So Laurie was out of Ruby's house and we wished her well, but I already missed her. I started to voice my feelings, but when I looked at Ruby, I knew something was up. Ruby said she didn't tell Laurie what was about to happen because she was afraid Laurie might change her plans. She didn't want Laurie to stay around just for her sake. The big surprise was that Ruby was planning to get married! She had been seeing the local banker for several years, and he decided he wanted to make it legal. I should have suspected, because Ruby had been using less face powder, and lip paint. She had let her natural blonde hair grown in, which had a few streaks of gray in her temples. It was quite becoming. I guess respectability was getting to be a habit around Ruby's house!

Ruby had been proud of all of her girls, but Laurie had been her favorite. Now Laurie was gone and the house was nearly deserted. That last evening we had a few of the gentlemen who had frequented the house for several years drop by. They ate dinner quietly and afterward sat in the parlor sipping their brandy and smoking, but it was not the same as being in

the music room listening to Laurie play and sing. No one said
it at the time, but Ruby's house would soon be a thing of the
past. Finally each man said good-bye, paid his respects, and
left. As Ruby, Myrna and I looked at each other, we knew our
life together was over forever.

That night after the men had gone we three sat for one last
visit in the kitchen sipping our coffee and warm milk. Big
Black lay as usual under the table near our feet. It was Ruby
who brought up the subject of what to do with him. She knew
he meant a great deal to me, but she too had become fond of
him. "Lilly," she began, "you know how I've always felt about
Big Black. I think he's more my dog than yours and I was just
wondering if you would be willing to part with him?" I could
see she couldn't bear to let him go. After all, it was bad enough
saying good-bye to her girls and then to have to give up Big
Black was just too much.

So I answered her. "Well, I don't know Ruby, I think that's
up to Big Black. He's always been happy around here and he's
been fond of you, so I guess he'll be better off wherever you
are.

At first, I was upset, but decided since I did not know where
I was going or where I'd be living, I had better give him up.
Letting go of that big dog was like letting go of a child of
mine. I guess he felt my sadness, because he came right over to
me, licked my hand, and then went back and settled down at
Ruby's feet. It appeared he had already made his choice. I would
miss the old fellow but he never really was mine. In fact, I'm
not sure he was Ruby's either. He had been Jim's puppy, had
grown up on the wagon train trail and when he lost Jim, had
followed me to Ruby's, but I suspect he belonged to nobody.
He was one independent animal. The day I left Ruby's was the
last time I saw Big Black, but I never got over missing him.
Sometimes even now I think I see him flash in front of my eyes

trying to get my attention.

The very next day Ruby put her house up for sale, to be used, as she said, as a school for young ladies or something like that, which made us all chuckle. Before the house sold, Ruby decided to rid it of some of the old furniture, pictures and household items. She held a big auction and it was a sad day for the three of us. Emma, in her fashionable business suit, came walking in like some big tycoon and scooped up many of the better items. Then she was off again with not so much as a word to Myrna or me. It was like she was better than we were and couldn't give us the time of day. She spoke with Ruby, but the way she treated Myrna and me was shameless. After that I didn't care if I ever saw her again. I was puzzled and confused.

Ruby, on the other hand, saw all this as an end to an adventure. She was ready to begin her new life with her banker husband, Melton F. Benson, who was a wealthy old widower. He had been married in his youth and had one son. His young wife had died in childbirth so he had raised the boy by himself. Mr. Benson was older than Ruby, but that didn't matter. He was crazy about her and had been true to her from the first time he came to the house. She had felt the same way about him, but each time he mentioned marriage she only laughed and said it wouldn't be proper, besides, she had a business to run. He had tried to convince her to give up the house and marry him, but she said she felt responsible for each of her girls and would not think of leaving them. Finally, he just gave up and never mentioned marriage again. However, when the girls were turning respectable he decided to ask her once more to be his wife, and to his surprise and delight she agreed!

When the house was empty of most of its furnishings, Ruby had the Justice of the Peace come and officiate at her wedding. It was a small gathering in the parlor. The invited guests were

Maggie and Mr. Jed, Peaches, Charley and their young son
Jamie, Myrna and me, and Emma and Robert, who came strut-
ting in like they owned the place. The Justice of the Peace had
brought his wife along to sing. As I recall, it wasn't very good.
I remember I couldn't help thinking how wonderful it would
have been if Laurie had been singing instead of that old crow.
All I wanted to do was cry. Without Laurie's piano there wasn't
any music to accompany Mrs. Roseabell or whatever her name
was, but it was such a short ceremony it didn't really matter.
Ruby just wanted to get it over with and get on with her life.

We were happy for Ruby and Mr. Benson, but we were not
sure what was going to happen to us. Ruby had been our secu-
rity too long. Before the wedding, Ruby had moved her bedroom furniture and Laurie's piano into Mr. Benson's beautiful
two-story house, on one of the most prestigious streets in town.
It all happened so quickly that Myrna and I could hardly catch
our breath. After the ceremony we had a small gathering in the
kitchen to celebrate. A lot of toasts to the bride and groom
were made, and a good meal was shared before Ruby and Mr.
Benson left. My kitchen was still in good working order and
the long table had not been moved. We decided to leave all the
kitchen things for the new owners.

When the festivities ended, Myrna and I stood on the gracious front porch, which now had flowers growing everywhere.
Morning-glories and honeysuckle vines twined around the
porch columns and out on the front fence. There were several
vases of flowers sitting on little tables here and there on the
porch. Myrna and I watched as Mr. and Mrs. Benson drove
off in his fine carriage headed toward the train station. Their
plan was to go back East for a month of fun, shopping, and
sight-seeing. All was arranged. Emma would take care of the
sale of the house as well as Ruby's business holdings, and Myrna
and I would remain there until it was sold and the new owners

arrived.

Big Black would stay with Peaches and Charley. They decided he would be a great playmate for Jamie. I agreed, but not until we actually pulled out. I wanted Big Black to stay with us, because the house felt so empty. He was getting older and he needed a family to love him. We knew he would truly be happy with Charley's family until Ruby returned. And so it was that Myrna and I found ourselves alone in Ruby's house, with only Big Black to keep us company. So much happened in those years at the house — good events and bad ones — but there are later stories yet to be told.

Nine

Death Is So Final

I had experienced seeing death before - Ma in the terrible flood, and Pa in the dead of night, which I didn't really see. I did remember seeing countless small animals on our farm die, but nothing prepared me for what was about to take place.

Peaches and Charley had a happy marriage and a pleasant life with little Jamie, but it didn't last. As I recall, this is what happened. It was about seven o'clock in the morning, a few days after Ruby's wedding. Myrna and I were in the kitchen getting our cups of coffee when Peaches came flying in the back door screaming at the top of her lungs. She looked wild with pain and grief. She kept yelling our names even though we were standing in plain sight. I think she was in some kind of shock. She was a mess, with her hair falling down around her face in matted ringlets, as sweat ran down the sides of her head and neck. Her eyes were filled with fear like that of an animal caught in a trap. She was trembling and was as white as a snow-capped mountain.

I grabbed her by the shoulders and gently shook her as Myrna pulled up a kitchen chair for her to sit on. At first, I thought Peaches was going to faint on us. However, by then she was crying convulsively and her words seemed to be stuck in her throat. Finally she got hold of herself well enough to blurt out. "Jamie! It's Jamie, he's sick! He's got the fever! This is the third day! The doctor came, but Jamie isn't getting any better. Oh, Myrna, Lilly, what can we do? We've done all we know how. Charley is with Jamie now. Please come. We need you. We need you badly!"

Saying this, Peaches jumped up, ran out the door, and across the fields to her house. It would have been easier to have taken the buggy, but Peaches was nearly out of her mind, and not thinking properly, just ran. We could see her racing across open spaces with her skirt flying at her heels. Not to be left behind, we joined in the race - Myrna in her red silk robe, bloomers and chemise, with her red hair streaming out and glistening in the morning sun. She was as barefoot as the day she was born. If her feet hurt, you couldn't tell it. She ran like a jackrabbit, side-stepping any rock or protruding stick in her path. She ran more like an Indian than a parlor house girl.

I kept my eyes on Peaches and followed close on Myrna's heels. I was fully dressed, as usual, in an everyday long blue jumper that was belted at the waist, and a long-sleeved white blouse with a white petticoat and drawers underneath. In my high top shoes I ran with unsteady leaps and bounds, my skirt and petticoat getting in my way. Finally I reached down between my legs and pulled up my skirts and tucked them in my belt. I am sure it was a strange sight, three crazy women racing across the fields with Big Black in hot pursuit. He was yapping at our heels because he could feel our fear. He didn't know what was happening, so he kept racing up and down and around us enjoying the chase, but I'm sure he was puzzled at our break-neck pace.

As I ran I thought of Jamie and how Big Black loved that little boy and how patient he had been when Jamie was learning to walk holding on to his fur. Jamie just couldn't be that sick, and if he were he would get well. I just knew it!

We finally cleared the last fence and crossed the road to Peaches and Charley's house - three frantic figures entered the door calling for Charley. We found him sitting in the bedroom near their large wooden four-poster bed. Jamie was lying in the middle of the bed looking very small and helpless. His cheeks were flushed a bright pink, almost red. He was drenched with sweat and kept mumbling. His small body turned from side to side. His eyes closed. When we came into the room he seemed to know we were there, because for an instant he opened his bloodshot eyes, and then they rolled to the back of his head. It was frightening. I thought he was dead. As I looked at him I remembered the Jamie we all knew and loved. He was the little boy who had won our hearts. All of us had been there to share his first steps, and watch him learn to drink from a cup and feed himself. He was like Peaches, cheerful, inquisitive, alert and full of energy. We had watched him and Big Black romp in the parlor of Ruby's house. That child was the joy of all of our lives, and now he was very sick, if not dead.

I stood there dumfounded. Charley looked at us with questioning, red-rimmed eyes, lined face, and rumpled clothes which looked like he had slept in them for a week. He looked totally whipped. Peaches was hysterical as she knelt at Jamie's bedside. She began praying with fervor for she was desperate, the words tumbling out of her mouth. "Oh, Lord, save my baby. Don't take him from us. He's all we've got! We need him, Lord. Please, Lord, I'll do anything. Please forgive me my sins. I'm the one you should take, not this precious, innocent little boy. Oh, God, what can we do? Help us Lord!" As she prayed her words rose and fell in the quiet room, and we all knelt beside her feeling her pain and sorrow.

At one time Peaches had told me that she saw Jamie as a gift from God, showing His forgiveness for her past. All her hopes and dreams rested in her son. She said if Jamie ever died it would mean that God had not forgiven her and she would not be able to bear it. I wondered if this was the time of testing?

Myrna got up from her knees, took a good look at the situation and began giving orders. She sent Charley out to fetch cold water from the well and Peaches to the kitchen to make us a pot of strong coffee. Then she turned to me and asked me to help her uncover Jamie. After we removed the patchwork quilt we took off his sleep shirt. When Charley arrived with the buckets of cold water we soaked the bed sheets, rung them out and then gently wrapped Jamie's frail body in an attempt to lower his fever. He shivered and trembled but didn't open his eyes again.

As soon as the sheets warmed and Charley had returned with more buckets of cold water we repeated the treatment. Finally Myrna stopped and told Charley he had better go get the doctor and the preacher. Myrna was beside herself with grief and frustration because we could not get Jamie's fever to come down. It never did break. At long last, Jamie opened his eyes, looked around the room and when he spotted his mother he reached out to her. She was standing near the bed clutching her hands in prayer. He looked up and reached his little pale arms toward her. Then just as she reached for him he spoke his last word, "Mama."

To our shock his eyes became blank and his arms fell silently on the bed. Just as he died his daddy, the doctor and the preacher came rushing into the room. The doctor moved toward the bed, leaned over Jamie, and placed his ear over the boy's mouth and nose. Hearing nothing, he gently closed Jamie's bright blue eyes with his fingertips. Peaches screamed and Charley grabbed her by the waist and held her tightly, as they both almost fell over the bed and the body of their little son. It was one of the saddest sights I have ever seen. I know it was truly one of the worst days of my life.

I didn't know what to do. I looked at Myrna and saw her bite her lower lip until blood appeared. She mumbled something about if there was a God, where was he now when we needed him. Abruptly she turned and ran out of the room through the front door and retraced our steps to Ruby's. I remained with Peaches and Charley. The doctor said how sorry he was and left, but the preacher stayed and prayed with us. His prayer touched my soul. He spoke of heaven and that we would meet Jamie again someday.

Soon the neighbors became aware of what had happened, and were coming in the house asking what they could do to help. One neighbor said we needed to get Jamie bathed and prepared for the undertaker, who would come and get his body. I agreed, but since I had never done that I admit I was scared. I had never touched a dead body, and really didn't want to touch the lifeless body of that little boy. Peaches stopped crying and came to grips with what had happened. She knew it was no one's fault, Jamie had died of a childhood illness, so she took over washing her son for the last time. I watched her as she gave her son back to God, all the while singing a sweet melody. She was not bitter. She believed she would see her son again in heaven.

The undertaker, Carl Sanders, arrived and took the little

body away. He was a skilled carpenter and promised to put him in a special casket. True to his word he came the next morning with Jamie in a beautiful hand-crafted casket, which looked very much like a large treasure chest. It was made of pinewood, sanded, stained and rubbed with wax. He was laid out in his overalls, and a blue cotton shirt. He didn't have any shoes on his feet, because Peaches wanted him to be free in death like he had been in life. He never wore shoes and complained loudly when he was told to do so.

The casket sat for three days in the parlor of Ruby's house. We would not have had it any other way. It didn't seem to matter what the house had once been, because all of the town's people came to pay their respects anyway. On the fourth day we buried Jamie in the cemetery, on a sloping hill overlooking the town. There were a few small trees and some grass here and there, with several well-tended graves near by. As the preacher spoke, I felt my heart would break. He told about how Jamie and his dad would come to town to get peppermint sticks at Maggie's and Jed's store, how he laughed all the time, and how he started talking when he was just a wee little thing. He remembered the many times he had seen the boy come by the church hanging on to Big Black. Hearing all of this was almost more than a body could stand. When we stood over his grave and sang "In the Sweet By-and-By," the words got stuck in my throat and I couldn't finish the hymn.

We didn't know where to reach Laurie and Mr. Clark, or Jesse and her cattle Baron, Mr. Weber, so they didn't know that Peaches and Charley had lost their son. We tried to send word to Ruby, but somehow she never received our message. She would learn of it when she returned from her trip.

Maggie and Mr. Jed were there with their baby boy, Tillsey, who slept cradled in Maggie's arms. Emma and Robert came and stood with us, Emma in her elegant black silk dress with parasol to match, and the latest black leather high-top button shoes. Robert looked ill at ease in his black store-bought suit and black cowboy hat. I have never seen a man cry so hard before or since. He had remarked several times that he would like to have a son or a daughter, but Emma was just too busy to raise a family. I thought, (and too selfish too!) I guess when Jamie died; it was like Robert had lost his own son, for he had spent a good deal of time with the boy. The man was plain heartbroken.

There was a slight breeze whispering our good-byes as we lowered Jamie's casket into the cold ground. Peaches was the first to throw a handful of dirt over her son's casket. Then each of us in turn picked up a handful of dirt and tossed it into the grave. When it was over we slowly made our way out of the cemetery. Peaches and Charley remained behind kneeling at the grave as the last of the dirt was pitched in. I stopped, turned around and saw Peaches looking toward heaven saying a silent prayer. At that moment I realized she would be just fine. She and Charley were still young and they would have more babies. What must it be like to have a child and then lose it? It was more than I could understand.

After the funeral Myrna and I returned to Ruby's. Both of us felt an even greater desire to leave Carson City and our old way of life in the house. It was time to move on.

Ten

What Path Will They Follow?

yrna and I decided we had better go some place where we could make a living. I wasn't sure I wanted to find employment as a cook or a housekeeper, but if I could find nothing else, I would do it. Myrna told me she had made up her mind not to get horizontal for any man again. When she was working at Ruby's she had called as little attention to herself as possible and entertained quietly upstairs when required. Myrna was a good singer, not like Laurie, but in her own different way. She was a fantastic dancer and a serious actress. She had a secret dream that none of the girls or Ruby ever knew. She truly wanted to join a company and become a legitimate actress on the stage. When she shared this with me I was not surprised, because I had often caught her dancing around in her room and reciting lines from plays.

One of her favorite plays, "The Two Orphans," by Eugene Corman and Adolphe Philippe D'Ennery, she knew by heart. As I recall, the story is about two young sisters, who journeyed to Paris to find a doctor to cure the younger girl, Louise, who was blind. Henriette, the oldest was taken off by Antoine who pretended to be their guardian. When Henriette shrinks from him, he stifles her. She cries and he carries her off, leaving Louise helpless. Louise is taken away by beggars and made to sing in front of a church, as an object of pity to get money from the parishioners. Louise is miserable. In the end, all is well. Both sisters are saved from the villain, and the doctor heals Louise of her blindness. The Countess admits that Louise is her child. Pierre, the hero, saves them from the villain, and the rest is in the hands of heaven! A true melodrama.

I would sit on Myrna's bed as she recited the part of Henriette, and applaud loudly when she was finished. She was really a convincing actress. This frustrated young woman, in the past always seemed to feel that Laurie was the one who should be noticed. Many times Myrna would hang back when Laurie was singing and playing her piano. It was apparent she was trying to give Laurie center stage. Laurie, on the other hand, never recognized Myrna as talented or near her equal. I'm sure Laurie's only thought was of herself. When she sang she was aloof. But when Myrna sang she looked right at you, making you believe she was singing only to you and for you. There was no pretense in her. She laughed easily and often, yet I sensed a deep sadness inside her, a part of her life she did not wish to share.

I believe the reason she was always smiling is because she had a mouth full of pretty white teeth and liked to show them off. Her hair was natural auburn with red highlights, and her eyes were sparkling green. That spoke of her Irish background.

When Ruby found Myrna she was working in one of the local saloons. She didn't respond when Ruby asked her to join her house, but eventually she came around seeking employment. Ruby knew little of her past and that is the way Myrna wanted it. She never asked questions of others and never gave any information about herself.

I guess since we were going out on our own she felt the need to confide in me about her young life, when she had been jerked around by her stage mother. Her father, who was a drunk, had been a reasonably good actor. He had traveled all over the country in his youth doing bit parts in plays at the local opera houses, and had played the big time in New York. Because of his drinking he had been fired from most of his jobs, so eventually he tried his luck at gold mining in Alaska. When his mine played out he gave it up, saying the work was too hard and that he was ill-suited for mining. That is when he joined a troupe of actors in Fairbanks and began following the troupe wherever they went. It was in Alaska that he met and married Myrna's mother, and it was there that Myrna was born. Her mother, Jose, followed her actor husband by wagon train, stagecoach, and the new railroad for several years. They ended up in Carson City. He believed he could get a new start on the stage there, and then go back East to resume his acting career in New York.

But it never happened. He was killed while drunk, trying to cross the street. It was a busy time of day when he stepped out from behind a carriage and staggered right into the path of a racing fire wagon. He was knocked down, and dragged for quite a ways. When they got to him, they found him dead. Guess he never knew what hit him. Jose was now destitute and at the mercy of the community. But the town didn't have much use for drunken actors, or their wives and children for that matter. She didn't receive any help from the town's people, so she hung around the theatre, hoping to get a bit part for herself or trying to push Myrna into some singing and dancing role on the stage. That action didn't last a year, because her mother started hitting the bottle pretty hard. Finally in desperation she took Myrna to an orphanage run by the church, and left her. The last time Myrna remembered seeing her mother was the day she told her to be good, stay with the sisters, and she would come back and get her someday. She was barely thirteen when this happened. Year after year Myrna waited for her mother to return but she never did. When she was sixteen, the priest put her into service with a large family who practically starved her to death, and treated her like a slave.

When she got her fill she ran away with only the clothes on her back. She didn't know what to do or where to go. After sleeping in a barn one night, she was surprised to meet a young man and woman who were also sleeping in the barn. They were with a troupe of actors playing in Carson City, so they invited her to come and join them. She had a little experience in the theatre, but that was when she was a child. Hoping to secure employment with the troupe, she told them that her parents had once been great actors, but had fallen on bad times and had been killed in a riverboat accident on the Mississippi.

The stage manager saw right through her story and told her to get lost. She walked around the city and finally made her way to one of the local saloons, where she offered to sing and dance for a room and something to eat. She was just the kind of girl the owner liked - young, pretty, innocent and talented. He gave her a place to sleep and all the food she could eat. He dressed her up in a fancy costume, gave her some sheet music, and put her on the stage.

Her first appearance was in front of rough cowboys who gawked at her like she was a piece of meat. She said she was so frightened she almost wet her pants. But she was a tough little gal and didn't let that bunch of bad-mannered men get the best of her. She sang an Irish ballad like an angel and the cowboys were almost shedding tears before she was through. The owner of the saloon liked what he saw and heard, so he hired her. Once the word got out that they had a new Irish gal singing ballads at the saloon, she packed them in. Her red hair, green eyes, and beautiful white teeth didn't do any harm either. All was going pretty good for her, until one night Billy Jack, a rather rich young man and somewhat of a bully, saw her performing and laid his claim on her. He let it be known no man had better talk to her, much less touch her. Myrna became his personal property whether she liked it or not.

The sad part was the way Billy Jack treated her. Myrna was fond of him, but at the same time she hated his guts. He smothered her with trinkets and fancy clothes, making her feel obligated to him. But he demanded her services upstairs like any other prostitute, and let her know she had better not refuse him or let any other man in her bed. He beat her up more than once, and told her if she didn't do what he wanted he would get her thrown out on the streets. Billy Jack was a tall, lean, hard-muscled man who always wore fancy suits and a smirk on his face. He was handsome in a strange way, but he was unreasonable. It was common knowledge that he kicked Myrna around, but no one lifted a finger to help her. All the men were afraid of Billy Jack and his wild pals.

Working in a saloon and living under Billy Jack's thumb was not the life Myrna would have chosen, but it was better than sleeping on the street or in a hay loft. Billy Jack was a regular gambler and a heavy drinker, so he was in the saloon almost every evening. Being a loud talker he could be heard bragging about his silver mine. He spent a lot of evenings making big deals, because he did have another passion, and that was constructing homes and buildings. He talked about his dreams of getting rich in the construction business. Then, like so many men of the time, just when things were looking good, the bottom fell out of the economy and there were a lot of unemployed people in Nevada. His silver mine played out and there was little need for new homes or buildings. Lots of folks just packed up and moved on.

The only good thing about Billy Jack is that he was a one-woman man. No matter how bad he treated Myrna he stayed clear of the other girls. He was determined to break Myrna's spirit, thinking that if he controlled her, he would own her. Wrong! One day he was mean as hell to her and the next, as sweet as honey. The more he tried to dominate Myrna the harder she fought him. The black eyes were bad enough, but when he nearly knocked her pretty white teeth out of her head, that was the last straw. She knew then she had to leave him or he would kill her someday.

She sent word to Ruby telling her she was in bad trouble, and needed her help. When Ruby got the message she went to that saloon real fast. She just told Myrna to get her things and get in the carriage. As usual, she said she would take care of everything. Whatever Ruby said to the barkeep, Myrna never knew. But she heard a lot of yelling and language that would have scorched the wings off a dove. When Billy Jack found out she was gone he was furious and swore an oath to close Ruby's house down. He probably would have if he had lived. It was a stroke of luck that he had an accident.

After the price of silver dropped, Billy Jack had to let some of the workman in his mines and in his construction business go. This caused him to do more of the work himself. He was constantly going out alone, working on a project or just looking over the job. Being a hard man to work for, he had few friends and a lot of enemies. One day during a heavy rainstorm, he went out to one of the building sites - and that is where they found his body. Apparently he had fallen and hit his head because he had a nasty gash on the back of his skull. It was considered an accident, but some people said one of his own men had killed him over some back wages. That was never proven. Some of his bully pals tried to find the man who did it, but since there was nothing in it for them they soon went on to greener pastures. If Billy Jack was murdered, no one was ever charged.

It was a terrible thing and it nearly drove Myrna crazy. I guess, in some strange way she really loved that man. It was a love-hate affair. She worried about him being killed and yet, was relieved that she would never have to see him again. She admitted it was a good thing she was with Ruby. Anything was better than working in a saloon. The dancing and singing had been all right, but cleaning spittoons and dumping stale beer mugs wasn't any fun. Using her body didn't bother her, for she certainly had done it before, and not for money. At least, this way she would not be at the mercy of Murphy, the saloon owner. At Ruby's she had the chance of sleeping with decent gents, and being treated well to boot. To have her own bed-room was pleasing to her, and eating good food at a proper table appealed to her.

She loved pretty clothes and jewelry. Her father had given her several good pieces that she had carried around for years, expensive stuff with real gemstones like rubies and diamonds. Nothing she owned was cheap. She kept it hidden, figuring that it might come in handy some day. She wouldn't wear any of the ugly stuff, as she called it, so she wore very little. I did not know this until we were ready to leave Ruby's. I never did understand why a woman would not wear the real thing if she had it.

She said the real reason she went to live and work in Ruby's was because she had something in common with the other young women. She knew there was safety in numbers and Ruby's house had a good reputation for attracting the best clientele in the state of Nevada.

Another thing about Myrna is that she liked her sherry. I never saw her drunk, but sometimes during the early morning hours I was aware of her coming downstairs and sipping a glass of her favorite wine on occasion. Ruby wouldn't have liked it, but I kept my mouth shut, because it wasn't any of my business. Myrna indulged in the sherry and Laurie liked her brandy. So what?

Myrna and I had saved a little money over the years working for Ruby, so the prospect of having no place to live and no job didn't bother us too much. Ruby had been generous. We could have lived very comfortably for a year or more on what we had saved, but we needed to be busy. I decided to go with Myrna wherever she went, and if she joined a troupe I would too, even though my acting ability was certainly limited. I knew Myrna would head for a high- class establishment that provided entertainment as well as good food. I figured I might even be able to take a job doing wardrobe for the actors and actresses. I certainly was skilled enough to be a seamstress. I could even sing if I got the chance. We found I had a fairly decent voice, and I knew a number of old tunes my mother had sung to me when I was a child. They weren't exactly theater songs, but I knew I could learn new ones. I had paid attention when the girls entertained in the parlor and had practiced with Laurie when she had been in a good mood, so I had some training of sorts. Now when I think about it, I was fairly good. I just needed a little courage to sing alone in front of people.

We made our plans, packed our trunks, said our goodbyes, and took the train out of town.

Eleven

Sudden Death

*O*ur plan was to end up in Cripple Creek, Colorado. We wanted to go where all the fuss was being made over gold mining. We reasoned where there was gold, there were hotels - and where there were hotels, there were opera houses and even saloon owners who hired singers and dancers. And besides, we figured where there was gold there would be plenty of men who didn't mind being separated from their riches by a good looking girl.

Since Myrna had decided to try working in a respectable establishment, she only considered seeking employment at the opera house or one of the better gambling houses. If things got bad she said she could always go back to her old trade, but she would rather become a respected actress. I would look for a singing job or whatever came along just hoping I would succeed, because I was alone in the world and so was she. I needed Myrna and she needed me.

When we finally arrived in Cripple Creek we did indeed join a group of actors who played the circuit: Cripple Creek, Colorado, Calico, and that far-away city of San Francisco. Those were hard trips which wore us out, but the fun and excitement of it kept us going. We took all types of transportation, stage-coach, buckboards with farmers, wagon trains where people were still headed West - and finally even the railroad.

We weren't a wonderful troupe of actors, but we were good enough for the small opera houses and beer gardens. Myrna and I did make a living and that was what counted. And we didn't have to do it lying on our backs. I loved being able to entertain and not have to spend my time cleaning and cook-ing. I soon began to get more singing roles and some bit parts with other performers. I found doing routines was fun, espe-cially comedy. It became quite clear I had the ability to make people laugh. Goodness knows I had enough material to draw from. Mostly, I talked about funny things that happened while living in Ruby's house. Of course, I never mentioned where the house was or who owned it or that I had been part of it.

It was in Cripple Creek that I met Gerald LaBraun, known as Gary to his friends. He was quite a musician. He played the piano better than anyone I'd ever met, even better than Laurie. We had a great time together traveling with the troupe. He taught me a lot about singing and how to please an audience. In fact, he helped me get my start with the company, but I really never got over being afraid of singing alone. While I played around in the chorus line of dancers and in the sketches, Myrna excelled in the dramatic roles and singing parts. The ballads of the day were well suited to her voice; "In the Evening By the Moonlight", "After the Ball," and "She's Only a Bird In A Gilded Cage." With songs like these she began to realize her potential.

Gary and I spent many evenings after the show or during the late afternoon going over music which had been sent to him from back East and even from Europe. He played that high-class music so well we often pretended we were in the great opera houses of Europe. I would sing like a bird and he would play like a master. In front of him I had little fear and was always a performer. He always planned on going to Europe, but was never able to save enough money to get there. He enjoyed his drinking and playing poker too much, so most of the time his money was gone before he earned it.

As we three traveled with the theatrical troupe we gradually left the dingy hotels and moved up to more respectable places. We acted, played, sang and danced our way through many shows. Some theaters were better than others, and sometimes they were no better than tents pitched in the middle of town. We were well aware of other troupes visiting most of the larger cities throughout the country and here in the West. We heard of Sarah Bernhardt, that great French actress who toured most of the United States. Her appearances in "Camille" were outstanding. It was said she always left her audiences in tears after a performance. How Myrna wished she could make a name for herself. She talked endlessly to me about Miss Bernhardt, and wished desperately to see her.

One time her wish almost came true. We were booked into Maguire's Opera House in San Francisco. Miss Bernhardt had been there the week before. As I say, we were a small company and used to fill in between the famous visiting stars. A little taste of the big time thrilled us all, and Myrna was very excited. It was from one extreme to the other - great opera houses to beer gardens. But we were performers and never turned down any work. Finally, the troupe burned out and disbanded.

When this happened, we decided to settle in Cripple Creek,

Colorado and get steady jobs. Myrna had accepted the fact she was never going to make it big, so when we arrived in Cripple Creek we took the first jobs available - as maids in a hotel and entertainers in the hotel theatre. We cleaned rooms in the morning and rehearsed our numbers in the afternoon for the evening performance. It was an easier life and I would have enjoyed it more, but for what happened to Myrna. I am not sure why, but she was often late and sometimes did not show up for rehearsals at all. I really never knew where she was, but I suspected she was sleeping around or maybe drinking more than she should. I was even aware of a bottle of laudanum she carried around, saying she used it for headaches. I worried about her for fear she would end up like her parents. Anyway, it was her life and what she chose to do with it was her business and certainly not mine. But somehow I felt responsible for her and I was very fond of her.

Just how much I loved her became evident one night when we were performing in a show with a large cast of characters, singers, and dancers. We were decked out in our fanciest costumes. I wore a bright blue ruffled dress to my knees with several short petticoats underneath. It was low cut revealing my bare shoulders. We all wore black stockings and black hightop button shoes. Myrna had on a bright red dress with ruffles around the skirt and also off the shoulders. She had added a crazy feather plume stuck in the back of her hair, which bounced when she walked in her saucy way. I remember seeing her walk past me several times, flashing her beautiful smile and showing off her pretty white teeth. She was a tease and loved to work a crowd.

It was a rowdy bunch we had that evening. She talked and flirted with each man present and they loved it. This was not unusual, because to calm the audience several of us often went out, talked, told jokes and tried to get their attention before the show began.

As usual, I was nervous, because it was my time to sing a solo. I was trying to get myself ready with deep breaths and thinking of the words to the song. I had just taken my place on the stage and Gary had played the first few bars of my song, when I heard a commotion down in front of the stage. One rather giant of a cowboy was unwilling to be quiet. He was throwing his weight around, cussing and kicking up a fuss. Full of liquor, he was raring to go! This made Myrna mad, because she knew how hard it was for me to sing alone anyway. She sidled up to him with her sweet talk and pretty smile, trying to calm him down. It didn't work. The more she talked to him the louder and more belligerent he became. I continued to sing while watching what was going on. I think I messed up on the lyrics but Gary just played on like everything was normal.

Myrna walked away from the man the first time and then I guess she really got angry. She went over to him a second time and asked him to sit down and be quiet. Finally she pushed him down into a chair. He was so drunk he went into a wild rage. He jumped up and threw her over one of the tables and began choking her to death, right there in front of everybody. Before anyone realized what was happening Myrna was dead. I don't think he planned to kill her, but she was no match for such a powerful man. I grabbed my own throat and ran down the side steps of the stage to get to her side. I tried to pull the drunken cowboy off of her. I jumped on his back and yelled for help. Nobody moved. I think they were all shocked at what was happening.

As I held onto his back, I was beating him with both of my clinched fists, and he was trying to fight me off. Pretty soon he knocked me to the floor where I fell with a mighty thud. My mouth felt like I had been kicked by a mule, but the truth was that I had a broken jaw. After awhile, the cowboy was dragged off to jail by several men sitting near by. They had witnessed the murder and assured me the cowboy would hang for what he had done.

I managed to stand up, with blood running down my chin while I held my jaw with my hands. My mouth was cut and my teeth felt like they would fall out. My head throbbed and I shook all over as I looked in disbelief at my dear friend Myrna. I wanted to scream and never stop, but I could not control my mouth. At that moment, I hated the theatre and all the men and sleazy women who were there. My heart broke, seeing Myrna lying so still and dead. I knew how unhappy my Ma would have been to see me at that moment. I was ashamed. I had the crazy notion that Myrna's death was my fault, because she was trying to keep that cowboy quiet while I sang. I vowed then that I would never sing again and I never have.

Twelve

Recovery and Marriage

Gary did everything he could to help me during my recovery, but nothing soothed me, because I felt so guilty about Myrna's death. I continued to repeat my damnable vow many times. Looking back at Myrna's death, I knew it was not my fault, but I could not get over the pain I was suffering. That night after the men took her murderer away I passed out and was unconscious for several days. One minute I was lying on the theatre floor in a pool of blood, and the next I was in the local doctor's office down the street. It was all like a bad dream. The doctor did what he could to set my jaw, leaving a small opening so that liquids and mashed food could be spooned into my mouth, then he sent me home.

Home was a small hotel room from which I would soon be

evicted if I could not pay the rent. Well, Gary took care of everything, He was very attentive, but since he was younger I didn't see him as anything, but a good friend. Certainly he was not a sweetheart. He continued playing the piano at the hotel, but soon tired of Cripple Creek and moved on. When he said goodbye, he told me he was leaving me in good hands. Derrick Coleman, Gary's friend, was a man who worked as a card dealer in the hotel. Derrick was extremely handsome, a fast talker, and always on his feet except when he was playing cards. He was the nervous type. He talked a lot about going back East, and said he wanted to see the great Mississippi, and even go to the wide-open port of New Orleans. He imagined himself as a riverboat gambler. I had to agree - he was definitely that kind of man.

As we visited each day, he told me he had heard there was plenty of work on the paddle-wheelers for good card dealers, and he was one of the best. I'll say one thing for him he sure wasn't a modest man. He began talking about taking me with him. It was easy for me to imagine since I was sick of the West and all it stood for. All the promises and hopes I carried with me as a child now had faded away.

I didn't have much money, but I did have Myrna's jewelry well hidden in my trunk. I sold some of the better pieces and got enough money to buy a few clothes and a ticket on the train. You'd think that by now I'd have learned something about men, but I was still naïve and had never been bedded. I was eager for that experience. I wanted to find a man who would marry me and raise a bunch of children. I guess Derrick appeared at the right time, because I saw him as my prince in shining armor. I was blind to his faults.

We took the train as far as we could go east, but true to most card dealers Derrick played in the smoker on the train and lost most of his winnings. When he was out of funds he dipped into mine, and because I trusted him to pay me back when his luck changed I gladly loaned him the money. We were young. I was nineteen and Derrick over twenty. I believed his luck would soon change - but it was a big mistake.

After many months, we arrived in New Orleans in the year 1884. It was one of the largest cities in the country, with a population of over 116,000. The excitement of the city was beyond my belief. Trade was the city's lifeblood. Large clumsy barges and steamboats paddled down the Mississippi to New Orleans carrying the goods of mid-America. Some years back in 1859 the city had had a siege of yellow fever, malaria, and cholera. This was when over seven thousand people died of these diseases.

In 1877, after the Civil War with reconstruction there was a complete recovery of the city. A Mr. James B. Eads designed a series of jetties to prevent sand and silt from blocking the mouth of the Mississippi. These jetties made it possible for large ocean-going steamships to dock at New Orleans, so the excitement of the city was never-ending.

We watched the massive sailing ships take on cargoes and sail off across the oceans. New Orleans was truly the Paris of America. Now it was 1884 and the city was the host of the Cotton Centennial Exposition, a big world's fair. Derrick and I were full of wonder and excitement at being there. We spent a lot of time in Jackson Square, the heart of the French Quarter. I often said my prayers in the tall, gray-spiral Cathedral of St. Louis, built way back in 1794. It was not like the small church my family attended when I was a child but it felt more like a church to me than any place I had ever been.

I loved strolling along Canal Street shopping and enjoying the view. It was fun observing the people coming and going. Many of those I saw were descendants of the original French and Spanish settlers. The Spanish descendents were called Creoles. Cajuns were descendants of the French settlers from the Acadia region of eastern Canada. Negroes made up about one-third of the population.

Derrick and I found an apartment in the Pontalba building, which suited Derrick just fine. We were near Royal Street and the French Market, close to the river. Never have I enjoyed seafood so much. We dined on wonderful dishes like fresh oysters baked on rock salt with spinach sauce, and pompano fish baked with shellfish sauce wrapped in a cloth. There were also delicious soups made with fish and other salt-water delicacies. However, my favorite was the black coffee made from the root of the chicory plant. I had always liked strong coffee, but this stuff was the best. As Pa would say, "It was so strong it could grow hair on your chest." I figured Ruby would have been very fond of it too. She also liked her coffee strong and black!

During the times when Derrick was away playing cards or pursuing other interests, I always found something to do. I visited the local Library which was founded in 1843. Reading had always been important to me from the time I sat at my mother's knee and learned my letters. By taking daily walks in the park I became familiar with every square inch. It was big, about 135 acres in all. I was fascinated with the fact it included an area where part of the battle of New Orleans was fought in 1812.

During our early stay in New Orleans I wore the prettiest gowns money could buy, and I didn't have to turn a hand. I just enjoyed the scenery and shopped in all the delightful little stores. Evenings were filled with lovely dinner parties at the most stately homes, with me visiting the ladies while Derrick gambled at the poker table.

We loved each other's company, but there was just one problem between us - I wanted to get married and Derrick kept putting me off. Now when I think about it, why should he marry me? He was having all the fun with none of the responsibility. I knew I was living in sin and needed to make our arrangement legal, but when I mentioned it to him he always said he would marry me when his luck was better. Well, as far as I could tell he was doing all right at the poker tables and his luck was at its best.

In fact, things were looking real good. He had acquired a lot of money while living in New Orleans. One night after a very good evening at cards we decided to take a walk through the balmy night to our apartment. We really didn't need a carriage, and the walk would feel good. I suspected that I was with child, and I knew I had to tell him before I started showing. I had not had my time of the month for three months. I wasn't sure how he would take this news. As we walked I approached the subject cautiously, because I knew he was not ready to settle down with a wife and child. We would be a burden to him, but as we walked I finally blurted it out, that I was going to be a mother. He stopped dead in his tracks like he had been shot, looked at me and said nothing. We walked along in silence for a time, but I could see he was considering what to say or do next. He was never good at hiding his thoughts from me. For a poker player he wasn't very good at masking his feelings - period!

When he did speak, it was with an unnatural voice, one I hardly recognized. "Well, Lilly, now I suppose you want me to marry you?" That was a dumb question, of course I wanted him to marry me. After all, he was the father of our child and I believed it was his duty to make our union legal.

So I answered him. "Derrick, our child needs a father and a name. What do you think I want? You promised me that when your luck changed and there was enough money, we would get married - and now certainly is a good time, especially with me being in a family way. I didn't plan this you know, it just happened. I can't help it if you don't want to be a father."

He looked at me with a puzzled look and mumbled, "Lilly, it's not like I don't love you, but I never figured on having a child around to get in the way. However, if you want to get married we'll do it. We'll do it right away. I know of a preacher here in New Orleans who will marry us real quick, and then I can take you to my parents in Virginia. You can stay there until you have the baby. I'll come back here, get a dealer's job on one of the paddle wheelers, and send for you when you are able to travel." The more he talked the more excited he became. "It will all work out, you'll see. You'll love my parents and they'll take good care of you." I couldn't really believe my ears. We were actually going to get married, and I would at last have a family. I was so excited that I couldn't really hear the odd tone in his voice.

Then it hit me. He was planning to get rid of me, but I wasn't sure how. I knew he never wanted any children and now that there was one on its way it would spoil everything. As long as I had a perfect figure, and could wear pretty clothes and be on his arm as a prize possession, he was happy. But now all that was going to change. I would get fat and be an embarrassment to him. Yet, he had said we would get married. What I wanted to know was, when?

As we continued to walk I thought back to Laurie and how she had loved a man who had not loved her. I could see that Derrick was using me and always had been. He had never loved me, but I decided it would be better to marry Derrick even if he did run out on me. It was better to give our baby a name than to have a bastard child. At least I would be with his parents somewhere in Virginia, and that gave me comfort. Then I grasped the situation. Virginia was miles and miles away and in a place I knew little about. I was sure it would be a long hard trip, and one I wasn't looking forward to while carrying a baby. I don't think Derrick believed I knew where Virginia was located, but I knew all right. It was north and just about as far East as we could go. I should have suspected something was wrong with his plan then, but I still trusted him in some crazy way.

Two days later we were up early. We dressed hastily and by sunup we're at the preacher's house. Derrick said he wanted to get an early start on the day. We were married in a small wedding chapel. It was not the type of wedding I had always dreamed of, but it was a wedding. There were no friends invited. We were alone except for the preacher who smelled of tonic water, his frail wife who kept squeaking around like a church mouse, plus a couple of servants who were more asleep than awake. All the old lady wanted was to get the ceremony over and us out of the house - in preparation for the next couple, so she said. I guess they ran couples through there like cattle through a slaughterhouse. But I didn't care, I was married to Derrick.

Thirteen

Married Life and Old Friends

After we were married, things settled into a strained routine. Derrick was on one of his winning streaks so all was going well with him, but he was spending as little time with me as possible. One afternoon when he was in good spirits he rented a carriage and driver to take us sightseeing around New Orleans. Since I was not showing much he consented to be seen with me. It was on this day during our carriage ride that I happened to see Jesse again.

We shouldn't have gone to the waterfront, because there were some pretty rough places around there, but Derrick was feeling cocky and wanted to test his luck in a few of the gambling places. He liked to show off in his fancy clothes, and believed himself to be one of the best gamblers in the world when he was on a winning streak. There were a lot of taverns in this part of town, and that is where Derrick told the coachman to take us. One gambling house was especially notorious, but that didn't bother Derrick. It was just what he wanted. He told the driver to remain in the carriage with me while he went inside - never mind that it was a dangerous place to stop. There I was sitting in an open carriage with a coachman who couldn't care less about what happened to me.

Young hoodlums hung around on the street, and whores wandered up and down advertising their trade looking for takers. It was then I spotted Jesse. I became aware of this drunk, poorly-dressed, half-breed woman stumbling up the street hanging on the arm of a drunken seaman. She had dark circles under her eyes and was as thin as a rail. I knew it was Jesse. Her blue eyes were hidden by her hair, which was hanging limp around her head. Without a thought to my own safety, I half flew, half jumped out of the carriage and ran to her aid. At first, she was stunned, and in an ugly voice uttered some very unkind and blasphemous words at me. When she saw who I was, she pushed the seaman away and bolted. I chased after her through the busy streets calling her by name. I knew she was too weak to go very far.

When she was about to fall to the ground, I overtook her and grabbed her by the arm, pulling her to me and hugging her tightly. She yanked herself away and told me to go to hell. She said she didn't want to see me, and she didn't want me to see her. She just wanted me to go away. I grabbed her shoulders and shook her since she wasn't making any sense. She needed help, and there I was.

She looked at my face, and large tears began to run down her cheeks. She nearly collapsed in my arms. Finally, my frightened coachman responded to my calls for help and caught up with me. He secured the horses and came to my aid. We lifted

Jesse into the carriage and I told him to take us to my apartment. He protested, saying I should not take a common whore into my fine apartment. He told me it would not be proper for me to be seen with such a woman. Drunk or sober, this was Jesse, my friend, and it didn't matter what she was or in what condition.

I insisted he drive the carriage to the side entrance of the apartment building, and I assured him that this woman was my friend. She was in need of help. He could say what he wanted, but it would not change my mind. I didn't care for the reputation of the other tenants, or about my own for that matter. My home would always be open to an old friend. I had forgotten all about Derrick. When the coachman mentioned we had left my husband behind and asked if he should return for him, I told him to forget it. He had been paid for the afternoon so he might as well return to the livery. Then I cautioned him to keep his mouth shut about this woman. I'm sure he expected more money for his efforts, but that was too bad. I carried none in my purse. I helped Jesse out of the carriage, and told him to go.

As we approached the side entrance several people gawked at us. I led Jesse upstairs and helped her undress. She was a mess - dirty clothes, long black matted hair, with a dirty tear-streaked face and rough, dirty hands. I rang for my maid to prepare a bath for Jesse, after which she slept in Derrick's and my bed for many hours. It did cross my mind at the time, what had happened to Derrick? He did not return that night or for the next two days. I didn't know where he was or what he was doing - I didn't care. During his absence I was absorbed with Jesse. The next morning when she finally came around, she was somewhat appalled at where she was and again wanted to run away from me. She was ashamed that I had found her in such a low condition. Her Indian pride was still intact so I figured she would survive. I would not let her run away even if I had to tie her to a chair. We were going to talk, and that was all there was to it!

We spent the next two days catching up on the past, since she and I had left Ruby's. I told her about Ruby, and all the girls, and how I had come to be with Derrick. She told me of her adventures with Mr. Weber from Texas, and how he was never more to her than a companion. She told me that on their way to Texas he sweet-talked her and spun her many tales, filling her with anticipation of seeing his ranch. It took several weeks by railroad and then a wagon ride before they arrived at his home place in West Texas. The big house was three stories tall and looked like a lonely castle sitting out on the open range. Built of cold stone and logs, it looked more like a fort than a house. There were few trees around. All that seemed to grow on the endless flat landscape were clumps of sage grass, mesquite and tumbleweed. She said it was the most lonesome place she had ever seen.

They say love is blind, so with the promise of marriage in her ears she swallowed her doubts and rode proudly through the fine black wrought iron gates of the Circle W and on toward the house. They were met by a small group of people including some hired hands standing around gawking. An old couple lingered by the front door, a frisky young woman stood on the big open porch, and a mean shadow-eyed, hawk-faced man stood glaring at her, making nasty remarks - all of which Tex Weber just ignored.

Jesse came to realize that the frisky young woman, Berty, was Mr. Weber's daughter, and the hawk-faced man was his kid brother - a spoiled, ill-tempered bully who made Jesse feel real uncomfortable. Since she was experienced when it came to judging men, she knew he was a bad one. The servants were an old couple who had been in Mr. Weber's family for many years. They spoke of his father as if they had known him well. The little group welcomed their father, brother and employer home and never even glanced at Jesse. It was as if she did not exist. They treated her like a servant. When Mr. Weber told them about bringing Jesse home to be his second wife, and overseer of his house, Berty began yelling at the top of her voice that she didn't need or want a stepmother. Then, she added, "Not some half-breed Indian woman especially." She proceeded to yell insults at Jesse until Mr. Weber stepped in and tried to set her straight.

"See here, Berty, don't get so all-fired carried away. Your ma has been dead for eight years now, and it's high time you had a new ma. You need a woman to help you learn to grow up, and to teach you how to talk about what women-folk talk about. This damned place is as much a home as a circus tent. You and Luke fight all the time and I'm fed up with it. You scrap like a couple of wild mountain lions, always itching for a fight, but never settling anything. Leo and Minny are getting too old to put up with your shenanigans. You two are just too much for them to handle. It's time for some new blood around here and a new face to boot. Besides, look at her. She's a real beauty - straight off the reservation and smarting to work. Aren't you, Jesse gal?"

This was her first meeting with her Texas household and not a very happy one, I'm afraid. It was clear that Tex did not really want it known where he had found her or what her pro-fession had been. Before Jesse had time to catch her breath or say her howdy-do's, she was ushered to the servants' quarters at the back of the house. Berty pranced down the long hall with Luke carrying Jesse's traveling case. With his free arm he took hold of Jesse's arm like he was the boss man, squeezed hard and looked down at her. He had a wicked grin on his face as he pulled her close to his side and whispered in her ear. "You and me, honey, are going to have us some fun. I like an Indian woman with shiny black hair and a white man's blue eyes." Jesse pulled away from him, and for the first time realized she was never meant to really become Mrs. Weber or anything of the sort. It was all a big lie, and she was stuck in a bad situation.

Jesse was never one to make any fast moves, so she just bided her time and decided to see what would happen next. She kept her mouth shut, took her case from Luke and went into the small room bolting the door behind her. That first night she slept lightly for fear Luke would break in and rape her. She had seen that look in his eyes.

After a few days on the ranch, it became quite clear to Jesse she had been duped and she wasn't going to help Mr. Weber run his ranch. She was instead to be a slave to all who lived in his house - and especially to Berty and Luke. Berty never allowed her father near Jesse from the day they arrived at the ranch. When Jesse tried to approach Tex Weber, Luke always stepped in and dominated the conversation. Luke was somewhat handsome, but in a cruel dark way, and he knew it. He never missed an opportunity to make lewd remarks toward Jesse, and always looked at her in a lustful manner. That look Jesse recognized. She had seen it many times before. It was just a matter of when he chose to come to her room.

The strange thing was that Mr. Weber seemed to be afraid of his kid brother. Luke had a nasty disposition and no one wanted to tangle with him. It was also quite evident that Tex Weber was being controlled by his spoiled daughter. She and Luke made all the major decisions concerning his ranch. Berty was headstrong, and determined to be the boss of her father's house.

The old couple was timid and afraid to talk to Jesse. When Jesse was able to do their jobs they left the ranch "in search of a more simple life on the prairie," according to Luke. He used very abusive language when he spoke of them and never mentioned the fact that they had been the ones who had bathed him and cleaned his bottom when he was a baby.

He was an ungrateful pup! Jesse said she always felt that the old couple had been dismissed because of her, even after their many years of loyal service to the family. Luke was a heartless man, and had turned them out without so much as a "thank you" or enough money to sustain them on their way. That is how he paid them for years of loyal service. The pain and suffering of others meant nothing to him. She knew it was partly her fault, because Luke didn't want anyone to have anything to do with her - except himself.

It was a pitiful sight, according to Jesse, the day the woman and old man left the ranch. Jesse had watched from the upstairs window. The old woman sat in a worn saddle on a nag that should have been put out to pasture years ago. The man walked stooped over leading the horse. They both carried a weathered leather traveling bag, with a couple of blankets tied on the back of the saddle. She never saw them again and had no idea where they had gone.

When she confronted Luke and protested at what he had done, he told her to shut her mouth. He slapped her across the face and told her it was none of her business what went on in his brother's house. When the blood oozed out of the corner of Jesse's mouth and dripped down her chin she didn't say another word, but looked at Luke with blue menacing eyes. She said at that moment, she had never hated another human being as much as she hated Luke.

The strange part was that Luke liked seeing Jesse this way. He moved toward her with quick determined steps, and before she knew what was happening, grabbed her around her slender waist, bent her over backwards, and planted a hard open-mouth kiss on her still bleeding lips. He then sucked her blood into his drooling mouth, pulled her to the floor and proceeded to pin her down. She fought like a wild panther, but it was of little use since he was a big man. She was no match for his ferocious energy.

Mr. Weber and Berty had gone to town for supplies and the hired hands were out on the range checking for strays, so no one heard the scuffle. She knew to scream was of no help, and her Indian breeding would not permit it anyway. She came from a tough breed of people, who were taught from childhood to be quiet when in danger. Pain wasn't new to her either. She had suffered much as a child and as an adult, so now it was her Indian blood running strong in her veins that caused her to take action.

What Luke didn't know was that on Jesse's right leg she wore a garter which held a small lady's derringer. As Luke tried to hold her down and fight off her clawing left hand, her right hand was busy under her skirts searching for the gun. At one point when her skirt flew up she drew the derringer, pushed it into Luke's ribs, and pulled the trigger. The shot sounded like a thud against Luke's taunt body, but the damage was done. Luke exploded with fury and surprise. As he tried to stand up, he grabbed his side and swung his fist at her. Missing her, he fell headlong across the floor with blood flowing out of his wounded side.

Jesse felt no guilt that she had shot him. In her mind he needed killing! Her blood boiled with hate and she was glad he was dead. But she knew, her life wouldn't be worth a plugged nickel if she didn't get out of there and fast. She went directly to her room, gathered a few things and threw them in her traveling case. Having done this, she ran to Luke's room and pulled out a pair of his pants and a shirt. Then she went to the old couple's room and grabbed a black dress and bonnet the old woman had left behind. Putting on the traveling suit she had worn when she first came to the ranch, she decided she was ready to leave.

Once outside she realized there was not a soul around, so she saddled the fastest and best horse in the stable, which happened to be Miss Berty's mare. Then she high-tailed it out of there on a dead run. She knew she would be followed as soon as someone found Luke's body. So when she could, she turned the mare lose and took off on foot. Jesse had strong memories of being an Indian child. She remembered the teachings of how to survive on a trail. The first thing she did was to shed her white woman's suit, then cut Luke's pants off several inches and put them on along with his shirt. She put the old man's large felt hat on her head, slung a shotgun and water tin over one shoulder and her small traveling case over the other, and took off hoping to find a place to hole up for a time while she decided what to do.

It was sundown on the second day when she spotted a cattle-drive moving east. It wasn't Weber's men, but some other outfit she hoped wouldn't know who she was. She figured she would try pretending to be a man and set out after the herd. The cattle boss, Hank Bedwell, spotted her and wasn't fooled a minute by her men's clothing. It was a good thing he was a decent sort of man. When he saw her he rode out to talk, but he had no idea who she was. If he had ever been at the Circle W he probably would never have noticed her anyway. As he moved closer to Jesse and really got a good look he said he thought he recognized her as a woman he once had seen at Ruby's Parlor House in Carson City, Nevada - but perhaps he was mistaken. Of course, she didn't answer him.

It didn't take Hank long to see Jesse was in some kind of trouble, so he didn't ask her any more questions. He decided she would tell him later what she wanted him to know. Hank saw her as one angry, fire-spitting crazy Indian female, so full of fear she was nearly out of her mind. He saw the fresh cut on her mouth and her swollen lips. Her red/purple black eyes made it clear she had been beaten and that she had won the fight. After looking her over he told her one of his men could do a little doctoring, so best she go over to the supply wagon and get her face taken care of. He then told her she could ride with them to the railroad cattle-loading station. He surprised her by asking if she could cook. Their chuck wagon cook had shot himself accidentally while cleaning his rifle, so Hank offered to pay her fifteen cents a day to make the meals for them, and promised to give her a stake whenever she went on her way. This offer was like having money in the bank. It was a good deal she couldn't refuse, so she signed up.

That was how her acquaintance with Hank Bedwell began. However, being a confirmed bachelor, he was no prospect for marriage. He said he did miss the company of a woman, but he had no intentions of getting married. He'd had his fill of married life years ago and it had left a sour taste in his mouth. Hank and Jesse became good friends and that was all. Jesse felt safe with Hank and he felt no threat from her. On the trail, after their evening meal when the tin plates and cups were washed, Hank often spent time talking to Jesse by the light of the silver moon and shimmering stars. Sometimes they talked for hours while keeping the campfire going.

It was on one of these pleasant early-morning talks that Jesse blurted out the whole story of her life, ending with her confession of having shot Luke. Hank said he had heard of the Circle W Ranch, and he knew of Luke's bad temper and evil ways. He said he didn't blame her none, because Luke was a bad sort devoid of any compassion. However, Hank suggested Jesse change her appearance, take the first train she could get, and just lose herself in a big city some place back East. That was good advice because he knew Weber and his men. They were the kind of men who would hunt her down if she was anywhere in Texas. She was as good as dead.

Soon after that Jesse tried to make herself over. She put her long hair in a bun on the nap of her neck, covered her head with a bonnet like other women did, and dressed in the ugly long black, high-necked dress. She powdered her face to make her skin look lighter and wore no jewelry. Hank said it didn't do her justice, but it did help hide her identity. He swore all of his men to secrecy and told them to say they had never seen a woman answering to Jesse's description.

When the drive reached the railroad, the cattle were loaded into cars. She rode in the only car available to passengers. The president of the Cattlemen's Society was en route to the East to sell the cattle himself. Since he was alone he welcomed the company of a woman in his private car. At first, she said nothing, but finally admitted being a widow woman going to be with her family who lived in New Orleans. She played the role well. He was a kind man and felt sorry for her, so he arranged for Jesse to get to New Orleans.

When I ran into her it had been less than a year and she was really down on her luck. When Jesse arrived in New Orleans she had gone to a fancy hotel, and while sleeping a deep troubled sleep, she was robbed. She was left with nothing but the clothes on her back - her nightgown, and the old black dress and bonnet. She tried to get a job cleaning houses or cooking, but because she didn't have the proper clothes Jesse was not hired by the influential families. That's how she ended up on the waterfront. Her black dress had seen better days, and her bonnet was a sad looking thing. Her black hair hung in two long braids down her back. She was dirty and in general, a mess. At this point, it didn't take her long to decide what her next move would be. She watched from behind an outbuilding as one of the servants of a big house hung wash on a line to dry - a dress, undergarments, hose, white gloves and even a nightgown. It wasn't long before Jesse was under the line grabbing the clothes. With them tucked under her arm, she slipped off without anyone seeing her. She said it was a hard decision, but one she had to make. She never planned to steal, but reasoned it was better to steal than to die in some hole on the waterfront stabbed by some drunk. Her next plan was to bath in the river, dress in the clothes and make her way to the best brothel in New Orleans. When she showed herself to the madam she was immediately put to work. Again, because she was so beautiful and interesting-looking, she was highly sought after by the many gentlemen callers. Although the madam tried to choose for her, it was still Jesse who chose her clientele. Apparently all went well with this arrangement, and they both made money until one evening when Jesse heard a familiar voice in the parlor. It was Mr. Weber. He was in New Orleans. She did not know why, but suspected he was looking for her in the most likely place. She listened briefly at the door and then quickly scampered to her room. There was no time to pack, she just crawled out the bedroom window and ran away as fast as her feet would carry her.

So here she was again with only the clothes on her back, but she didn't care. It was better than being dead. Her only thought was to get lost in the crowd of merrymakers wandering the waterfront. It was easy, because New Orleans was in the middle of a week-long celebration. People were dancing in the streets while vendors sold their wares. New Orleans was full of strangers and home folks to celebrate the holidays. It wasn't long before Jesse fell in with a fast-stepping seaman who happened to be an old client of hers. She told him she was on the run from a murderous man and needed to lay low for awhile. He didn't seem to care, so he slung his arm over her shoulder and off they went. It was after this that I spotted her in the crowd.

When I heard her story I wasn't about to let her out of my sight. I suggested she get dressed in one of my dark dresses with a lovely cape and bonnet to match, powder her face and once again leave. She protested about all the clothes I had given her, but when I showed her I had plenty, she hushed. Besides, before long I would not be able to fit into any of them. The next morning I hailed a closed coach and Jesse and I headed for the railroad station. I wanted to put her on a train heading north. She needed to get away from New Orleans, Mr. Weber, and his men, as soon as possible. Whether the madam talked with Mr. Weber we would never know, but it was best not to stick around and find out. Most madams were pretty closed-mouthed when it came to discussing their girls.

I believed that with the dress, shoes and hat, plus the money I had given her, she would probably make it all the way to New York. I never heard from her or saw her again. To this day I still think about Jesse, and remember standing on the platform as the train pulled out. I stood there for a long time waving good-bye and saying a prayer for her. I felt sad for Jesse, because life had not been good to her. Then I thought about Mr. Weber and I remembered he had seen me at Ruby's too, so I stayed out of sight for several days. I didn't want to have anything to do with that man.

When Derrick returned I shared nothing about Jesse. Knowing him as I did, I was afraid that during one of his card games he'd have too much to drink and tell all he knew about my visitor. I didn't trust him, even though he was my husband, and the father of my baby.

Fourteen

Betrayal and New Life

*J*esse's exciting romance with Mr. Weber had failed. In fact, it never got off the ground. She had been promised a new life and had gotten only heartache and murdered a man. Not a happy thought. I was beginning to feel the same thing was going to happen to me. Derrick was getting more and more restless and unhappy with my condition. I was sure my marriage was about to fail, and there were times I had murder in my heart. Finally we packed all our trunks and left New Orleans. We took the train to Montgomery, Alabama, where we stopped for several weeks so Derrick could investigate the various poker games in town. Then we went on to Atlanta, Georgia, where he repeated the same thing, always using me as an excuse, saying I needed the rest. He spent his days in the saloons and his nights playing poker. God only knew where. I spent most of my time in a hotel cooped up like an over weight chicken.

I wanted to keep going and not stop until we reached Virginia and his parents, but that did not happen. When we arrived at Charlotte, North Carolina, we were helped off the train with our trunks. I stood there round and full with a baby inside me that was doing somersaults. It was hot and I was miserable, but it did not bother Derrick. I was bewildered as to why we had to get off the train with all our trunks, but he explained the problem. It was as far as we could go, because he was out of funds. He said he could not afford to buy us tickets to go on to Norfolk, Virginia. We would have to get there by some other cheaper transportation. Were we to walk, ride a horse, or pile in a wagon? None of those choices sounded too pleasant to me.

Those high-stake poker games had taken all of his money and even some of mine. We needed to get to Virginia where his parents were, because my time was getting near. He asked me for more of my money. Then he told me to sit on a bench at the station, and he'd see what he could do. I don't know what possessed him, but he came back with a wagon, a team of horses, and the supplies he thought we needed to travel across country. Derrick did nothing to help me once we were on our way. I did not like the idea of traveling alone and especially without a woman around to help with the birth of our child, in case it came early. However, Derrick wanted us to be alone and deliver our child ourselves. I thought he was crazy, but what else could I do? It was either climb up on that wagon or stand there until I delivered on the platform. So with a slight boost from the ticket master, who had come out to give us a hand, I pulled myself up on the driver seat next to Derrick.

We each had our trunk of clothes, and several other trunks packed with household items. When we were still in New

Orleans, I had also made a few baby clothes which were neatly packed away. I always dreamed of having a place of my own, so I had sewn some linens such as bed coverings, dresser runners, a beautiful table cloth and a set of lovely napkins. I was proud of the work I had done and loved the thought of sharing them with Derrick's mother.

By the time we reached Virginia I was in my eighth month and I was very uncomfortable. Riding in the wagon was impossible, so I walked along the side until I was so large I could not see my feet. I slept on the ground at night, because it was just too hard pulling myself up into the wagon. I was strong and healthy, and I was getting fuller and rounder. The baby inside me never stopped moving or kicking which made me think the baby was quite healthy too. Because of all this movement, rest was near impossible, and I was getting weak from the lack of sleep. Finally, I had to ride in the wagon all of the time, and I felt so big I thought I surely would explode if the baby didn't come soon. I wore large flowing cotton dresses that were gathered under the breast, and hung straight down, blousing out in front. Not very pretty, but they served the purpose, and were quite functional.

We had followed the old trails north, taking our time, which added to my anxiety. We passed many old settlements and new towns, and eventually arrived in Greensboro, where Derrick became even more restless. One evening he left me alone at our campsite with only the horses to keep me company. I was scared the baby would come and I would be alone. I wasn't sure I even knew what to do if the pains did start. I guess I should have suspected something was wrong then, but I was too miserable to think about anything except getting on to Derrick's parents. This time he spent several days in town, and when he did return he didn't explain where he had been or what he had been doing. In fact, he said nothing to me at all.

I think he hoped I had died while he was gone. Then his troubles would be over. He loaded the wagon, hitched the horses and told me to get in. I tried, but it was impossible without a boost so he begrudgingly got down, came around the wagon and pushed me up and onto the waiting seat. I was beginning to see that he was a very impatient man, and was not the least interested in what happened to our baby or me. I started to cry and then I was obsessed with the desire to get to his parents. When I mentioned that to him he just ignored me and went on driving, sullen and quiet.

One evening just after we passed over the Virginia state line somewhere near Danville, it started raining and I began to have a deep ache in the small of my back. As the rain gathered into a storm my pains increased. Finally, seeing we were too far from the last town we had passed through, I begged Derrick to stop somewhere, anywhere, because I needed to rest. I knew my time was getting near, but I figured it was at least a week or two before the baby was due. I had hoped and prayed we would arrive at Derrick's parents before I went into labor. I was so afraid the baby or I would die on the trail with just Derrick to attend us. I was sure he would not be able to handle it. He probably would pass out at the first sight of blood. We needed help and I knew it.

Going around a bend in the road we saw a beautiful little green valley stretching out before us, and sitting on one side of the valley was a farm house, barn and out buildings. The rain stung my eyes as I strained to get a better view. It was at twilight when we entered the valley, so by the time we reached the farm it was dark. I insisted that Derrick pull into the barn and not disturb the people living in the house. I was too tired to care. We could talk to the people in the morning when the storm was over. I was sure they would not mind giving shelter to a man, and a woman expecting a baby very soon.

The canvas top of the wagon was soaked and so were we. Derrick agreed to stop, so he jumped down, opened the barn door and drove our team and wagon right inside. It was a big warm barn with a hayloft almost full of hay. It smelled wonderful to me. There was a cow in one stall and a couple of horses in two others. They merely looked up at us with curiosity and then continued munching bits of hay. At one end of the barn and high up in the loft we could see an open place where the hay was not stacked very high. Derrick unhitched the team, rubbed them down and led them to an empty stall. Then he looked around for a place to put me. There was a ladder directly below the spot where the hay was not stacked so high, so we decided to climb up, eat a little, and rest until morning. I don't know how I ever climbed a ladder in my condition, but by this time I just wanted to get dry and rest. Somehow I made it up and never thought about the climb down. I couldn't see my feet, but I could feel the strong rough ladder steps below them. When I reached the open place in the hayloft I was exhausted. Derrick spread out a blanket and we proceeded to take off our wet clothes. I wrapped my shivering, full body in another blanket and he changed into a set of old clothes.

Derrick brought our food basket up into the loft and we had an indoor picnic by the light of a kerosene lantern. It was a warm and comfortable place. There were no chickens in the barn, so there wasn't any bad odor. I never was fond of chickens. When I was a child Ma would send me out to the hen house to gather eggs, and when I reached in the nest those big old hens would eye me and peck at my hands. Thinking of those chickens now brought tears to my eyes. My thoughts were on my Ma and Pa. How happy they would have been to be grandparents, but I'm sure Ma would have been disappointed seeing me now. Looking around I could see the corn crib, but it was so dark that little else was visible.

After eating a small amount and getting warm, my pains diminished and I fell asleep, listening to the soft breathing of the animals and Derrick snoring beside me. I guess I was so tired nothing could have awakened me. I slept hard and soundly through the rest of the night.

As the first rays of sunlight began making their way into the barn I began to stir for I needed to relieve myself. At first, I was not sure what was happening, but then I realized I was beginning to experience a deep pain in my stomach every few minutes. I had the sensation of small cramps getting stronger each time the pain occurred, and I had the desire to push down. The pain slowly increased and I knew I was really going into labor. I called out to Derrick, but there was no answer. I called again and again, but he didn't come to me. I knew in my heart that he was not around, and I hated him at that minute more than ever. I wondered where he had gone. All I could think of was that I needed help. I wanted to scream and cry all at once, but I knew it would do little good.

I half-walked and half-crawled to the edge of the loft where the ladder stood. I could see where we had ventured up and I was amazed that I could have climbed up without falling. Now I saw it was impossible for me to get down. I was higher than I had thought last evening, and the worse part of all was that Derrick had taken the wagon and horses, our household trunks and left. All was gone except my personal clothes trunk. It sat on the floor of the barn with hazy sunlight and bits of dust dancing all around it. That was all he had left? I sat there weeping, with my blanket wrapped around me. He hadn't even bothered to leave my nightshirt. I was naked as a jay-bird.

I couldn't believe that I was alone. Then I laughed out loud, because what he didn't know was that I had always hid some money in my laced-up boots. Looking to where he had helped me remove them, I saw even my boots were gone and next to where we had been sleeping was a piece of paper. Could it be a letter from Derrick? Surely not!

I managed between pains to return to the blanket and seized the letter and read it. I can still remember every word like it was only yesterday.

Dear Lilly,

It pains me to tell you this. We had some good times, you and me, but to tell you the truth, I am not willing to take on the responsibility of a wife and child. By the way, I owe you this much. We are not married and never have been. The wedding was rigged to make you believe we were married and to make you think everything was legal. I had to take the other things to make it out of this place, but I'm sure the good farm folks will help out. You never have been at a loss for words so go to it. Oh, yes, my parents are both dead and they never lived in Virginia. That was just a way to get you out on the trail. I thought for sure the hard trip would cause you to lose the baby and we could go on like before. These last few days I have been driving aimlessly looking for some place to leave you. Good luck and don't expect to see or hear from me again. Sorry things turned out this way.

Fondly, Derrick

I sat there looking at that awful piece of paper, and all the bad things that had happened to me came to mind. Really, when I thought about it, I had made it through my life fairly well, and this was another card I had been dealt in the game of life. I thought about Derrick and wanted to cut his heart out. I hated his guts at that moment. How dare he abandon me? It wasn't just me he had left, but also our child. I found it hard to believe that anyone could be that heartless, and that we had been living a lie all this time.

My pains were getting closer and I was sweating, but my mind kept going over what he had said. He had planned to leave me somewhere. My God, where? In a ditch some place or the side of the road? What kind of man would do such a thing? It was bad enough that he left me, but it was unforgivable that he took almost everything I owned, even the baby clothes I had hand-sewed. The worse hurt of all was that he actually hoped the hard life on the trail would cause me to lose our baby.

When the next pain hit I screamed and became angry just thinking how he had deceived me about our wedding. As I recalled that day it seemed quite real to me. The old Justice of the Peace had married us and his wife stood up for us, but I didn't remember signing any papers. If they were acting they certainly played their parts well. I wondered how many other women had been deceived in the same way? I suppose Derrick had paid them well and I wondered what the price was. Was it thirty pieces of silver or what?

I crumpled the piece of paper in my hand and pulled my blanket tighter around me. Then a deep cramp hit me across my back and I knew I would never make it anywhere. I decided if I died, I should at least be found properly clothed, so I put on the one thing Derrick had overlooked, my dry dress. I pulled it over my swollen body and eased down onto the blanket, trying to think. I reasoned, if I was going to have this baby now I had better do something to help the poor little thing. When I tried to rise from the blanket I found I could not. My body reeled with the pain I was experiencing. So I slumped down on the blanket once more, stretched out and prepared to die. Then I screamed again and again until I passed out.

I'm not sure how long or how loud I screamed for help. It was like I was awake and someone else was yelling her head off. When I did become aware of what was happening around me, I heard someone coming into the barn. I tried to yell again, but the words would not come out of my throat. My throat was raw and dry. My pains were about three minutes apart and I felt a pulling sensation down my groin. I knew it was time for the baby to be born. I just prayed I could remain awake long enough to bring it into this world. In my clouded state I tried to remember all the things I had heard about the birth of babies. There was something about tying off the cord and keeping the baby warm, but I couldn't remember. I began to sweat more and heave with each cramp. My water broke and I don't remember what happened next.

Unknown to me at that time, the old man in the farmhouse thought he had heard a woman scream. He told his wife he had heard a team of horses and a wagon pulling into the barn during the rain storm, and leave in the pre-dawn hours. He wondered who would do such a thing without letting someone in the house know they were there, or at least come to the house first and ask permission. Being curious he put on his rain slicker, picked up a lantern, a milk bucket and made his way through the oozing mud to take a look, in case he had not been dreaming. The streak of sunlight I had seen earlier was now gone, replaced by dark storm clouds overhead. He said he needed to check on the animals anyway.

By the time he reached the barn it was extremely dark inside the building. He could hear the rain peppering down on the old tin roof. The cow and the horses were quietly chewing their hay. The cow gave a good morning moo as he approached her stall to milk her. Then he thought he heard the sound of a woman moaning and calling for help. It was a woman's voice somewhere off in the distance. Then a light scream and a few muffled groans followed. When he realized the cries were coming from the loft he walked swiftly over to the ladder nearly falling over my trunk sitting on the floor.

The old man was very agile for a man in his sixties, so he swung himself quickly on the ladder and climbed up. At the edge of the loft he spotted me in a heap of pain and suffering. He came closer and saw at once what the problem was. The old man had fathered several children and had helped deliver farm animals. He suspected I was about to deliver, but he was afraid to touch me for fear he would startle me. Seeing I needed help quickly, he turned to go down the ladder. But before he was on the floor his wife was coming through the barn door. He yelled to her what was happening in the loft, and before he could say another word, his wife almost knocked him down getting up the ladder to attend me.

Just as I had given up hope, I saw the old woman looking down at me. She was saying something, but I was so racked with pain I could not respond. I felt her soothing hands on my forehead and heard her giving instructions to her husband. She knew what was needed, and that it was too late to send for the doctor or move me, because the baby was already coming. She called to her husband to bring clean linen, scissors, and some hot water and strong soap. Kneeling she peered at me and I let out a little yell.

One mighty push and I felt a searing pain run up my stomach and down my legs. The baby was out! Thank God! It let out a sharp cry as the woman slapped it on its rump. A few minutes later she told me to push again. I was tired of gritting my teeth and pushing, I wanted to stop. Then the old woman gave a whoop and holler, and I heard her say. "Don't worry honey, there's another baby in there! Push down!" I was shocked, but pushed as hard as I could - and out it came. The woman gave a shout as she held the second baby in her arms. Then holding it up by its feet she gave it a gentle slap on the bottom and it, too, let out a cry.

That explained why I had gotten so big early in my pregnancy and why my baby was never quiet inside me. I guess the two of them were rolling around with each other all the time! The babies were both small so the delivery was rather easy, so she said. Easy for whom, I thought? Maybe for you, but Lord-a-mercy, that was just plain hard work and I was exhausted. Then it hit me. I had two children instead of one. I was almost in shock! By this time the old woman was on her knees working with the babies and completely ignoring me. Her husband had brought what she had asked for and then disappeared. I turned my head and saw her working over my babies and I was scared thinking something was wrong. I was so weak I couldn't speak or move. Then I heard her say, I had given birth to two perfectly healthy, beautiful baby girls. They had black curly hair, blue eyes, and were identical. They looked like two little dolls. I was happy and surprised at the same time! The old woman washed each one carefully, wrapped it in a soft blanket, and then turned her attention to me. She sponged my face and my sweating body until I felt clean once again. When she put a baby in each of my weary arms, I looked down at them, overwhelmed with both joy and sadness.

I remember thinking of Derrick with a lot of bitterness in my heart. How terrible of him to have left me in such a condition, depending on the mercy of strangers. Still I longed for him to see his daughters. The tears came flooding down my cheeks and I couldn't stop. I guess the old woman understood, because she told me to rest, and said she would take special care of my babies. The last thing I remember before passing out was seeing her kindly face, the face of an angel. It was with her assurance that I drifted off into a deep sleep.

Sometime later that day I awakened inside the house lying on a wonderful, soft featherbed. As I slowly opened my eyes I became aware of my surroundings. The pleasant bedroom was filled with massive wood furniture. There were samplers on the wall, pretty cotton curtains draped the windows, and to my right sat a young woman keeping watch over me. She shifted in her chair the minute I stirred, ran out the door, and called her mother. Quickly the old woman came into the room. She looked down at me, smiled and patted my cheek. Her hand felt cool and pleasant. As I gazed up into her face I imagined her hand was the hand of my mother and almost broke into tears once again.

"You are a good little mama. You made us all very proud today. How do you feel now, dear? Are you up to answering some questions?"

Questions? What did she want to know, I wondered. Well, certainly they deserved some explanation, but this just wasn't the time, at least not in front of the child. Looking at the young girl, I asked the woman if we could talk alone. "Of course dear," she answered moving toward me and sending Missy out of the room. She told her there was work to be done in the kitchen and she should get busy, helping Bess. The girl looked disappointed but answered, "Sure Ma." Then she skipped out of the room, but not before looking back at me full of curiosity. And what girl her age wouldn't be?

The old woman pulled a chair closer to the bed. As I tried to raise up she gently pushed me back onto the soft pillow and said, "Now honey, don't try to get up. You have had a busy day and you need your rest. We can talk just as well with you lying down as sitting up. Now, how did you come to be in our barn? Pa thought he heard something in the night, but it was raining so hard he couldn't see a thing. He decided it was his imagination, so he waited until this morning to check the barn. We saw nothing of a wagon when we looked out, but the barn door seemed to be ajar and pa knew he had closed it tightly after he fed the stock last evening."

I answered her, "Ma'am, I don't know where to begin. I feel so terrible. Oh, I'm not in any pain, but I am hurt, sad and just plain mad. I was left in your barn by a no-good son of a— well, you know what I mean. I even thought I was married to the bastard. We had a wedding and all that, but he said, in that hell of a letter he left me, we were not married. Now I'm confused. I can't believe it. He left me cold - and me about to have his child. He took all the money I had left, and my other trunks. He left me at the mercy of strangers. I know you are good people, but this is not the way it is supposed to happen. He told me he was taking me to his parents, but that was a lie too! They are dead and never lived in Virginia. Now I have two beautiful daughters, but no husband, no money and no home. I have nothing. What am I going to do now? How are we supposed to live?" Looking up at her again I sobbed uncontrollable tears. "How can I ever repay you for all you've done for us?"

"Repay me? Oh, land's sake, dear. You don't have to pay me. I did what any good Christian woman would have done. You were in trouble and needed help, but you are safe now, my child. Just relax and don't upset yourself. We'll talk again some other time." And with that she stood up, patted my cheek, leaned over and kissed me, then left the room. I was grateful she had not persisted in asking any more questions. As I lay there my mind raced with all the plans we, or should I say, I had made. Obviously, Derrick had different ideas.

For ten days I lay in bed while others fed me, bathed and treated me like a beloved daughter. They were wonderful people. I was allowed to stand, and walk a few steps each day. I soon recovered my strength with the loving care I was getting. The twins put on weight and grew fast. They were delightful, with their ivory skin and black hair which curled in little ringlets all over their heads. One twin was quiet and very passive. She watched as her sister screamed her head off, as if waiting for someone to come take care of them. The "screamer," as we called her, was never still unless she was asleep or being fed. She wasn't sickly, but was perfectly normal. We finally decided she had a strong set of lungs and wanted to use them. She demanded to be held all of the time. When we were working with her twin, she would scream and cry.

I named our little darlings, Virginia and Tiffany. I planned to call them Ginny and Tinny, because they were born in Virginia under a tin roof. I would never forget their births and I would never forgive their father for leaving us. I often dreamed of seeing him, and what I would say. But I never could resolve the problem in my own mind. Would I welcome him if he came around again - or would I want to shoot him? Finally, I had to put it all behind me and quit worrying about Derrick. I decided to leave it to chance. That was one problem I would handle when it came to my door!

I stayed for over a year with Sarah, Bess her sister, Theresa her daughter and Martin her husband. We were like a big happy family, the family I had lost and so often longed for. Martin was a fine man who delighted in his household of women. Soon the twins were just like Sarah and Martin's grandchildren. I could see them growing very attached to the girls. Theresa was the age I was when Ma, Pa and I had left the East for California. I could see all the youthful hopes and dreams in her, and remembering my own, I felt rather sad.

My dreams of California had never come true, and here I was almost back where I had started. I had traveled with my parents to Utah, and watched as Pa got sicker and finally died. Then I watched Ma drown in the flood, and yet somehow I had survived it all. I had worked for Ruby as a cook. I sang my way through countless shows with Myrna, and watched her being killed. I married a man whom I thought was a fairly decent person, who turned out to be a loser. Well, all that was water under the bridge.

Now I was on a farm in Virginia with two babies and nothing to call my own. Of course, I did have my adopted family. I loved them dearly, but I needed to move on with my life. If I ever got ahead on my own, it would be by my own two hands and plenty of hard work. I finally called my adopted family together and told them I was going to leave. I felt I must raise my daughters by myself - I could not live beholden to them forever.

Sarah and Martin protested and said I didn't have to leave, but they did understand my desire to be on my own. I was young and needed a life where there were more people around - someplace where I could find a husband, even though that was the last thing I wanted. I was prepared to support the girls and myself. I told them I had decided to open a seamstress business.

Fifteen

Independence

When I decided to leave the farm, Sarah and Martin insisted the twins remain with them until I was settled, and they were a mite easier to handle. This was a great help, because I would never have to worry about their care.

I chose to go to a nearby town where I could buy a house and hang out a sign. I was good with a needle and thread, and I knew I could make a handsome living if I worked hard. There was always work for a good seamstress. Patterns were plentiful and I had a good eye for design. With the new treadle sewing machine, I believed I could do quite well. I borrowed some money from Martin and bought myself an unpainted clapboard frame house, a sewing machine, and a few household goods. I applied for a loan at the local bank and was turned down, because I was a woman and had no husband. I was furious, but it didn't matter - rules were rules. Women were just not reliable, and they were not considered the head of a household. This made me steaming mad. I decided it was a dumb law and one that needed to be changed.

Women's rights were non existent at the time this happened to me. I was aware of the National Women's Suffrage Association, which was founded in 1869. I also knew there was a great crusade going on to promote women's rights. I for one believed our country needed to give all women the right to vote so we could change any laws discriminating against women.

Since I could not obtain a loan Martin put the house in his name, but it belonged to me, and I knew I would pay him back as soon as possible. He even helped me set up my business. At his suggestion, I created a ledger to keep track of the money I received and the money I paid out. I was grateful for his help, but a little resentful too. I knew if I'd been given the chance, I could have done it myself.

Anyway, after a few months I was established with a number of ladies dropping by regularly. My house sat on a slope overlooking the town and I had a rocking chair on the front porch. It made me feel settled and quite content. I had a parlor, dining room, kitchen and one bedroom, with an added attic room upstairs. There was a hall leading from the front door back to the kitchen. I used the dining room for sewing so it was always piled high with bolts of fabric, laces, ribbons and hat forms. We never considered eating in that room. The house was rather small, but adequate and a very good place for me to start a new life.

For the next three years I worked to establish myself as a seamstress - hardworking, polite, quiet, and very capable. The ladies knew little of my past. I figured that way they were less likely to talk about me. I didn't want anyone to know what had happened before I came to their town. I passed myself off as a widow woman with two small children, and no questions were asked. Many women were in the same situation, so my story was easily accepted. I wasn't ashamed of my previous life, but I did have to think of my children since they would be growing up in this town.

When I visited my daughters on the farm, I told my clients I was going to their grandparents, who were keeping the twins until I was able to care for them properly. It was on these visits that I got to know my children. Ginny and Tinny were such darlings. They were quiet, polite and never caused much trouble. They played together in their own little world, and tumbled around on the floor like two kittens.

When I brought them home they were quite happy, and slept in my bed with me. Theresa, Martin and Sarah's daughter, came along to help with them since they were still too young to be in the attic room alone. She slept up there and watched over the girls for almost a year. She liked living with us and would have stayed, but there just wasn't enough room, so she returned home. However, she came for visits quite often, and the girls loved having her stay with them.

The twins played together in the attic room most of the time, so many of my customers never saw them. I made Ginny and Tinny clothing fit for little princesses from the scraps of the fine dresses I sewed. When they were dressed they looked like two Chinese porcelain dolls, and I often referred to them as my little dolls.

Ginny was determined to have her own way. She never gave up when she wanted to do something. She was the stronger of the two, physically and perhaps mentally. She had been born first, so was older by several minutes. She always tried to tell her sister what to do, how to do it, and usually won. Tinny was willing to follow her sister and accepted whatever she was told. As they grew older, I began to see that Ginny had a mean streak in her while Tinny was gentle and kind. Ginny would catch a butterfly and pull its wings off while Tinny cried and told Ginny she was bad for doing it. The twins may have looked alike, but were as different as night and day.

Our lives didn't change much for a while. Then the rains came. It rained solid for several days and I knew what to expect. It was getting worse and there was certainly going to be a flood. It was like history repeating itself. I wondered what I would do if it did flood our house, but we were on a slope, and I just couldn't believe the water would ever reach our place. I knew I had to have a plan. I didn't own a buggy or a horse, so to get out of town I would have to rely on others. I never asked for help from strangers, except Sarah and Martin - and that was different because they had just taken over out of necessity.

It was about dawn on an early spring morning in 1891 when the water did start rising. The girls were four years of age. As my neighbors pulled out one by one in search of higher ground, I watched them leave still too stubborn to believe the creek would raise high enough to flood the whole area. It got so quiet I finally realized we were alone. It was very quiet and scary!

The storm grew worse, and rain pelted down in sheets. I watched the out-house slide down the slick ghostly white mud slope. By then I knew I had better do something and quick. Had I waited until it was too late? I wondered where I could take my little dolls that they would be safe. Where was there a place strong enough to withstand the flood?

Here I was alone in the world, with these precious little girls with a chance of losing our lives. I could hardly bear it. I knew many of the ladies in town, but I did not have one close friend. They didn't seem to know we even existed. I will admit I was rather puzzled when none of them came to see if we were safe or even to offer us a ride out of town. Most of my clients knew I owned no transportation, but I always appeared to be a rather self-reliant person. It was possible they'd assumed we had left with the rest of our neighbors. All of that did not matter now because we were in one heck of a fix, and I was the only one who could do anything about it. At that moment I hated myself for being so full of pride - and most of all I hated Derrick. I blamed him for all that had happened to us. My hatred had not surfaced in a long time, but now it drove me into action.

It came to me what I should do. We would dress in some of the finest clothes I had sewn, and pack our canvas bags with the best garments we owned. I'd be damned if we would be found dead dressed like servants. I pulled out one of the gowns I had finished for the mayor's wife, which she had not yet paid for. It was a beautiful dress of royal blue velvet covered with small beads. It had a high stand-up collar, a fitted bodice with long sleeves, and a long flowing skirt. It had taken me months to sew on those beads, and now it was what I needed to wear. I told the girls to put on traveling suits and stuff their canvas bag with the prettiest things they owned. They obeyed me without question, but I am sure they did not understand. Why would we get dressed up to go outside in the rain?

I threw some hardtack biscuits in a tin, put some water in a fruit jar, a small blanket in my bag, and called Ginny and Tinny to come to me. We put on coats, threw an oilcloth table covering over our heads and set out. Before we left the house, I made the girls promise they would never tell where we had lived before the flood, or that I was a seamstress. I told them we were playing a game that we were rich and never poor. No matter what happened they were to keep our secret! You have to understand, I wanted to belong to somebody and be from a rich family, so this would be the final fantasy.

When I had first arrived in town I remembered seeing the jailhouse being built, and I reasoned it was probably the strongest building around. I knew if any structure remained standing after the water drained off, it would be that one. It wasn't too far from our house so I dragged the girls down the street to the main part of town. The rain beat down on us making our walk through the water extremely hard. Tinny cried and Ginny kept telling her to shut up and move along. If I weren't pulling Tinny, her sister was. Ginny was a tough little girl and had a strong survival instinct. She never slowed her pace, but dogged my tracks with Tinny in tow. Because the water was deep and it was raining so hard, it took us a least an hour to get to the place where I remembered the jailhouse stood. Sure enough we found the jail, and not a soul was around. We were literally in a ghost town. Leaving the girls standing on the porch, I pushed the door open and walked inside. The cell doors were open and the black pot-belly stove stood alone in the middle of the deserted room. It hadn't been lit for at least a day or maybe two. I looked for some stairs leading up to the second floor, but there were none. I had to get us on the roof somehow, because as we stood there the water was still rising and sloshing around my ankles. God only knew how high it would eventually get or when the rain would stop.

Going back outside, I discovered there was a second story with steps leading up on the outside of the building. We made our way up these stairs to find the outside door was locked. Peering in I could see nothing through the small smoky glass pane. Next door stood a similar building with stairs facing the opposite direction. Below us standing on the ground and leaning up against the side of the building were some old two-by-fours. I told the girls to stand on the landing up against the door. Because of my soaked velvet dress I had to work my way down the stairs. When I returned I brought one of the boards up to the landing. I did this twice. I laid the boards across one railing and over to the other. Then I climbed up on the boards and tested my make-shift bridge for strength. It would hold me so I stood up and reached for the flat roof. My fingers held tight as I pulled myself up and crawled over onto the roof. It was not full of water as I had expected, but was built so the water would run off the back edge of the building. Over in one corner was a makeshift tent made with strong waterproof canvas. I was sure it was where the man who guarded the prisoners took up his watch during the night. I realized if I could get the girls up there we would have a chance.

I leaned over the edge and told Ginny to boost her sister up on the two-by-four boards. Then I told Tinny to stand up. She was afraid and screamed she would not do it. Ginny must have pinched her and said something, because quickly and without another word Tinny did as she was told. She stood up on her tiptoes and nearly fell off, causing my heart to almost stop, but she quickly righted herself. With my strong grip I grabbed her gloved hands and pulled her to safety. Without a word Ginny was up on the lumber. She handed me our canvas bags one at a time, and then reached up for my hand. As I pulled her over the edge I saw she was drenched, as we all were, but her eyes were sparkling with determination. She was not a quitter.

Once on the roof I directed the girls to the tent and quickly let the flap door down. It was surprisingly dry inside the small area. The canvas roof had kept the rain out so far. It was almost dark and the rain had not eased a bit. There was an old oil lamp sitting on top of a wooden box, and matches inside. I lit the lamp and we all felt much better. We sat down in the cold damp tent with our light burning brightly, eating our hardtack and drinking some of the water. Ginny had put some dried fruit in her pockets, which was now soaked, but the wet fruit she pulled out tasted wonderful.

As the girls began to get sleepy, I heard Tinny crying again and Ginny telling her it was all going to be all right. After all, they were with mother, and she would keep them safe. I wished I believed that too, but I was not sure at the time if we would get out of there alive. Perhaps in the morning I could come up with a solution, but for tonight I decided we all needed some sleep. I had taken their clothes off, as well as mine, and wrung them out as best I could, but we had no choice but to put them back on. We all were shaking so I suggested they sit one on each side of me so our body heat would help keep us warm. Before we settled ourselves I remembered the small blanket I had stuffed in my canvas bag. I used it to cover us then I tucked one girl under each arm. It was Ginny who finally spoke.

"Mama, are we going to die before morning?"

"Not if I can help it Ginny. I promise I'll find some way to get us off this roof and out of the rain, but for now just go to sleep and things will be better in the morning."

Well, Ginny wasn't about to be put off or go to sleep. She had some questions she wanted answered and as usual she was persistent. Looking into my eyes she asked me, "When we die, do we go to heaven like Theresa told us?"

No doubt Ginny was concerned about death because she had been told by Theresa many times, that when she was mean to her sister or would not do as she was told, she would go to hell and not heaven. This frightened her, and I guess even Ginny, at her tender age, knew she had often been a bad girl. She looked worried as she studied my face waiting for an answer. Tinny looked at me with her trusting eyes and snuggled closer. Her eyes had black circles under them and were haunting as she gazed at me. I wondered what she was thinking and seeing her weakness I wondered if she would ever have any fire in her. Would the day come when she would challenge her sister? Finally they both went to sleep.

As I closed my eyes I found myself pondering Ginny's question. "Would we go to heaven?" I certainly hoped so! Neither of us had slept very long when Tinny began coughing a deep rasping cough. I realized she had a fever. Even though Ginny never said a word, I knew she felt sick too, but she coughed little. I could see Ginny blamed me for our plight - her eyes were very accusing. I knew I would never be able to reason with her. Therefore, I began talking about the animals and birds I used to see around our home place when I was a child. I told them about my parents and our trip out West. Soon both were fast sleep. I again dozed off while watching the oil lamp sputter, and the rain gently falling. Finally, I slept for a time.

The next morning I awoke stiff and disoriented. I eased out of the tent as the girls leaned on each other. The rain continued all morning with Ginny and Tinny moving very little. The sun came out around noon and beat down on us all afternoon. Its warmth felt good - my aches went away. Then I looked around on the roof and found nothing of use. When I looked down at the way we had climbed up I saw the boards were missing. They had fallen during the night. I knew I could probably swing down to the landing, then catch the girls as they lowered themselves down to me. However Tinny was very weak and too sick to move, much less walk. The fever, which had made her sleepy, had stayed about the same during the night. But looking at her closer, I realized she was burning up. I would have to get her cooled down as soon as possible. When she opened her eyes they rolled back into her head and she passed out. There were still a few puddles on the roof, so I sent Ginny to soak my petticoat in the water. Then I wrung the water out over Tinny's head and shoulders. I needed help and I needed it quickly. Ginny did as she was told, but she looked at me with anger in her eyes. I was puzzled what to do next. Until Tinny was better, I decided it was best that we remain. I had a little drinking water left, and there were a few puddles on the roof. We still had some hardtack and the dried fruit, so we could survive another day. The sun grew hot on the jail roof. Now I prayed for more water to help cool Tinny, and cool our dry throats. Tinny was very thin and now she looked like she was dying. I sat there helpless, with my daughters, one weak as a mouse, lying listless, while the other sat with crossed arms and feet glaring at me. Her angry eyes said, *"Do something,"* but I did not know what to do or say - so I said nothing.

Sixteen

Rescue and Respectability

On the third afternoon the sun's rays were relentless. We sat huddled together in the shade of our makeshift tent, with our faces dirty and our lips cracked from the penetrating hot sun. I had given up hope of ever seeing another human being. Tinny's fever broke during the second night while we were stranded on the roof. She was very weak, but still alive much to my surprise. Ginny moved about on the roof restlessly like a caged animal. She was angry with me because she was so hungry. Every time our eyes met it was as if she was accusing me of getting us into this situation. I've never felt so helpless in my life.

As we sat there hopelessly waiting for some help to come, I heard the sound of a wagon nearing the jail. At first I thought

I was dreaming, but sure enough it *was* a wagon and it was moving in the muddy street below us. I knew at that moment we would be saved, but then I remembered how unsafe we really were. I had heard tales of men who came into deserted places and stole anything in sight, and also how women were treated if they were unlucky enough to be found by such men. I couldn't worry about that now! I had to get help for the girls as well as for myself. I started to run to the edge of the roof and found I was too weak so I crawled to the edge and peered over the top. What I saw was a surprise and I gasped in disbelief.

Standing up on the seat of the wagon was the most handsome man I had ever seen. He was dressed in a pure white suit, waving his hat, and yelling as he looked around at the deserted buildings. At first, I don't think he saw me. He yelled again, and this time I understood his words. "Anyone out there? Is there anyone around? Hello there, on top of the jail. We saw your light early this morning. Show yourself!" Hearing this, I stood up and called to him in a muffled cracking voice. "We're here. Thank God you came!" When he saw me he looked startled. He jumped off the wagon and moved toward the jail, sinking in the thick mud and water, which splashed around his ankles spoiling his white suit.

It occurred to me that he was dressed in white, just like an angel come to save us. Then I thought him foolish to go around rescuing folks in a white suit, but it didn't matter. Here we were and there he was! With all that yelling going on the twins awakened and crawled to my side. They were a mess, with tangled black curls falling over their grimy faces. Both were very pale, especially Tinny. We lay there looking down at our knight in his white suit and wondered what would happen next. I guess the three of us must have been quite a sight hanging over the edge of the roof - very helpless female creatures staring down at him.

The man took one look at us and asked how we had gotten on the roof. When I told him he smiled and started coming up the stairs. A lock of his thick black hair fell on his forehead giving him the appearance of a young man. He was extremely good looking and brimming over with strength. He asked me to carefully lower each girl down to him, which I did as quickly as possible using every muscle in my body. Neither child said a word. They were wide-eyed and scared, however they relaxed and let him carry them to the wagon - then sat there looking bewildered. When he came back for me I was so weak that I was ready to faint, but somehow I managed to let myself down into his strong waiting arms. He carried me as if I were as light as a feather. I leaned my head against his warm strong chest, and I could hear the beating of his heart. I felt safe and knew somehow that everything would be all right. I don't remember much after that, because once I was in the wagon with my children, I simply fell asleep on the soft quilts that were spread in the wagon bed.

I'm not sure how long I slept, but when I did awaken I found myself in a beautiful four-poster hand-carved bed. I was lying on a fluffy feather mattress that felt like a soft cloud cradling my tired body. It was wonderful! As I looked around the room I saw it was decorated with white curtains on stately narrow windows, with dark green window shades rolled to the top. The bright sunlight came streaming in through each window. The furniture was dark finished wood, and massive. When I was fully awake, I pinched myself thinking surely I was dreaming. I couldn't believe my eyes. I wondered if I had died and gone to heaven. I was in a richly decorated house and there didn't seem to be anyone around. I was confused and couldn't remember how I had gotten there.

I tried to get out of bed, but found I was so weak that my body would not obey. Just as I was trying to figure out what had happened, an older woman entered the room. She was wearing a blue cotton dress with hair piled high on top of her head. There was a hint of gray at her temples giving an angelic look, and following her was the slightest scent of lavender as she moved through the room. She had very few wrinkles in her creamy white skin, and her blue eyes sparkled with delight and laughter. I liked her at once! She was obviously the mistress of the house.

As I watched her she moved closer to the bed with the smile of a saint. Then she spoke to me, "How are you feeling, my dear? You have been sleeping for a long time and we were beginning to worry about you. You must have had a terrible time during the flood - and being on the roof of that building for God only knows how long. What is your name, dear? And where do you come from?" I answered her by saying the first name that came into my mind. "I am Lilly Clayberry, from the Clayberry's in Richmond, Virginia, and I am most grateful to the man who saved me and my daughters." At the thought of the girls, I bolted straight up in bed and tried to get out. When I asked where they were and if I could see them, she laughed and said they were fine after being washed and fed. In fact, they were now soundly asleep in a warm comfortable bed and I need not worry about them. I was so relieved that I fell back on my pillows, weary to the bone.

As I lay there, the woman continued to speak to me. "My name is Martha, Martha Anna Kingsley - Mistress Martha to you. Your daughters are precious little things. They've come through this ordeal better than you I fear, but they aren't talking much. Your sick little daughter is recovering nicely though she still is mighty peeked - looking. What are their names? We've tried everything to get them to tell us, but it's as if the cat's got their tongues." Mistress Martha gave a chuckle.

She studied me real good, commented on the dark circles

around my eyes, and suggested I remain in bed until I felt a lot better. I wanted to see Tinny and Ginny and told her so, but she ignored me and said I needed to rest and get my strength back. We could talk again later. As she turned to leave, she added, "Now honey, don't worry. We'll take good care of your little girls, and when you feel better we'll see about contacting your kin. I'm sure they are worried sick about you and the little ones. However, I'm afraid we won't be able to get in touch with your family for a while, because all the bridges have been washed out and the roads can't be traveled." I was relieved, and told her I understood, and thanked her for taking us into her home. I guess she knew I was curious, because she told me the man who had rescued us was her son Bart - Bartholomew Stewart Kingsley. She said he would be around later to check on me. Just as she left a young girl came into the room carry- ing a tray - a tray with a bowl of steaming chicken soup and some homemade bread. I didn't realize how hungry I was, but that chicken soup tasted wonderful! When my stomach was full I began to relax and was soon fast asleep.

When I awakened, I studied on what had happened to my daughters and me. I was grateful that these good people had taken us in, and could not contact my family until later, espe- cially since there was no family to contact. I hoped that before the roads were ready for travel and the bridges repaired, I would be able to figure out a story as to why the Clayberry's were no longer living in Virginia and why I did not want to tell them what had happened to us. I could say we had a falling out perhaps, or a death of one or both parents, or the last resort, the truth? But heck, I didn't want anyone to know we were alone in the world and penniless - or that I was never married to the father of my daughters. It would bring shame on me and on the girls as well. Besides I figured they never need know the truth. We would not be with the Kingsleys much longer anyway. I had told the girls that their father had died of consumption and that was that. When Ginny asked me where he was buried, I simply told her in a little cemetery outside of Carson City, Nevada. Ginny and Tinny were so young I assumed it didn't really matter what I told them about their father. I prayed they would never meet up with him or even see him as long as they lived.

Thinking about the lies I had told made me feel uneasy. I knew lying was wrong, but sometimes a body just had to stretch the truth a mite. I realized Ginny and Tinny were old enough to tell these people I was a dressmaker even though I had made them promise they would never speak about our past to anyone. I guess they were doing just that, and it made me laugh to think they wouldn't even tell Mistress Martha their names.

Then it came to me to tell our rescuers that I had run away from home to marry Derrick and my family had disowned me because Derrick was a gambler, and my father did not hold with gambling. He said gamblers never amounted to anything and would sooner or later lose everything, even the shirt off their back. My father believed gamblers caused a lot of grief for the people who loved them. Truer words were never spoken even though they were not really spoken by my real Pa.

As I lay in that beautiful bed I thought of Pa. I believed he would have said the same thing, and I knew he would have never approved of Derrick in the first place. Pa was a smart man and could see right through a person. He would have spotted Derrick's deceitful ways right off. He was a good judge of character and rarely taken in by strangers. Now I wished more than ever that Pa and Ma were still alive. At that moment, I missed them more than words could express, and it seemed so unfair. They would have been proud of their granddaughters. I could imagine how Pa would have bounced the girls on his knees, and carved toys for them. I knew Ma would have made pretty clothes for the babies and sung her sweet melodies in their ears. I'm sure she would have enjoyed reading from the Bible, and teaching them moral and spiritual truths as she had taught me.

Well that was in the past and I could not change what had happened before, so for the present I meant to make the most of where we were. I had to make some kind of life for the girls and myself even if I had to bend the truth to do it. I didn't want to be poor anymore. I wanted wealth, to wear pretty clothes and live in a stately house. I reasoned I had worked hard all my life and deserved better. Had I not been responsible most of my life none of this would have bothered me— but it did. I could only hope I would do what was right when the time came. I slept fitfully after that, and dreamed of Bart, my knight in a white suit.

After a lot of thought, I decided what my story would be. I would explain that I had learned dressmaking from watching our servants sew my dresses when I was young, and decided it was an honorable profession for a woman in my circumstances with no husband and two daughters to care for. All women wanted and needed new dresses. Those of means were not willing to sew for themselves, so I made myself available. It was a good story and one which could easily be believed. If the girls mentioned I was a seamstress the stories would fit. At least, at the time, I thought it was a good story.

I had been very fortunate in the small Virginia town where I had set up my house and called myself, "Lilly the Dressmaker." None of my previous acquaintances knew where I was, and if the truth were known they probably were busy building new lives of their own to be too concerned about me. I was sure they would want to let the past be forgotten and that was the way I felt.

I had never mentioned to the girls anything about Ruby or

anyone else from my past, except Ma and Pa and the people I had known back East when I was a child - and of course, Sarah, Martin, Bess and Theresa. They had been like family to us. Now even they did not know what had become of us, so I felt safe from the past. I knew I must contact them again someday, but that would have to wait. I wasn't exactly ashamed of my life up until that time, but I was tired of being poor and having to scrape by for a living. I wanted something better for my daughters. I wanted us to live in a fine house like this one, and have servants. I was not afraid of hard work, and resigned myself to the fact that I would resume the seamstress profession when we left the Kingsleys. However, at this point in my life I wanted and needed to be cared for.

Later that day Bart returned to the house and came to my room to check on me as Mistress Martha had promised. When he stood before my bed I surely would have fainted dead away had I not been in bed. He was a prince among men. I believe he was as smitten with me as I was with him. Though he did not say so, his eyes betrayed his thoughts. I knew his mother was fond of me and was delighted with Ginny and Tinny. Now I found comfort in knowing her son also found me attractive.

At that first meeting he told me we were welcome to stay until we regained our strength, and not to concern myself how long that might be. Soon after that, I began to recover and everyday we breakfasted together with the family in the main dining room. In a few weeks, Bart and I were going for horseback rides around the grounds of the mansion. In the evening after supper we took long leisurely walks.

As I observed my new surroundings, I realized the wealth of "my prince in shining armor." There were plenty of servants, inside the house and gardeners outside. They were not slaves as I had been told about in the South before the Civil War. They were paid servants. I knew I was in a rich man's house, and I hoped the girls and I could remain there as long as possible. I felt terribly spoiled and found I liked it! I was curious how the Kingsley family had come by their money - but that could wait.

Since we were so happy I tried hard to become part of the household. I wanted to fit in. I was agreeable to everyone, and as soon as I recovered completely I made myself useful. I found my way to the sewing room and offered to help with the mending and sewing. Martha, at first, didn't want me to turn a hand. But later when I told her I just couldn't sit around and do nothing all day, she agreed to let me try my hand at making her clothes. She still wanted all of her clothes to be made on the plantation and hand stitched. Even Bart owned very few store-bought shirts. Martha accepted my talent with needle and thread and asked me to make her a special dress. I was delighted because this was one way I could repay for her kindness.

I mentioned the new treadle sewing machines and how much better they were than hand sewing. Well, it wasn't long before she was the proud owner of one of the new inventions. I was so pleased, because once again I was able to create beautiful gowns for my lovely daughters and Mistress Martha. When she saw the speed with which I sewed, she insisted I create a whole wardrobe for the girls and myself. This I did eagerly.

Even though I saw Bart at breakfast and for our walks in the early evening after supper, he was rarely around during the day. Bart was a good prospect for a husband and I couldn't figure out why he wasn't already married. He and his mother were very close, but not overly so. I was told that after his father passed away several years earlier, he had taken on the responsibility of the plantation. This left him very little time for a social life while he was at home. Yet I had observed him leaving the house each night and returning in the early morning hours. Mistress Martha nor the servants mentioned Bart's nightly departures to me, so I gave it little thought.

Looking back I now realize Mistress Martha adored all of us from the beginning. I became the daughter she never had, and Ginny and Tinny were like her own grandchildren. When I said something about making an attempt to contact my family nothing was said. It was as if Mistress Martha was afraid I would take the girls away from her, because by this time they were fast friends and they even called her Grandmother Martha, which she relished.

The days grew into weeks and the weeks into months and then I had been with them over a year - and by this time Bart and I began to spend more time together. Our walks through the green lush woods surrounding the plantation became longer and longer. I was told many times how their mansion had survived during the Civil War. The fighting had not come directly through their area so they had somehow been spared the destruction. Martha's father had freed his slaves before the war, and when it was over and things had settled down he hired both white and colored workers.

After the war, the taxes they had to pay were enormous, but due to Bart's grandfather's careful planning and good business practices the plantation continued to flourish. The tobacco crop was good and the cotton did well on the open market. The business of the plantation was now handled by Bart, not a hired manager, therefore Mistress Martha never worried about the details of how the place was managed. She trusted her son and never questioned him. Money was drawn on a New York bank and from a European account. How this was handled at the local bank I never did know.

It was true that Martha's husband had seen what was happening, and like his father before him had kept his securities in those Eastern banks and in Europe. Bart's father died a wealthy man, not scarred by the war like so many of the other plantation owners. Bart's grandfather had properties in England when the war broke out, so it had not totally destroyed his way of life. His family was among the lucky ones. I didn't really care how they had gotten their money, or how they were able to keep it after the war. I just knew I wanted to be part of this family and the wealth I had never known.

My desire was to be part of a family and I thought that would make me happy. I decided if I happened to acquire a little money along the way, it would be fine with me. After all, that had been my dream when I started to California with Ma and Pa so many years ago. The way I looked at it, the dream had just been delayed.

As Bart and I grew closer the horseback rides became buggy rides and Sunday afternoon picnics. The girls were always being cared for by their Grandmother Martha or a servant so that gave me plenty of time to spend with him. Ginny and Tinny had several nursemaids, but their favorite was Dolly, a little black woman about four-feet ten-inches tall, with snapping black eyes that never missed a movement of the twins. She had cared for the girls since the first day we arrived and was well aware of their differences. She was a deeply spiritual person and at times I wondered if she didn't preach too much to the children. We all loved her and were pleased she was so bright and capable. As a child she had learned to read and write from Mistress Martha's mother Rosemary. And from Rosemary she had learned much of her Bible teachings. There was little doubt in my mind that the girls were being well cared for by Grandmother Martha and nursemaid Dolly.

Since I had little responsibility it gave me more time to concentrate on Bart. There was one Sunday I will always remember. And looking back now, I wonder if it was not part of a well-conceived plan. Bart had insisted that he and I miss church that morning and go for a long ride in the country. We would leave the girls in Martha's care while we enjoyed a pleasant picnic by an old mill. When we left the plantation it was lovely and warm, but not hot. It was just one of those lazy relaxing summer days. Birds chirped high in the trees and the buzz of insects broke the stillness of the air around us.

At first, the two of us rode along in silence and then Bart began talking about the first time he had seen me, his delight when two other little heads appeared over the edge of the jailhouse roof. He said he had been a bit puzzled to find the three of us there, but was enchanted with our dark hair hanging in cascading curls about our shoulders. He said we were an unforgettable picture - three little princesses in need of being rescued.

By late afternoon we were still at the mill sitting under the shade of a big tree, near a small pond formed by the river which flowed gently by us. We had taken off our shoes and let our feet dangle in the cool water. Once in a while a big fish would jump up, making a splash in the pond trying to catch an insect. Later we sat on a quilt made by Martha for the buggy. I loved its rich colors and texture and thought it a shame to be sitting on it. But Bart didn't seem to notice. His thoughts were somewhere else. He kept looking off in the distance with an expression I could not read. We sat for a long time and began eating our late lunch without saying a word. I tried several times to engage him in a conversation, but he looked away. I didn't know what to say so I sat there wondering what was on his mind.

Finally, he spoke to me, "Lilly, there is something I would like to say to you. You know I am fond of you and your daughters. I even think I might be in love with all three of you, but I have been a bachelor for a long time and I have had my freedom to come and go as I please. Do you understand what I am trying to say?"

I thought I did but if he was proposing marriage I wanted him to say so. I wanted him to say what was really in his heart. He kept looking up into a graying sky where in the distance we could see a storm was brewing. Heavy rain clouds were gathering in the east and would soon be over us. We sat there in silence just looking at each other for a long time, and then large droplets of rain started falling around us.

My lunch was half eaten and his was hardly touched. Tollavor, our black servant was sitting a distance away from us, busy "sinking a hook," as he called fishing. Then there was a large clap of thunder and the rain hit with huge drops that soaked a body before you could move. Tollavor came running and helped us gather up our things and ran for the buggy which stood under the protective branches of an oak tree. About that time a sharp flash of lightning and another clap of thunder hit, and off galloped the horses pulling the buggy with Tollavor in close pursuit. It was a funny sight, but seeing the rig gone we ran inside the mill and found shelter from the rain. Bart took off his coat, put it around my shoulders, and we sat side by side waiting for the return of our servant. When he did not come back in a reasonable time we assumed he had run all the way to the stable. There was nothing to do but wait there until the rain stopped.

I was shaking because I was so cold. Being a gentlemen, Bart offered to put his arm around me. It was the first time he had ever touched me, except for the day he plucked me off the jailhouse roof, though we had been within touching distance many times. It felt good being so close to him. I could feel his warm breath on my cheek as he watched me, and the odor of him made my head swim. He was such a handsome man, a man of the world and one I was sure was not a saint. Yet I found myself falling deeply in love with him. I knew he had his women, but none had been the kind he would have chosen to bring home to meet his mother. He was getting older and I think he felt part of life was passing him by. Much to Martha's sorrow he had not found a proper wife and he had not produced any children. I didn't know if he missed having a family, but I knew he wished to please his mother.

I sat there taking him in, trembling as he gathered me closer, looking into my eyes. I knew he was struggling for the right words. I sensed he wanted me, but I wasn't sure he loved me. He might be in love with me and he might love my daughters, but he loved his freedom too. As my heart raced even faster another roll of thunder pierced our ears causing me to cling to him even closer. At that moment, I remembered such a night long ago when I had listened to the rain from my bed in the loft of my parents home. I was young then with my head full of dreams. Now I didn't care, I wanted his arms around me - his full lips upon mine. As I thought this his lips brushed my cheek, while his hands moved expertly around my body drawing me even closer until I felt I could not breathe. I felt the dampness of his cheek, the stubble of his beard and his tongue exploring mine. He was kissing me with a passion I had never experienced before. Derrick had been an experienced lover, but he had used me only for his own pleasure never concerned with how I felt or my enjoyment. This was different. This man touched me in a way that drove me crazy. I wanted more, much more.

I had not had a man in my bed or as much as looked at one since Derrick. I began to feel dizzy and could not collect my thoughts. Bart was persistent and I was hungry. I knew I should hold back, but my desire was too great to stop him. My clothes were peeled from my damp body by the hands of an expert. I thrilled to his touch feeling pure pleasure at knowing he desired me. His mouth closed hard on mine and I felt his tongue probe deeper into my mouth. I felt his fingers touching my most private parts and soon the inevitable happened. He was inside me with a fullness that tore at my body, a sensation that made my legs tingle and my back arch. With our clothes off and our bodies locked in each other's embrace we rolled and turned with raging desire. As the rain hammered down outside our passion knew no boundaries. It was as wild as the storm that howled around us.

I had never experienced this kind of lovemaking, but somehow I knew it was right. It was as it should be. The feelings that rose in me for Bart would not be denied. When our needs were satisfied we held each other for a long time without saying a word. As I lay my head on his chest I once again could feel his heart beating and hear the murmurs of pleasure escaping from his lips. We were one now and it was very natural to us. We had a sense of belonging to each other. It was like being made whole, knowing it was the way one should feel - satisfied and complete. "Lilly, does this tell you what I am feeling? That I love you and I want you. These last few months have been the happiest and best times in my life. I am a man of few words, but I know what I want and right now I want you. Will you be my wife?"

What could I say? My dream had come true, not in California, but in his arms. I had found happiness. I told him yes, of course I would marry him, but there were a few things I needed to tell him about my past. However he quieted me by saying the past didn't matter. He said we both had a past and he vowed to ask me no questions if I would ask none of him. I was so relieved that it never dawned on me that he might have something to hide. He said we would be a family, but that he didn't want any more children. Tinny and Ginny were like his own daughters and he felt he was too old to start raising a family. I looked at him at that moment, and believed we could have a wonderful life together. The thought of not having more children didn't bother me, I was content with my beautiful twin girls.

Seventeen

Marriage and Heartache

After the episode at the old mill it was clear to Bart and me that we should be married. When we announced our engagement to Martha she was extremely happy about our decision. She immediately set about arranging everything for our wedding, and I was all too willing for her to do it. She knew the proper etiquette for such an occasion, all the rich southern traditions. I was unschooled in such matters, although I had learned a lot about proper manners from Laurie and Ruby.

Our wedding day was set and it took months for all the preparations to be made. Martha wanted every detail to be perfect. After all, this was her only son and heir. It was decided we would be married in the stately old house and not a church.

The mansion was a graceful southern colonial home with tall columns across the front and windows perfectly balanced on each side of the entrance. It was built on a grand scale. An open foyer led to a graceful curving staircase. On either side of the foyer were halls leading to various rooms. On the right there was a parlor, small dining area with another room for preparing plates to be served, followed by a larger room containing cabinets, workspace and a small cooking stove for family use. On the left side was a sitting room, library, elegant ballroom with mirrored walls and a spacious dining room. There was even a separate water closet, and a wash area next to that which contained a large imported bath tub that looked quite expensive. Looking up from the foyer you could see the hall and doors leading to a number of bedrooms. Beyond the bedrooms you would find a sewing room and a delightful nursery with a private sitting room. It truly was a magnificent mansion!

The reception would be held on the wide porch and on the lawn, with its majestic old trees, box hedges and formal flower gardens that were carefully planned and cared for. Behind the house was a group of separate buildings - a summer and winter kitchen, the servants' quarters, a smokehouse for curing meat, a carriage house, a tool shed and stables. The barns were placed quite a distance from the house. There were even separate shops for the blacksmith, carpenter, cooper and tanner. By all standards, it was a most gracious way of life - a place where some of the pre-war customs continued, but without slaves. It took a lot of money to maintain the house and grounds, but according to Martha there was plenty in the bank. I never mentioned money, because the Kingsley resources seemed to be limitless.

Of course Ginny and Tinny were agog at all the preparations. It was a spring wedding with perfect weather. The sun rose early displaying brilliant golden rays with pink streaks stretching out over the horizon. A breeze wafted the scent of honeysuckle through the house. Windows were opened to the fresh smell of cut grass and blooming flowers. As I stood in my bedroom before the ceremony I looked closely into the imported, gilt-framed glass mirror. It was then and only then I realized I had acquired my dream. I was to become Mrs. Bartholomew Stewart Kingsley, the mistress of a plantation and wealthy beyond all imagination.

When the music started, I came down the winding staircase. The oil paintings of Bart's ancestors stared out of their frames, as if looking at me. The beautiful wallpaper on which the portraits hung was actually hand-painted silk, that had been imported from China before the war. It was elegant with a gold and white floral motif. My dress was a pale yellow. It had a tight-fitted deeply pointed bodice with a drape ending in a long train. I wore long white gloves with a golden tiara in my hair. My dark hair was curled with most of it on top of my head and a long curl cascading down one side.

The stairs were spectacular - highly polished steps with a wooden banister and railing decorated with ribbons and bows for the occasion. As I came down those stairs two little black servant girls carried the train of my wedding dress. They'd been born on the plantation to members of the household staff. Their hair was braided in tiny braids all over their heads and tied with little satin ribbon bows. Their yellow rose pattern cotton dresses were highly starched. The girls looked delicate and brittle.

Ginny and Tinny entered before me, dainty and lovely. Their dresses were soft flowing cotton similar to mine, with a slight train, but no drape, just a length of material puffed out in the back. For Ginny, we had chosen a light blue dress trimmed in tiny ribbon roses. Tinny wore the identical dress in petal pink. Each wore a matching bow on the back of their heads to keep the cascading curls from falling forward. They looked like my two precious porcelain dolls, just as they had when we left our house during the flood. Seeing them dressed so beautifully was like seeing a flashback of our past.

We had come a long way and I had kept my promise. We didn't perish on the jailhouse roof. Everything was so beautiful that I had to pinch myself to see if it was real or just a fairy tale. My happiness at that moment was complete. I was alive, excited, and desperately in love!

Following the wedding there was a carefully planned lavish reception with a multitude attending. I felt like I would suffocate from all the attention. Members of many of the old families were there. I received a number of approving glances, though once in a while a statement was made concerning my family, or lack of one. Neither Martha nor Bart offered any explanation. Several ladies approached me in the formal wedding party line with comments about how fortunate I was to be marrying Bart. Apparently he had been the most eligible bachelor around. I felt their jealousy plain enough, but refused to let their comments ruin my day. One rather beautiful woman approached me and whispered in my ear that she had been after Bart for years with no luck. Then she dropped my hand saying, "I guess I'm not one of his kind of women!" What she tried to imply I was not sure. When at last I retired for the night I lay exhausted in our bed. It had been an exciting day. All had gone well except that Bart was not in bed with me. He was still downstairs with the single men drinking, smoking, and being a reluctant bridegroom. It wasn't like I didn't know what to expect, because I did. What I was not prepared for was his lack of eagerness to be with me. Because my feelings were hurt, I was mad!

As I lay in bed I could hear a lot of noise coming from the

library. The men were carrying on something terrible. They were talking, swearing, and hollering loudly in their drunkenness. Later in the early morning hours I heard gun shots. I was frightened so I ran to the window and looked down in time to see the men getting on their horses, shooting off their guns. They told Bart good night and teased him about his bride waiting patiently in the marriage bed. I was embarrassed, but pleased they were finally leaving. I was not sure if Martha heard all the commotion going on in front of the house, but I imagined the whole household was awake.

Bart finally came up stairs. I was glad that he was not really drunk, but in a happy mood. He came in the door flinging his clothes here and there looking like a conquering general. When he approached the bed he yanked the cover off of me, picked me up and swung me around several times like we were dancing. My gown slid off my body and with one swift movement we were locked in each other's embrace. What followed was pure pleasure, ending with more contentment than I had ever known. We both slept like babies until mid-morning when the real world came crashing in upon us.

Both girls came running into our room and jumped onto the bed with us. They were puzzled why we did not get up right away, but we were stark naked so we kept the covers tucked tightly under our chins. Bart was chuckling all the time.

Soon Grandmother Martha appeared with a twinkle in her eye, and a smile as big as all outdoors. She was amused by the whole situation. She grabbed the girls and off they went in search of breakfast, leaving Bart and me to our own desires which were still unsatisfied.

When our love-making was over and Bart returned to sleep, I lay letting myself think about my daughters and their personalities. I wondered if they would always be so different. As infants they were happy babies. Ginny was the stronger of the two and had been from the beginning. When they were little babies they would cry if they could not see each other, but when I put them together in one baby bed, in fact a dresser drawer, they were content. I remember how sweet it was to watch them sleep with their arms entwined. They were very dependent on each other for warmth and comfort.

After my marriage the three of us were not as close as we had once been. I can see it all started when Bart plucked us from the roof of the jailhouse. I had become obsessed with him. He was the center of my world, and Ginny and Tinny must have sensed this change in me. I was no longer hovering over them as maybe I should have been, but at five years of age they were relatively sweet-natured girls so I was not concerned.

In fact at times I was oblivious to what was happening in my own household during their growing-up years. Grand-mother Martha employed a governess and several servants to care for their needs. I saw them at breakfast in their room. We talked briefly about their plans for the day and I responded with the usual, "Have a good day and enjoy yourselves. Obey your Grandmother," and so forth. Each morning they were off on some adventure. In the afternoon they would take a nap. When they awakened I often went into their room and we talked. Occasionally we would play dolls. We often ended our visit with a tea party, real cookies and weak tea. Ginny always poured the tea while Tinny served the cookies. They were de-lighted to use their exquisite miniature china cups and saucers Bart had brought to them after one of his business trips. Never did we discuss serious matters nor did I inquire much about their day. If they offered information, I was more than willing to listen.

They never had supper with the family until they were in their teens. Their meals were served and eaten in their own sitting room. It was an old southern custom according to

Grandmother Martha. She believed children should be fed away from the rest of the family where serious matters were discussed. They learned proper manners for young ladies from their governess. Grandmother Martha taught them how to embroider and do needlepoint. Secretly, I think Ginny hated it.

Tinny loved being around her Grandmother and did everything she could to please her. She tried to be a good girl, always doing whatever Martha told her. However, she was not an angel by any means - nor was her sister. Like most children they had the usual childhood problems, and frequently got into mischief. One episode I remember is when they pulled all the buds off of every flower in Martha's garden. Both had done the deed, but refused to admit it. Martha was furious because she was sure it was Ginny who had planned the mischief. When questioned they both lied and would not admit to pulling the buds so both were punished. Usually Tinny was sorry for what she had done crying big tears if caught in some naughty action. But Ginny would stand looking straight at you and stick out her chin in defiance. She would lie when the truth would have been better. I worried about how to get her to stop, but it was a habit with her. I think she wanted to test the adults around her. I could find no reason for her to lie, except that she just never wanted to admit doing anything wrong. She would rather take the punishment.

Martha always favored Tinny letting her get away with more than she should have. She said it was because Tinny was weaker in body and was subject to catarrh and all the other childhood illnesses. The whole household catered to Tinny when she was sick. They dressed her in lovely nightgowns and brought her breakfast in bed with special foods. She was constantly watched over by Martha or the governess, while Ginny was hardly noticed by either. Ginny resented her sister enjoying all the attention especially as Tinny didn't recover quickly. This made Ginny mad.

Ginny was the picture of health with a wonderful constitution. When she was sick the illness never lasted more than a day or a week at the most. She wouldn't stand for it. She hated weakness even as a child complaining loudly that she would rather be outside playing. It was quite evident she hated our tea parties, playing dolls, and even the extra ruffled dresses Grandmother Martha was so fond of. She would rather play rough games with the servants' children, and come home a mess. The servants often caught her wading in the stream near the house in her fancy dress, shoes and socks. She could climb a tree as well as any boy, and often did, so her clothes were most always dirty and torn. Tinny, on the other hand, looked like she had just stepped out of a picture book. She was never caught wading in the stream or playing rough games. She would just watch her sister while telling her she was going to catch a cold or get into trouble - but Ginny never listened.

During their growing-up years I visited them each evening just before they retired, and as my Ma had taught me, I taught them to say their prayers. After prayers we shared a bedtime story. This was a pleasant time for all of us. It was in those twilight hours I forgot about Bart, Martha, and the big house. I gave my daughters my full attention. Looking back now I remember when we said our prayers together Ginny was very uncomfortable. She almost cried every time we asked forgiveness of our sins. Whether she or Tinny really knew what sin was I was not sure, but I knew both of them were getting into mischief and telling lies. I figured it was childhood behavior and that eventually it would pass.

Both girls feared punishment with good reason. Martha loved Tinny so much she had a hard time scolding her, but Ginny was different. She was stubborn and would not apologize for anything. Quite often her Grandmother would put her in the closet and tell her she could not come out until she learned how to behave. All this did was make Ginny angry and less apt than ever to give in. Tinny tried to reason with her grandmother, but Martha would tell her that her sister was naughty. And since Ginny had caused the problem she was the one to be punished. Ginny would never cry a tear.

I didn't realize until much later that when Bart was home he would appear in Martha's sitting room, open the closet door and allow Ginny to come out. He then proceeded to give his mother a strong lecture on how to punish children, as if he had lots of experience. The truth was he felt sorry for Ginny.

I don't know why I said nothing at the time. I had never believed in that kind of punishment for children. A switch on their legs or a swat on their bottom would have been better in my mind. But I was still afraid of being left alone in the world without a place to call my own, and I guess I didn't trust Bart's love enough to run the risk of interfering. I suffered a tremendous sense of guilt because I had lied about my past and told my daughters never to disclose our humble beginnings. So in a sense I had taught them to not tell the truth. How do you explain to children that a white lie sometimes is all right as long as it doesn't hurt anyone? I wanted desperately to fit into this new life.

I became increasingly involved in ladies' organizations like the Ladies' Aid Society and other worthy causes. Also being active in church work gave me the sense of being a good person. It helped me feel like I was making up for my past. So I guess I gave little notice to what was happening in our own home. Ginny had become ill-tempered most of the time and went around with a sour expression on her face. Tinny was very sensitive concerning her sister and tried to comfort her not really knowing what the problem was. I was vaguely aware that something was wrong during those years, but I was too happy with my life with Bart to pay much attention to their needs or the fact that they were maturing young girls.

As the years passed both seemed to grow an inch a year and before long they were showing budding breasts. By the age of twelve they had started their periods. Tinny came running to me in great distress and wondered what was happening to her, complaining of stomach cramps. Ginny started within a few days of her sister, but took it as a sign of growing up, so she was filled with questions. She wanted to know why she was bleeding and what she could do to stop it.

We talked about being a woman, having children after this happens, and how that occurred. Ginny was disgusted with the whole subject and said she never wanted to have children, especially any girls. Tinny said she was afraid of how it might make her feel, but she thought it would be delightful to have a baby to call her own. She was the nurturing sort, so I was sure she would make a wonderful mother. Ginny was another matter. She wanted to know how she could manage to never have any babies. I couldn't tell her all she wanted to know about men and women, but I was sure she would become aware of the truth soon enough, though I never dreamed how it actually would happen.

Bart was away a lot handling plantation business and I remained at home. To keep me busy in the winter months, Martha and I enjoyed hooking rugs made from old clothing decorated with designs of bright colors. The rugs were used in the kitchen and in the servants' quarters. I became interested in quilting and often attended the local bees as much for the gossip as the quilting.

After the war, the market for cotton had gone sky-high and tobacco was equally in great demand, so the Kingsleys never wanted for anything. They simply planted more cotton crops. Bart followed in his father's footsteps. He hired whites and free blacks to do all the work. To me our income seemed limitless. I was content living with a devoted family in a beautiful home with its graceful gardens.

Those years passed swiftly. As strange as it was I never ran into anyone from my past, except on one occasion. Bart and I had taken the train from Norfolk, Virginia to New Orleans on a business trip. While we were there I saw a woman who looked like Ruby. She was wearing a fashionable dress with a matching bonnet. Although she was heavier than I remembered, her profile was unmistakably Ruby's. I wanted to run up to her, give her a hug and catch up on old times. However, I decided it would only open up a "can of worms" which had better be left in the past. Of course, as most of us find out, sooner or later the past always comes back to haunt us. As I have said, I wasn't ashamed of my life with Ruby and the girls, but having even lived in a parlor house was enough to cause tongues to wag. This would bring unnecessary grief to my family.

The Kingsleys were an old family, well respected in the community, and I did not want to spoil their image. It had occurred to me it wouldn't do Ginny or Tinny any good either to find out their mother had once worked in a social club, even if I was only the cook and housekeeper. And besides, who would have believed those were my only duties? The saying is, "Birds of a feather flock together." Small communities love gossip, so I was in no mind to supply them with any information, good or bad about my past. As I recalled, it had been Bart who told me the past didn't matter. Also what had happened before we met should be forgotten. I figured it was good enough for all concerned to think I was once from a prominent family in Virginia. I was determined to forget anything that had happened to the girls or me before we became involved with the Kingsleys.

When they were old enough, Ginny and Tinny went to the same school Martha had attended. It was a private school run by the local minister. The Pastor, Steven Edgar Swanson, was a fine teacher. Mrs. Peabody taught reading, writing, cyphering, grammar and geography while the pastor taught algebra and geometry. He also offered the boys navigation, surveying, astronomy and other similar subjects. It was a well respected school, and anyone who had money sent their sons and daughters there. I was extremely proud that my girls were accepted and encouraged them to learn. I even found myself bragging about them to my lady friends.

Tinny did well in school. She was a diligent student, but Ginny wouldn't apply herself. She was smart enough, but delighted in getting into mischief at school as well as at home. I was sent a note, written by one of her teachers almost every other day. She managed to talk her way out of most problems, or Tinny would come to her rescue, even taking the blame for what her sister had done. They looked so much alike in those young years that people never knew who they were talking to, or which twin they were punishing. I realized the problem, because when I looked at them it was even hard for me to decide which twin was which. So as a result both girls were usually punished since neither would tell on the other.

Pastor Swanson did not believe in sparing the rod and spoiling the child. He used switches on the children's legs and even a "whispering stick" in their mouths if they talked too much. This stick made them look like a horse, with a bit between its teeth. The hardest discipline was when Ginny failed to get her lessons. The pastor would have her sit on a high stool and wear a cone-shaped cap with the word "Dunce" printed on it in large letters. It never bothered Ginny, it just made her angry. So she spent most of her time trying to figure out how to get even with the teachers.

When Ginny and Tinny turned thirteen they finished the eighth grade, rather mature young girls. Ginny was much aware of her beauty and teased the boys to get her way. I am sure her behavior was much like Derrick's at the same age. What else could it be? I certainly had never been wild like Ginny. I couldn't understand her. Like Derrick she was every bit as drawn to men as he had been to women. Somehow I think she felt a lot of contempt for men. Perhaps it was because she had been abandoned by her natural father.

Tinny always said she wanted to marry, live a quiet life with a special man, and have a number of children. She prepared herself to be a wife and mother while Ginny hung around with the boys as much as our society would allow. She didn't care about the girls with their pretty dresses and fluffy curls. Every girl was just competition to her. Ginny wore rather loose-fitting dresses without a corset, to free herself for a more active life, she claimed. She refused to be uncomfortable and wore riding clothes more often than not. I knew she was cunning. It was obvious she was forward with the young men, though I could not really prove it. When I approached the subject she would laugh at me, turn away and stomp off. She was even so brave, or should I say disrespectful, as to tell me it was none of my business how she acted since it was her life and she would do as she pleased. I did not know what to say to her. Bart, of course, was of no help. Ginny was his pet.

Tinny lectured her sister on proper behavior with young men. She tried to teach her good manners, but she got nowhere. Tinny wasn't above doing something wrong, but she was concerned what people said about her behavior, so she tried to be a good girl. Ginny didn't give a hang about what other people thought about her.

As they matured, Ginny began to resent her sister more and more. Their arguments developed into fights that were downright mean. Tinny was usually in the right. To get even, Ginny would do whatever she could to make Tinny look bad in the eyes of our household-staff. Their grandmother made no concessions to Ginny and foiled her whenever she could. She warned me time after time that something had to done before the two girls got completely out of control. I did not want to listen to her, because deep down I wanted to see only good in both of my daughters. Besides, somehow I felt Ginny would outgrow her improper actions.

Tinny often wept at being tormented by her sister. She would come running to the sanctuary of my bedroom, with Ginny in close pursuit. It was there that both girls had to behave. Ginny always wanted to appear the perfect little lady, especially when Bart was present. She was a little angel when he entered our bedroom or sitting room. She would purr like a kitten entwining her arms around his neck, kissing him and making over him way too much. She always wanted to be his "little girl." It irritated me just watching her.

About a year after their eighth-grade graduation Tinny came to me asking if she and I might leave the plantation. She had heard of Bart's trips to New Orleans and wanted just the two of us to take a trip there. She admitted she could not stand to be around her sister for another day. I did understand her problem perfectly, so I decided to do something about it.

I announced to Bart, Martha, Ginny and the household staff that I was taking Tinny on a trip by herself. You should have heard all the commotion that caused. Ginny said that we absolutely could not go without her. She proceeded to throw a temper tantrum, but it did no good. I had made up my mind and simply ignored her. For once, Bart chimed in and agreed with me - Tinny and I should go on a trip. We made our plans and within the week we were on our way.

It dawned a bright clear morning in June when we left the

plantation. Never had a day been so beautiful. To tell you the truth, I was looking forward to getting away from the girls' fighting. We had not traveled far when, as often happens, the sky turned muddy gray and large raindrops spilled from the thick black clouds. I gave a sigh of regret, because now the day couldn't be perfect. I felt like the storm was a warning of things to come.

We were traveling in a one-horse buggy which had a flimsy top, and there was a piece of strong oilcloth covering our trunks which sat directly behind the seat. Our driver was squeezed to one side of the seat while Tinny almost sat in my lap. The three of us were crowded. Samuel was a white boy from the North who had been instructed by Bart to take us directly to the train station. Since he was a serious young man he wanted to please Mr. Kingsley, so he would not stop no matter what!

Well, when the storm became impossible, I finally convinced Samuel to pull over to a small log cabin we spotted beside the road. The old cabin sat on a rolling knoll looking down toward the road, but the back overlooked a stream. The roof seemed to be in good shape and we found it didn't leak a drop - for which we were most grateful. Since we were all soaked to the bone, I knew we needed a change of clothing and some hot tea. I asked Samuel to bring in our trunks and the food hamper. The cabin was not occupied at the moment, but a few things had been left for the use of any travelers who might come around - a table, two chairs, a rocking chair plus a small, but adequate bed. I decided a big roaring fire in the old rock fireplace would make us all feel better. Finding a stub or two of candles, I lit them, and soon the place took on a cheery atmosphere. When the water was boiling I made some hot tea and opened the hamper. I had packed a delicious picnic supper, so since we were apt to be stuck until morning, I thought we should indulge in the food right then and there.

Samuel brought in a rope, tied it across the one room and proceeded to throw a blanket over it which gave Tinny and me some privacy. He must have changed his clothes while we were on the other side of the blanket even though we never heard a sound out of him. Later he told us he had found a lean-to shed for our horse and fed the animal. I was aware of him bringing in several piles of wood to keep the fire blazing without being told to do so. I heated water in a kettle, which hung in the hearth on a crane arm mounted on the edge of the fireplace. When I looked at it, I could imagine a good pot of hot stew cooking in that same iron pot, but we would have to forgo that for our sandwiches and sweet cakes.

It was getting real warm and cozy so we were beginning to relax. I quickly unpacked my trunk, dried myself off, and changed my clothes. Seeing that Tinny was shivering even though wrapped in a blanket, I suggested she do the same thing. When we opened her trunk I was not prepared for what we saw. Tinny wailed, "Mother, look at this mess. There is mud in my trunk and all my good dresses are spoiled - besides the nightgowns and other things." She was in tears. "The special green velvet dress you made me is ruined forever!" And so it was. "How could this happen to my trunk and not to yours?" They were both covered with oilcloth weren't they?"

I was shocked, but I knew it had not been the storm that had caused this, because there wasn't any mud on the outside of either trunk. Of course I knew what had happened and after a minute so did Tinny. Only one person could have played such a mean trick, though for the life of me I could not understand why she had done it. Looking at those muddy clothes I could have cried, but instead I told Tinny I was sorry for what had happened and that her sister would certainly be punished.

"Mama, why does she hate me so? What have I ever done to her?" My heart broke as I watched big tears rolling down her beautiful sorrowing face. I knew that somehow I had failed my daughter.

"Tinny, it is all right. You can wear something of mine now, and when we get to New Orleans I will buy you a complete wardrobe of dresses, bonnets, and all that goes with them. Please don't cry any longer."

Tinny dressed in one of my gowns and snuggled down on the bed with some blankets. She drank her cup of tea quietly. I am sure she was wondering about what had happened. I could see it was bothering her, so I sat on the side of the bed waiting for her to go to sleep. When she began to drift off I removed the cup quickly from her limp hand. Then I ducked under our blanket curtain.

There was Samuel sitting patiently waiting for further instructions. I set about preparing some food for him. When he had finished eating I helped him fix a pallet in front of the fireplace. Almost before his head hit the blanket he was fast asleep. I began walking the floor, thinking of all that had taken place until I was totally exhausted. Then I sat down in the old worn rocking chair for a spell - rocking and thinking, rocking and thinking. Finally I let myself go to bed, stretching out quietly beside Tinny. Once there, I vowed to change things if I could between Ginny and me. But the question was - how does one change a person's behavior?

Eighteen

New Orleans

*A*fter a rather long trip on the train we arrived in New Orleans. As we approached the station I wondered if history could repeat itself. I was back where Derrick and I had had our good and bad times. It was as though Derrick had fallen off the face of the earth. I didn't try to find him. To tell you the truth I hoped I would never see him again.

Once on a business trip Bart and I had stayed with friends in a pleasant residential area near Audubon Park. On that trip I had lived in fear that we would run into Derrick, because there were so many memories of the places Bart and I had visited together. This time I dreaded being in the city without Bart, for fear Tinny and I might accidentally see Derrick. But I vowed my fear would not spoil our touring the city, visiting the little shops, and eating our fill at the exquisite restaurants. I reminded myself that Derrick, in my mind, was a dead man, and even if I did see him I was sure he would never recognize me.

Thinking back, I remembered it was here that I had put Jesse on the train, sending her North to New York. Recently I had heard about the popular beaded purses being sold in all the ladies' hat stores across the country. They were designed by a mysterious Indian woman in New York City called "Essej." That name didn't fool me, because I knew it was Jesse's work. She obviously had done well and now her designs were showing up everywhere. They were the rage! I was eager to purchase several of the beaded purses for my daughters and me. Would I tell them I had once known Jesse? I rather doubted it. Some things are better left unsaid.

Tinny was wide eyed with interest at everything we saw. She was glad to be away from her sister as well as the plantation. I know she was delighted to spend some time alone with me, and certainly I with her. I saw this trip as a chance to get to know my daughter. She charmed me with her excitement and joy at seeing the city. Her enthusiasm was infectious. I soon forgot about Derrick, becoming as much of a sightseer as Tinny. We did all the usual things. We walked down Canal Street and visited the French Quarter with its quaint little businesses. We passed under graceful balconies built of iron grillwork, and as we looked from the street we gazed through shady passageways into colorful patios. They were the features of French-Quarter houses. Through the gates we could see cool splashing fountains, bright blooming flowers, and leafy banana trees. The cool welcoming gardens gave relief from the sun to the people of New Orleans.

Seeing these houses gave me an idea. Bart's business often brought him to the city. It occurred to me that it would be nice to live here part of the year. Other folks did it, so why shouldn't we? Bart was very interested in improving trade relations with many foreign lands, and New Orleans was a natural meeting place for persons with similar interests. I was sure I would be quite safe here with my family. After all, no one from my past knew I was married to a wealthy man from Virginia and none knew my married name. I had changed physically too. I was still small in size with dark brown hair, though a few gray hairs were appearing at my temples. I was a mature woman with the air of an established society matron. Lilly Benton was dead and gone in my mind. I was Mrs. Lillian Kingsley of the Virginia Kingsleys - cotton and tobacco growers, with holdings in several states in both the South and North, and also properties in England.

With Tinny's encouragement I decided to purchase a small home in the French Quarter or possibly the Garden District. I set up a meeting with a gentleman who bought and sold houses in the city, and within a week we were looking at real estate in various areas. Tinny wanted one of the quaint houses in the French quarter, and that also suited my taste. I was sure that whatever we chose, Bart and Martha would be pleased. I sent one telegram telling them of our desire to purchase a place, and another describing the house we had picked. Bart responded saying he was pleased and had also often thought of buying property in New Orleans. Now I had made it easy for him. He told us to carry on with our plans, and said he would contact a local bank where an account would be opened. I had expected him to ask more about the place we had chosen and the cost, but he commented little. He believed if you had money you should enjoy spending it, and of course I agreed.

So it was settled! We selected a house of French architecture with a beautiful flower-filled courtyard that had a lot of iron grillwork on the fence surrounding the house and on the windows. The tall arched casement windows were set in stucco walls. And there were sidewalks around the garden inside the fence. The house was larger than I had planned to buy, but it felt like home, especially when Tinny pointed out there was plenty of room for her and Ginny to have bedrooms of their own - also a delightful cozy little room for Grandmother Martha. In addition, there was a large bedroom and sitting room with a dressing area for Bart and me.

Since I wrote a letter almost every evening to Bart and Martha, I'm sure when Ginny heard the news of our shopping trips, sightseeing days, house hunting, and actually buying a house, she was jealous - and that made me a bit uneasy. I was convinced she would try to figure some way to get back at us. I didn't share these thoughts with Tinny for fear it would distress her. Instead, I concentrated on the interior of our new home. It was entirely furnished with elegant furniture. The couple who owned the house had fallen on bad times. The man had taken ill with a fever and died rather suddenly, leaving a sick and childless widow. She sold the house to me and then planned to join her in-laws in the Garden District.

I loved the place almost from the beginning. When I met the previous owner I told her how I felt. She was so happy she cried, saying it had been a dream house for her and her late husband. She was delighted that we liked it so well and was sure we would be happy living there. She said her only regret about the house was that she and her husband had had no children there.

When the sale was completed we took possession, and the thought of returning home to Virginia was a letdown. Neither of us wanted to leave New Orleans because we were having so much fun. Martha made it quite clear she wanted us back at the plantation, and I am sure Bart missed us also, even though he did not express his feelings.

Even if we were needed at home I did not hurry our preparation for leaving. One evening as Tinny and I sat on our balcony taking in the night smells and sounds, she informed me we needed to talk. She said she had been thinking about her sweetheart, Harley, and how much she missed seeing him. She had been writing to him every evening. He had been her eighth-grade beau. She told me she wanted to be with him more than any person in the world. In fact, he had declared his feelings to her saying he was planning to ask for her hand in marriage. She felt this was the best time to approach the subject even though she knew I would think she was too young.

At first, I was shocked, but I knew she might really be in love with Harley. I had seen her at the play parties, socials, and even at church talking with him. Then I realized I had never seen her with any other young man. She was concerned about Bart giving his consent. I knew that would not be a problem. He and I had thought of sending the girls to an eastern finishing school which was really a dream of mine. We felt both girls were intelligent enough to succeed in further schooling, and perhaps even become teachers. However, it was clear to me that this was out of the question for Tinny. At such an early age of thirteen, Tinny was a very mature young lady to have the courage to ask me what I thought about her getting married. I could see she was deeply in love, so I was sure that nothing I said would entice her to change her feelings for Harley.

I couldn't help wondering if part of it was a desire to get away from home and her sister. I asked her and she said that was true, but really she was desperately in love with Harley. She told me she cared nothing about furthering her education. She just wanted to be his wife and have his children. Looking into her pleading eyes I knew she was telling me the truth, so I agreed. After all, who was I to stand in the way of her happiness? I gave my blessing, telling her I would deal with Bart when we returned home. She was not to concern herself about that any longer.

It was a sad day when we finally closed up the house and took our leave. We retraced our trip home on the train and then by carriage. It was good to be back in Virginia. We enjoyed seeing the sights and experiencing the familiar odors and sounds of the Virginia countryside. We were welcomed with open arms by Martha. She had missed us a great deal. Bart was pleased at our arrival. He gave us both a rather enthusiastic hug and kiss. He was delighted to learn of all the things we had done, the places we had been, and the people we had met.

Ginny avoided us like the plague. She was off in her room pouting, and showed no interest in the least that we had returned. It was only when we began to present gifts to the family and a few of the servants that she appeared. She was totally aloof as she came into the room with a definite chip on her shoulder. When Tinny began passing out the gifts Ginny was the one who came forward first, her hands out and looking rather smug. Tinny had chosen one of the beaded bags for her, and a rather charming spring hat covered with flowers and bows. At first Ginny was overjoyed at seeing the gifts, and then she stopped herself. She simply took the presents, saying "Thank you," and giving a little curtsy, whirled around and abruptly left the room. This behavior hurt Tinny, but she said nothing. I felt badly for both girls, but I knew that it was just Ginny's way of getting back at us. Nothing Tinny did or said would please her sister.

There never was a happy reunion between the girls, rather, a cold indifference followed. I didn't have to worry about them being together too much. After our return they never visited each other's rooms or went riding together. They didn't even like being at the same table. It was as though they were living with an unwritten truce, that would burst wide open if either were to be civil to the other.

Harley did ask Bart for Tinny's hand in marriage, and Bart readily gave it. She was only fourteen by the time the wedding took place. Tinny was happy during those months, helping Grandmother Martha and me make plans. Martha was so pleased to be putting on another wedding she made it quite clear that we were not to cut any corners. Tinny was to have the very best of everything, no matter what it cost.

Seeing Tinny enjoying herself and having her dreams come true, Ginny became more disagreeable than ever. At first, she teased and heckled her sister mercilessly, and then chose to ignore her completely. She would have nothing to do with any of the activities. Ginny had plenty of suitors herself, but when the eligible young men of the community came by, she bedeviled them. She used her beauty to tease them. These actions gave me cause to worry. I knew women who did that were asking for trouble. I had seen what flirting could lead to at Ruby's. I was sure Ginny would get herself into some kind of trouble, and you know the kind I mean. I tried to talk to her and she simply would not listen. In a rude way she said I didn't know what I was talking about. I got quite exasperated with her.

Ginny rode a horse like a man, refusing the sidesaddle and preferring to straddle the animal in a shameful way. When she rode her undergarments showed beneath her hiked-up skirt and petticoats. She spent much of her time in the stables, just as she had done as a child watching the grooms and flirting with anything in pants. When she became really angry she would get up early in the morning, saddle her horse and leave before breakfast. God only knew where she went. Late in the day she would come in looking exhausted, and head directly to her room. I watched her become a head-strong woman who spent less and less time with the family. It is hard to admit, but

I often found myself admiring her spunk and independence. Yet I did not like her actions. She reminded me so much of Derrick, selfish and inconsiderate of others.

Of course, Bart still took her part in any situation, refusing to see anything wrong. He spoiled her shamelessly, which made me furious. I knew he loved me, because he tried to spoil me too, but he over indulged Ginny. He gave Tinny very little of his time. I suppose he felt she received all the attention she needed. Ginny had an excuse to be with him a lot, because the rest of us were busy planning the wedding. I guess I should have realized she was playing a dangerous game, but I could never have believed my own daughter would do anything to shame me. She was beautiful, but had that coy yet cunning look about her. In general my daughter was a threat to me, though I was too blind to see it at the time.

My life with Bart was what I would call normal. He was attentive to me when he was at home. Our intimate times together were passionate and fulfilling. I never felt unloved by him or like a neglected wife. He was still very attractive and dashing with his tall lean figure, striking black hair, and endearing smile. I knew he cared for me, but somehow I felt a change in him ever since Tinny and I returned from New Orleans. Now his trips there became more frequent than ever. He liked the new house and made excuses to remain away longer and longer. I was hurt when he told me I need not accompany him on any of the business trips, because he would rarely have time to spend with me.

About that time Martha became ill. She needed constant care, which only added to Bart's desire that I stay home with her. We had servants to care for her, and Tinny was a wonderful little nurse, but Martha still insisted that I be there. During her illness she often reminded me she had been the one who had wanted us to stay at the plantation, and then she always added that it had not been Bart's idea to keep us, because he loved his freedom. She said she had reminded him he was not getting any younger and here I was with a ready-made family. We had these discussions in the afternoon when I was sitting with her. I only half listened, because I never wanted to believe Bart had not loved me from the very beginning.

Martha also shared more about herself. She told me things I didn't need to hear. She said that at the time we arrived she realized that she had been in mourning for her husband much too long. She knew her son was in need of a life of his own, but was afraid he would leave the plantation. She was desperate, so in reality when Bart saved us she saw it as if he had really saved her, as well as himself. Martha saw us as a blessing from above, sent to help her son settle down. She was determined to keep us there, with the hope Bart and I would fall in love.

She said she loved the three of us the minute she set eyes on me, and my beautiful twin girls. Ginny and Tinny had brought out her grandmother instincts, so she wasn't about to let any of us get away. She did all she could to see that Bart and I would get together. It was like we were being manipulated all along, but I didn't realize it. Yet as I recall it all now, I would not have changed a thing, because I truly loved Bart. I would have gladly done anything for him. But after Martha's confession I knew my marriage had been one of convenience, no matter what Bart had said at the time. So it was true. I came to the realization that no man had ever truly loved me, not Derrick and not Bart. I was sick at heart, but vowed I would never let Bart know that I knew the truth.

Nineteen

Grandchildren

Only one thing spoiled the day. Ginny! She of course had avoided Tinny for months refusing to be in the wedding, but just before Tinny put on her bridal gown, the heirloom dress her grandmother had worn, Ginny burst into the room. In a defiant manner she proceeded to tell her sister she had heard that Harley was seeing one of the Ashley girls down by the old mill.

Of course it was a lie and Tinny knew it. Ginny just wanted to bedevil her sister one last time. I was standing nearby ready to help Tinny dress, when I saw a marvelous change come over her. One minute she looked at her sister, and then to my surprise, yelled furiously telling her to get out of the room and never come through her door again. She even flung her hairbrush, nearly hitting Ginny in the face.

Ginny must have found it all amusing, because she just laughed, turned around, and slammed the door shut behind her as she walked out. I didn't know what to say. As so many times before, I was distressed by her actions and wanted to comfort Tinny, so I sat on her bed watching as the maids finished helping her dress. When they left we had our brief mother/daughter talk about her wedding night. I explained as best I could, what would be expected of her. I wanted to tell her so much about my past at that moment, but decided this was not the time. She only smiled at me with a twinkle in her eyes, and assured me she was aware of what a man and woman did on their wedding night. When she was ready, she stood looking in the mirror as I had done so many years ago. She was truly radiant, calm and poised in her lovely lace gown.

Giving me a sweet gentle hug she asked me not to worry about Ginny, for she had gone too far this time. She said she had always been aware that her sister had a mean streak. She had tried to love Ginny and overlook her behavior, but she had always been afraid of her. Now things had changed. She was going to be married and leave home, so she would not have to deal as much with Ginny. No one can understand how my heart ached at that moment. My precious baby girls were grown up. Yet they were as far apart as East from West. I wondered if that would ever change. Soon it would not matter, for Tinny would be with Harley in her own home.

There were over a hundred guests who attended the wedding. They were all dressed elegantly for the mid-morning gathering, women in their finest dresses made of satin, silk and polished cotton. The tea dresses were lovely with ruffles, lace and ribbon trim over delicate drapes that made their skirts full in the back. They looked very fashionable. Every woman wore a charming hat made of straw with ribbons, feathers and rosettes. The men wore fancy vests, trousers with matching cut-away coats, and high silk hats, looking very gallant.

The house had never been more beautiful with flowers in vases and bouquets tied over the mirrors and stair railings. The rooms were overflowing with friends and neighbors. Martha had hired an orchestra for the day, and their music filled the big old mansion. The elegant ballroom sparkled with a highly polished floor, mirrored walls and a dazzling crystal chandelier that almost hurt your eyes to look at it. The dining room furniture was shined to a high luster, and the side board was filled with highly polished silver serving dishes. Servants scurried around making sure all was ready for the happy occasion.

As I stood waiting for the bride with the other guests, I was transported back to my own wedding day, and coming down those same stairs. The portraits of the family were still hanging on the wall, but the wallpaper had been changed over the years. My happiness was overflowing for my daughter. I had never been more proud of her. Before she came down, two of her dearest friends entered side by side wearing lavender lace dresses, which showed off their contrasting hair. One was a lovely blonde and the other had dark chestnut hair. Their dresses were high-necked with fitted bodices and fluffy tiered overskirts that had bows cascading down the entire length of the slight flowing train. Tinny was glad when they agreed to be her bridesmaids. Even though she was happy, I knew in my heart she had hoped her own sister would be the maid-of-honor.

The girls came down the curved stairs first, followed by Tinny on the arm of Bart. I cried as most of the ladies did, and hung on every word the preacher said, reliving my own wedding. Bart gave her away, standing tall as a general and then returned to me. Seeing him so handsome made my heart almost stop. In my eyes he was every inch a gentlemen, beaming with fatherly pride. Of course all the ladies glanced at him admiringly. I was so proud of both of them I nearly popped out of my skin.

As the couple approached the preacher, who was standing before a large gold-framed mirror in the spacious entrance hall, I saw how handsome Harley and his groomsman appeared. Harley looked like he was going to sprout wings and fly. The anticipation was almost more than he could handle. I had to smile to myself seeing such young love and thinking of all the years ahead of them.

Ginny was there, but in the side parlor watching from the door. It nearly broke my heart. This was certainly not how I had pictured my daughter's wedding. I could see Ginny was sorry she was missing the big show, but being so stubborn, she would never admit it. She was wearing a pink dress, which was much too low-necked for a mid-morning wedding. It showed more of her breast than was necessary. I had tried to change her mind when she told me what she was planning to wear, but as usual she would not listen. In fact, when she saw me looking at her, she reached up and pulled the front of her gown even lower just to annoy me. She stood looking at her sister with daggers in her eyes, because she was so jealous. She fairly twitched with impatience during the ceremony, and even called attention to herself by coughing. I couldn't help wondering what mischief she was hatching up in that formidable mind of hers.

After the wedding, the ladies retired to one of the many bedrooms. The men gathered in the library for a smoke and a glass of sherry. When the women had rested, they changed into their ball gowns, which had either been sent ahead or brought with them. In the evening a formal meal was served to the many guests at several sittings. The dancing began when the first candles were lit with Harley and Tinny leading off a Virginia reel followed by a lovely waltz. The music swelled as the dancers moved across the floor like flowering petals open-ing and closing. It was a lovely evening, and our guests left reluctantly. This would be one wedding not easily forgotten.

The next morning Harley and Tinny left the plantation for their own place, saying their good-byes to us as we stood waving from the stately front porch. I caught Ginny looking out of her bedroom window with the most sullen expression I had ever seen. It is a terrible thing to be almost afraid of your own daughter, but I was. The girl was so angry after the wed-ding that she was hateful to all of us except Bart, and she doted on him. She was rude to her Grandmother and to me, so within a week Bart offered to take Ginny to New Orleans with him on another business trip. I was hesitant, but finally agreed that she would be better off away from the plantation. As yet she had not seen the new house. Bart planned to handle some important banking business and said he felt Ginny needed time away from us. I certainly knew we needed some time away from her. It was a relief to Martha and me to see her leave. They drove off in our carriage behind a couple of high-step-ping horses. Ginny never looked so smug in her whole life. She didn't say good-bye, turn around or even wave.

When they arrived in New Orleans we received a telegram, but after that few letters followed. Weeks slipped by and be-fore I knew it, almost eight months had passed. I was disturbed by the lack of communication and told Martha that I was up-set, because Bart had so little concern for his family. I had sent letters asking him to come home and had asked questions as to why they needed to stay away so long. There was no explana-tion except that he was busy with a number of pressing busi-ness matters.

Never mind that I had told him Tinny and Harley were expecting our first grandchild to be born in a month or two. I wanted him home when Tinny had the baby. This was one event that I hoped might even soften Ginny's heart toward her sister. I should have known better. They did return just a few days before Tinny had the baby. Both were tired and cranky. Not much was said about their trip home or the lengthy stay in New Orleans.

It was in March of 1902 when we received the exciting news that our first grandchild was about to be born. Bart and I went to Tinny's just as soon as we could get there. I stood outside the bedroom door as she gave birth. I heard the mid-wife say, "Push, honey, push!" She gave a big yell and he was here. While the mid-wife finished working with her, Harley came out carrying his son and proceeded to put him in my waiting arms. He was a fine healthy baby with chubby cheeks and blue eyes looking around as though he was trying to lo-cate where he was. They named him Charles Harley, and we were friends from that first moment.

I had come prepared to stay a few days, leaving Ginny to care for her Grandmother Martha and Bart. Ginny was all too eager to remain behind. The thought of having a baby repulsed her, and she made it clear she wanted nothing to do with - as she put it, "Tinny's tit-sucking brat." She never stopped amaz-ing me with her shocking statements.

I was ashamed of her attitude. I knew better than to expect more out of her, but I felt hurt that she regarded her sister and her first-born nephew with such a lack of respect. Why I should have expected anything more I don't know. Ginny made no pretense of liking any of us except Bart. After a few days at Tinny's Bart returned home and I stayed on to help with the baby.

As I cared for Tinny and our new grandson I tried to forget about my other daughter, but she was ever on my mind. Bart was also lacking in interest of the new baby. He did finally return to see the boy, but I could tell his heart was not in the visit for he was jumpy and wanted to leave. He insisted he was needed at one of our factories up north. On his return trip he said he would check on our place in New Orleans and perhaps remain there for a time. I was angry and didn't understand his need to be away so much. At least this time he wasn't taking Ginny. I really wanted her to stay at home with Martha. I had my hands full taking care of Tinny and the baby.

When Tinny was stronger I returned to the plantation and found things in an uproar. Martha and Ginny were fussing with each other day and night. Both were miserable. Nothing Ginny did pleased her grandmother, and Ginny couldn't have cared less. Finally Bart returned and offered to take Ginny away once again - and this time I really didn't care.

Time moved swiftly because I was very busy running between Tinny and Martha. I got used to Bart being gone though I was hurt at his spending so much of his time on business trips. But I had to admit I was just as glad that Ginny went with him. I felt badly about my feelings, but they were there and I couldn't change how I felt.

It seemed within a very short time Tinny was pregnant again, and the months flew by quickly. When she gave birth the second time it was to a beautiful little girl they named Melinda Ann. She was a perfect copy of her mother in every detail, except coming from her eyes was that same old defiant look of her Aunt Ginny. I hoped I was wrong, but there it was as plain as day. She was a spirit just itching to get going. I loved her instantly and vowed to be around in the future if a Grandmother's help was needed..

I returned home when Tinny was up on her feet and able to care for the children. I went immediately to check on Martha and finding her fast asleep I decided to retire. I fell into my bed exhausted, and as I drifted off to sleep I wondered where Bart was, and what was so important in his life that he did not bother to come home or even send a telegram concerning this second grandchild. What was more important than tending to his family duties? I knew he was crazy about little girls, and this one he would cherish because she looked so much like her Aunt Ginny. Then I realized, as much as I missed him, I had thought little about Ginny.

What really continued to puzzle me was his disinterest in anything connected with the family. When I began to think about it I realized he had been gone over a year this time and Ginny had been with him in New Orleans for the entire time. According to her few letters she was having the time of her life with social engagements. She said Bart was busy and away most of the time, but she was enjoying all the social life the city had to offer. The French Opera House was her favorite place to go. Bart had taken her several times. She said that anyone who was anybody was there. It was an elegant place where the women and men showed off the latest fashions. I could just imagine what a handsome couple they would be, with Ginny holding on to Bart's arm. The thought nagged at me, but I was too tired to think about it further.

The next morning we received a telegram stating they were coming home for a short visit. Ginny was worn out from the social season. Bart said he had a lot to check on and set right at the plantation. A short visit was not what I had in mind. I needed my husband! I was feeling neglected, unloved and taken for granted. Did he not understand that I was not too old to want a man? I also needed his help with the household and other plantation business. Martha was too ill to care about anything. I was not happy about the prospect of him coming back home and then quickly leaving, so I was determined to change his mind.

When they arrived we were all there waiting with much anticipation. Tinny was anxious to show off her little girl and

young Charles Harley. Motherhood, as I expected, had soft-
ened her toward her sister. She was excited for Grandfather
Bart to hold her baby girl and she talked continuously about
how she could see him cooing over Melinda Ann. And how
proud he would be of his grandson! I heard her, but I was not
convinced all would be that pleasant. You see, I was still angry
with both of them and was afraid I would not be able to keep
from showing it. As I expected, things were strained between
Bart and me. We had been apart much too long. Ginny looked
wonderful, much better than I had seen her look in years. She
was so grown up, but still distant from Tinny and me. She
spoke to me only when she needed to, and totally ignored her
Grandmother. Her mind seemed to be filled with horseback
riding in the countryside and visiting with her old friends.

She rarely visited with Tinny and Harley and again let it be
known she thought Tinny was disgusting for having babies so
quickly. She didn't approve of the children clinging to Tinny,
as she said, "Like suckling pigs." Her words stung and put her
at even further distance from her sister.

Bart was affectionate enough toward all of us, but he appeared to be holding himself apart from me. I was so unhappy
I could have died. He was sick when he came home and told
me he would stay in one of the guestrooms until he was better.
He didn't want me to get sick too. I thought so what? Coughing and sneezing were common around the house. What did
that matter? I wanted to feel his warm body on top of me and
experience a passionate night of lovemaking as man and wife.
I knew he was tired so I didn't protest, but I was as lonely now
that he was home, as I had been when he was away. After he
recovered he continued to stay in the guestroom. Instead of
going out every evening and during the day as well, he was
always under foot and was extremely anxious all the time. I
noticed the dramatic change in his behavior. I often found

him sitting in the library reading or just staring out the window. When I asked what was troubling him, he always brushed me off and would get angry if I pursued the subject. I saw him talking to Ginny in hushed tones and they would occasionally take long walks together. I thought nothing of it, because I assumed she needed a friend to talk to since she refused to speak to me or even her sister.

Months sped by after the birth of Melinda Ann and things settled into a routine. I continued to care for Martha. Bart adjusted to being home and took on more responsibility of the plantation. Before we knew it, it was spring and Tinny announced she was expecting again. I didn't know whether to be happy or sad. She was as strong as an ox, and she had delivered quite easily with the first two, but I was afraid another baby would be too much for her.

Grandmother Martha relished having great-grand children and was delighted with the prospect of another. She told Bart to hire some help for Tinny, and no way was he to plan to leave before this baby was born. I was relieved at both ideas. I certainly could use some help, and whatever it took to keep him home, I was in agreement. She had more control over him than I did. Also due to her illness he was reluctant to leave.

This time when Tinny went into labor she was early by almost a month and we were all scared, but the mid-wife was there and so was Dr. Drake. He fussed over Tinny touching her protruding stomach and saying, "What have we here?" I was alarmed, but he simply smiled and laughed. "Well, Mrs. Tinny it looks to me like we have more than one baby in there. I can feel two heads and tiny feet and fists seem to be everywhere! Guess you had better get ready for four children in your house." Tinny fairly beamed with joy even in her pain.

Well, history does repeat itself! My excitement was beyond anything I had ever dreamed. Twins? I guess they run in our family. By golly, what an exciting day this was going to be. I quickly sent word back to the house and soon the whole family arrived. Grandmother Martha was bundled up in the front seat of the carriage with Bart driving and Ginny wrapped in a blanket and half asleep in the second seat. We could hear them coming for a mile, hollering all the way, and they weren't alone. Every able-bodied person on the plantation followed by horseback, wagon or on foot. Word passed quickly, so some of the neighbors were tagging along. This was a day to celebrate!

The women gathered in the sitting room and in the kitchen, to prepare food for the day. The men joined Bart and Harley out in the barn - Harley white-faced and sick to his stomach. You'd think by now he'd be used to his wife having babies. The men were taking a little nip every once in a while just to help Harley keep up his courage, and Bart was striding back and forth between the barn and house. When young Charles Harley woke up he was quickly dressed and Melinda Ann too. They were passed from one want-to-be aunt to another and finally taken outside to play in the sun.

The day wore on and hours passed with our Tinny still in labor, but before sunset she delivered. The babies were boys! They were pretty good size for twins and both healthy as could be. We were all excited to see and hold them. Since twins had not been expected there was only one cradle, so both were placed side by side wrapped in light blankets. I shivered when I saw them, remembering the day I had first set eyes on Tinny and Ginny. I had been alone, but these boys had loving parents, grandparents and even a great-grandmother. I couldn't help wondering what kind of boys they would become. They were identical twins like their mother and Ginny. I prayed they would always be friends and not grow up to hate each other.

I stayed with Tinny for several weeks helping her once again, but when the new servants arrived I was all too ready to return to the plantation and take up my duties there. Bart left for New Orleans before I arrived home, again taking Ginny with him. He had told me nothing about this trip. I was so busy being grandmother that I didn't miss either of them. Martha sat in a rocking chair most of the time and was very limited as to what she was able to do. She could still walk, but she needed help. I became her constant companion. I was tiring out and really needed a rest, so I asked dear Miss Amy to come in and help care for Martha. Miss Amy was a maiden aunt of the Ashley girls and went where she was needed to care for the sick or newborn babies. She was about my age, and so she could fill my shoes very well.

When Tinny was able, she'd bring all her children over and let them entertain Great-grandmother Martha. Martha loved having the children around and received a good deal of pleasure just watching them play on the lawn. The boys crawled all over her, climbing up into her lap, making her laugh. She told Charles Harley and Melinda Ann stories, and I watched satisfied, knowing this time would not last. I was sorry Bart could not see the enjoyment we were having with the children. I will confess by this time, I missed Ginny and him both.

Twenty

Betrayal

*I*t was after Thanksgiving when Martha suggested she was well enough for me to take a trip to New Orleans. She wanted me to check on Bart and Ginny and thought a surprise visit would be wonderful. When I mentioned sending them a telegram she discouraged me. I decided it didn't matter since I wanted to go anyway to do some Christmas shopping besides spending time with my husband and daughter. I was fairly jumping out of my skin with the anticipation of seeing them. New Orleans was always fun around the holidays. The little shops and houses were usually decorated for Christmas with garlands, candles and lots of holly. I also looked forward to doing some plain old sightseeing.

We had been bitterly disappointed when Bart and Ginny had not returned home for Thanksgiving. But we planned to spend Christmas together, so we had a lot to look forward to. Ginny had written a couple of letters saying she was going to be away from New Orleans for a time, because she was to investigate a school for young ladies that she planned to attend the following year. Again, I had to laugh thinking of my innocent years when I had first arrived at Ruby's and thought I was in some kind of girls' school. What a misconception that had been. Now one of my daughters was actually going to go to such a school. I was delighted and eager to hear all about her trip and future plans. I knew a new wardrobe would be needed before she left for school, so I anticipated shopping with her.

As the train pulled in I became aware of the bustling activity on the approaching platform. I strained to look through the window, and the closer we got the more excited I was. I told myself I would enjoy a brisk walk from the train station to the house. I had been sitting much too long on the train and needed to stretch my legs. I had a key to the house so I didn't worry about anyone being there. I planned to send the servants to retrieve my trunks later. It was a clear, crisp winter day, cold enough to turn your nose pink, but warm enough to make the walk a pleasurable one. I was wearing my small fur muff and hat to match and an elegant dark forest-green wool cape, which kept me almost too warm. It was a very fashionable costume and I wanted to look my best when I saw Bart.

When I reached the house I found the front door locked so I used the brass knocker, but no one answered. I fumbled around in my travel bag and finally found my key, unlocked the door, and let myself in. At first, the house looked homey and inviting, but I soon realized there wasn't a fire going in the fireplace and no one was about. I did not hear servants anywhere in the house, especially the kitchen where they might be at this time of evening. The rooms were shut up and things were not tidy enough to suit me. I found myself opening the drapes and picking up objects that were out of place as I moved from one room to the next.

I reasoned it was a busy time of year and servants were not always easy to hire, so I supposed Bart had either not found any help or had chosen to manage for himself. I couldn't wait to see him. I wanted to see the look on his face when I arrived out of the blue. So I made little noise as I went upstairs and ran to the large double doors leading into our bedroom. I was hoping to find Bart resting before going out to dinner at one of the many fancy restaurants.

I flung the doors open, never dreaming what I would be walking into, a scene I have regretted seeing and will remember for the rest of my life. Ginny was lying across the bed with her black hair flowing over the pillows. Bart was asleep holding her in his arms, both of them as bare as the day they were born. My first thought was, why, that little slut is sleeping with my husband! Then I thought, how could she shame herself in such a way? And why would she do this to me, her own mother?

Looking at me she didn't so much as move a finger. She just looked up and smiled her sweetest and most mischievous smile. Then she spoke to me, "Well, fancy meeting you here. When did you arrive? Decided to check up on the old man, did you?" She laughed and added, "It's me Bart loves, not you! He has always loved me more and preferred me to you. You never did have what he wanted or needed in a woman. Mother dear, you were just a convenience."

You have no idea how her statement hurt me at that moment, but I was also very angry. When Ginny saw the expression on my face she shut her mouth. Just then Bart woke up and sat up in bed, with his eyes half-bugged out of his head. Staring first at Ginny, and then at me it was plain to see he had not quite grasped what was taking place. But Ginny must have been planning this scene for a long time. She had only waited for the right opportunity to present itself.

I knew in my heart she was a wayward girl, strong willed and often downright mean, but this was a whole new dimension of evil. This was my child, my flesh and blood, but at that instant I was close to hating her. I just clenched my teeth, walked over to the bed, grabbed her by that long black hair and tried to throw her out of the bed onto the floor.

"You little bitch! What do you think you are doing?"

She made a giggling sound that only increased my rage, but she pulled a coverlet up in front of her to hide her nakedness. Bart moved over to the edge of the bed not even bothering to cover himself, and even then I couldn't help noticing how very handsome his glistening body was. He reached for me and started to say something, but I was in no mood to listen. I just yelled at him, "You two-faced liar of a man, get out of my way!" I was so mad that if I had had a gun I would have put a bullet between his eyes. Sleeping with my child, he had gone against all I held sacred. "Bart, get your damned pants on and get out of this room. I'll deal with you later, you pig!" Not knowing what to do, he dove over to the chair where his pants were hanging, pulled them on and fairly ran out of the room, slamming the double doors behind him.

I turned on my daughter wanting to take her across my lap and beat the devil out of her, but instead I just looked at her. She stood there with the coverlet barely hiding her lovely curved body, which was glowing with sweat. Her eyes were wary as a cornered cat, but I was so angry my eyes must have been flashing. I believe, for the first time in her life she was really afraid of me. I made one fast move toward her and before she realized what had happened, I shoved her toward the dressing room.

"Put your clothes on, you little whore, and get out of my house. From now on you stay away from my husband!"

"He may be your husband, Mother, but he is my lover and

always has been. Why do you think he always liked me better than Tinny and why he detested you?"

"Shut your mouth, Ginny, before I slap you silly! Right now I'm in no mood to mess with you!"

When I raised my hand to take off my hat, she thought I was going to hit her so she stepped backwards, half falling over the coverlet and her own feet while making a hasty retreat to the dressing room. She put on the first thing in sight, a long black skirt that had seen better days and a dirty crumpled white blouse. She hadn't even taken time to find her undergarments.

As I looked around the room I realized her things were scattered everywhere. I began to see that this little affair had been going on for some time. I was so wild with anger it was a wonder I didn't kill her on the spot with my bare hands. Before I thought, I did slap her as hard as I could right across the face, nearly knocking her off her feet and causing my hand to burn and her head to snap to one side. As she recovered her balance she swung back at me, screaming obscenities I can't even repeat. She hit my shoulder with one hand and tried to sock me with the other. Finding that didn't work she reached up with both hands and tried to scratch my face. I had had enough so I grabbed her arm and pinned it behind her. With my free hand I grabbed her hair, jerking her head back as hard as I could. Even though we were about the same size, I was stronger.

Through all of this yelling and fighting Bart had watched in disbelief. I was vaguely aware of him coming back into the bedroom to try and stop us, but I just pushed him aside. He was no match for me. He stood by in shock not knowing what to do.

Seeing me as she had never seen me before, Ginny screamed in fear and it stopped me dead in my tracks.

Letting her go, I said, "You little whore, you'd better get

your ass out of here before I really hurt you."

She stood away from me but those brilliant blue eyes were defiant again. "How dare you touch me and call me names? You are no better than I, once a whore, always a whore!"

My jaw dropped, I was so thunderstruck. "Just who do you think you're talking to?"

"You!" she yelled.

I was stunned. Why did she say this? How did she know? Who had told her about my past? But wait a minute, it wasn't the truth, I never was a whore.

"And just where did you get that piece of misinformation?"

"Oh, I know all about you and Ruby's Social Club. You can't deny it either. You worked there didn't you?"

What could I say? I was too furious to explain and besides, she wouldn't listen to me. I realized that she must have told Bart about my past, too. Later he admitted that she had triumphantly told him he'd married a "damn whore." Of course, looking back I wondered if Bart really needed an excuse for the awful things he had done with Ginny.

But right then I was too angry to analyze it. I grabbed her again with a stronger hold, kicked the bedroom doors open and dragged her down the stairs with Bart following behind us, trying to grab my arm and pull me away from her. By the time he got even with us I was pulling Ginny across the floor to the front door where I literally threw her outside. She landed at the bottom of the steps.It was cold, but I didn't care. Running back upstairs I quickly gathered some of her clothes, brought them downstairs and threw them out in a heap beside her as she sat bewildered. My parting words to her were, "Girl, you get out of our lives forever. I never want to see you again as long as I live. You have always caused me trouble and heartache, but nothing worse than this. You'll never be welcome here again."

Bart stood back in shock as he looked at me with disbelief and accusing eyes. I really think he hated me at that moment. I closed the door and stood between it and him. "This is between you and me now! You better make your decision, I am either your wife and lover from now on, or I will get a divorce!" This was a statement he never dreamed I would make. It was unheard of for a woman to obtain a divorce and he knew it, but he also knew I meant what I said. And I wasn't through.

In a menacing voice I blurted, "You will be true to me from this moment on or I will tell the whole rotten story in court. I've always known about your other women, but I never dreamed my own daughter was one of them!"

He looked stunned like I had hit him. "Now Lilly, girl, don't get so fired up. It was just one of those things that happens sometimes. You know how crazy I've always been about Ginny. I've not done anything that other men haven't done. After all, most men have a mistress, and I've loved Ginny from the first time I saw her. When she grew into such a beautiful woman I just couldn't help myself."

"I don't care how beautiful she is! She's my daughter! It's the same as rape in my book. You dirty bastard!"

"At least, I'm keeping it in the family. Why, you know I'd give her anything she asked for, and this time I guess she asked for a little bit too much. Lilly, it just somehow got out of hand and I couldn't stop it. Ah, come on old girl, you can see how it is. She's so pretty, sweet and loving, and besides I was lonely here in New Orleans. I needed her comfort. You are always so busy taking care of my mother and the grandchildren that you never have any time for me. A man needs a woman, and you're always off some place. A lot of this is your fault."

I couldn't believe my hearing. "My fault? My fault? How in the heck can you say such a thing?"

Before I could say another word, he made matters worse. "Lilly, I didn't want you to find out this way. I do respect you, even though you did work in a whorehouse once. All is forgiven. I'm sorry you didn't trust me enough to tell me in the beginning. I would have understood, really I would have. And don't say another word. I know you have been a faithful wife to me, though I do think you have always been too hard on Ginny. After all she is your blood. For chris'sake, have a little compassion."

"Compassion!Ginny has always been hard to handle and I can't expect much from her. But you of all people! I've always wanted to trust you, and believed you loved me. I have loved you from the first time we met when you pulled the three of us off that jailhouse roof. How could you do this? Ginny can never be part of your life again!"

Hearing his weak excuses I was getting colder and colder inside, my rage like a great block of ice in my belly. "Bart, were you going to tell me? When - a year from now, next month or ever? Now I understand why you never wanted me to come here with you and why you were always so jumpy when you were at home. You were playing house with my own daughter, and you were afraid I would find out!"

By this time, I was exhausted and too close to tears. He stood there looking at me with his bare chest exposed, that lock of hair still falling over his forehead, and again I was reminded of seeing him for the first time. He had been my only true love. For a minute I almost weakened. But then in that maddening way of his, he spoke to me. "Sure, Lilly, you loved me, but not enough to tell me about your past." And he was the one who had said the past was best forgotten!"I'm surprised we didn't meet some of your old callers throughout our years together. That would have been something! I can see it all now. The lovely Mrs. Kingsley, one of Ruby's girls. Sorry I didn't meet you then, Lilly, we'd have had us a grand old time. You might have been more interesting then." He was speaking wildly now, I could see the hurt in his eyes. I had to tell him once and for all. What Ginny didn't know was that I was never one of Ruby's girls. I was only the cook. But after so many years how could I ever prove it?

What did it matter now anyway? The past was gone. I had given my husband an ultimatum and thrown my daughter out. I felt like my world had come to an end.

Twenty-one

Old Friend Appears

Leaving Bart standing below I walked slowly up the stairs, went into our bedroom and shut the door. I was shaking from head to toe. It took a long while before I got hold of myself enough to go back downstairs and make a cup of tea which I realized I needed. Like a sleepwalker I went to the kitchen. There was no heat coming from the fireplace or stove so I began putting small logs in the old wood-burning stove. Bart followed me into the kitchen. Neither of us said a word as he scouted around for something to eat and I looked for the teapot. When the tea was ready we both sat down at the small round table next to the window and just looked at each other.

Then I began to explain about my past, just a little, to tell him that I never was a working girl. "I would have told you years ago, but you were the one who didn't want to talk about the past. The truth is I never was one of Ruby's girls. I hadn't done anything wrong."

"Lilly, I'm sorry. I just don't know what to say to you."

"I'm not stupid Bart, I know what you feel for Ginny is somewhere between lust and love, but it still does not make it right. She is my daughter. I suppose blood is thicker than water, but I can't deal with any more heartache today."

He just looked at me, put his head in his palms and rested his elbows on the table. He said nothing, but slowly drank his tea looking deep into the cup, then rose and left the kitchen. I heard him go up the stairs, I assumed to our bedroom. I sat there for a long time just trying to gather my wits and finally retired to Grandmother Martha's bedroom, for I could not stand to go into our room where Ginny and Bart had been just a short time ago.

About an hour after I had retired there was a pounding at the front door. Someone was shouting at us to open the door. I put on a dressing gown and ran downstairs. Bart followed close behind me. When I opened the door a young woman stood there screaming for us to come with her quickly. She was hysterical as she talked. Ginny had gone to the Red Garter Saloon after leaving us and then proceeded to get drunk. The saloon was one of the wildest on the waterfront. The young woman told us that Ginny was causing a lot of trouble, talking loud and trying to pick a fight with anyone. One man had gotten tired of her drunken smart mouth and was knocking her around. Ginny was taking a terrible beating. The young woman didn't know what to do so she came running to us for help.

Without a word Bart went into the study, got his revolver and was out the door following closely behind the girl as she ran ahead. I threw a long cape over my shoulders covering my nightgown and hurried behind them for fear I would lose both Ginny and Bart. Though I had never been in the Red Garter Saloon, I knew we were headed for a rough place.

The girl stopped outside the saloon. When the odor of stale beer assaulted my nostrils, it brought back memories I would rather have forgotten. Hearing the sounds of a fight going on inside, all at once my mind flashed back to when I was young and on the stage. It was like Cripple Creek all over again, but I was not young and this was not Colorado. The noise was getting louder by the minute so the place was getting into an all –out brawl. Chairs were being thrown across the room, falling apart like so much kindling. Bottles were being broken and expensive mirrors smashed. Even getting in the door was difficult, but we managed to enter and slide down a wall past three burly men throwing punches right and left.

The room shook as men pushed, shoved, grappled and punched. A bone cracked and blood streamed down the face of one. I was frantic because I could not see Ginny, but then I spotted her! She was on the floor in a corner, lying very still with one side of her face covered with blood. I screamed and ran to her. As I knelt beside my daughter my heart broke. From my own experience long ago I knew what had happened. Her jaw was broken. I gently lifted her head, put it into my lap and began wiping her face with the edge of my nightgown. I thought to myself, history does have a way of repeating itself.

Out of the corner of my eye I could see the girl who had come to the house to get Bart and me. She was across the room pointing out a rough looking character. I supposed that he was the one who had beaten the tar out of my Ginny. Bart lunged and smashed the man against a table. Then he backed off, reached behind his belt on the left side and started to pull his revolver. The muzzle of the gun started up, but before he could get a shot off there was a loud crack and a bullet ripped through Bart's vest and thudded into his body. He spun backwards and landed in a heap on the floor with his head against a wall at a crazy angle. I thought he was dead. The big man had gotten his shot off first and then quickly disappeared into the crowd of brawling drunkards. Bart wasn't dead, but he was loosing a lot of blood.

At the sound of gunfire, the fighting stopped. Men with broken, bloody noses and ripped upper lips staggered around dazed. The place was in shambles. There was an uneasy calm as the owner came rushing from the rear of the building. He was a strong lean man who looked vaguely familiar to me. In one swift movement he gathered Bart over his shoulder and quickly carried him away to the back room. He put Bart down on the day bed and yelled to another man to go for the doctor.

I continued to sit on the floor holding Ginny's head in my lap. She wasn't able to speak to me, but as I looked at her it was plain to see that she had been struck several times. I could almost feel the pain she was experiencing. I had once been in a saloon with a broken jaw from a blow by a drunken cowboy. It was like I was reliving that terrible nightmare! In a few minutes the owner returned. He picked Ginny up with ease and carried her to the back room as I followed close behind.

"Follow me, Lilly. Old Jim will take care of you and your kin, jest like I done when we was kids on the wagon train."

My God, no wonder he looked familiar. It was Jim! After all of these years we had met again, but not under the best of circumstances. I wish it had been different. I looked at him not believing my eyes. It was like seeing a ghost from the past. I thought he had drowned in the flood so many years ago, but here he was alive. From what I could see, at least before the brawl, he was doing fairly well. I regretted Ginny had caused such a fight, nearly destroying his saloon. Right now there wasn't time to talk about the past, but I knew that sooner or later we would.

While we waited for the doctor to come, I sat on the floor between my daughter and husband thinking about Ruby. I was sorry I had not told them about her earlier, and vowed to do that as soon as possible. She was a darn good woman and had been a good friend. She took me in after both Pa and Ma had died. She gave me a place to sleep, food to eat and a job. I remembered the girls who lived there, and how different they were. Also the house was not as bad as people thought. Each girl, in time, either married or found new lives for themselves, and I liked to think, partly due to the fact that I was there. I came to Ruby's by accident, but I stayed by choice and saw the good qualities in her and all of her girls. Over the short time I was there I know I contributed to their decision to leave Ruby's in pursuit of a better way of life.

I have always felt it was better to go forward with one's life from where you find yourself rather than trying to struggle and fight with the past. But I saw then that the past does have a way of coming back to haunt you. I realized I needed to explain more about what my life was like in those early years. I needed to set the record straight about my working at Ruby's. Bart and Ginny might not believe me, but Ruby really did hire me as a cook and I was never one of her girls. I would tell them the whole story in time.

When the doctor arrived, he set to work on Bart first. He was losing too much blood and was very pale. The bullet had lodged in Bart's collarbone and his shoulder was now oozing blood. By the look on his face he was in a lot of pain. After some preparation the doctor extracted the bullet. Bart mercifully went unconscious. The loss of blood was a big concern, but the doctor assured me - Bart would recover in time.

Ginny was another matter. When she realized I was there,

she passed out which was a blessing. The doctor set her jaw by wiring her teeth together with hardly an opening big enough for her to drink water or even eat soft food. Then he tied a length of material around her jaw going up to the top of her head. She would need a lot of care and wouldn't be able to chew for several weeks. Her food would have to be mashed and forced between her teeth. I knew the routine, I had suffered the same thing.

Neither patient could be moved for a few days, so they would have to stay in Jim's back room until the doctor said it was safe to take them home. Bart was on the day-bed and Ginny on a small sofa. This put me in an awkward position. I had just said, less than an hour ago, that I never wanted to see Ginny again, but now that was not the truth. She was my child, and I knew I could not abandon her at this moment. Right now she needed my help.

When Bart and Ginny realized that they were in a small room together neither looked at the other. Anytime I came in they averted their eyes. Their guilt was so evident it almost made me feel sorry them, but their terrible betrayal was still fresh in my mind.

When the time came that they could be moved, we took them home to the French Quarter. I got Bart settled in Tinny's old room and put Ginny in hers. I left our bedroom empty since I could not go in there without reliving that ugly scene. Martha's room would be mine while we remained in New Orleans. I was beginning to hate that house, but knew I'd have to stay there until they both recovered.

Not wishing to upset the rest of the family, I sent word we would not be coming home for Christmas, saying we had decided to spend more time in New Orleans to enjoy the holidays with friends here. We would return to Virginia sometime in the spring. What they did not know wouldn't hurt them. There would be time enough to explain all that had happened here later. Also in a letter I suggested to Martha that she have Tinny and family move into the Kingsley mansion to be with her. Martha had always loved to have her family close around her, and knowing this, I was positive it would be a fine arrangement. Harley had proved himself a good manager of his own farm, so I was sure he would be glad to have the bigger house for his family and would welcome the responsibility of the Kingsley property. It turned out to be a good plan for everyone concerned. I knew Martha would feel safer with her family near. Also I would not have to worry about her, because with Tinny there she would be well cared for.

In New Orleans I hired two house servants so I could properly care for Ginny and Bart. One was a black cook and the other an experienced housemaid. The cook brought with her a little girl she called "Birdie". I never did get a close look at the child, but I realized her skin was almost as white as mine, and that she could have passed for white. She helped in the kitchen and ran errands for the family. She was small for her age and couldn't read or write, but that was not too surprising since most of the blacks could not read or write.

Anyway, after things calmed down and we were settled into a routine, I was determined to redecorate our bedroom, to try to erase the unpleasant memories it reminded me of. I knew I would never be able to sleep in that bed again so I decided to get rid of it. It was a massive bed, and probably had not been moved in years. Underneath it I found an old diary of Ginny's. I had not intended to invade her privacy, but there it was on the floor under our bed. I considered not reading it, but I couldn't help myself and when I did, I was not prepared for what I found. I was shocked as I read and found a reason for my young daughter's belligerent behavior. She must have been about eight or nine when she wrote about a tragic episode in her early life.

Eleventh of May

Dear Diary,

Tinny and I were playing in the barn today in the hayloft when Bart came in to saddle Cobra, his speckled horse. He asked us what we were doing, and we told him we were playing in the hay. My dress was torn and my drawers were showing. I was a mess and mama would not like me if she saw me. I told him Tinny never gets dirty because she doesn't play as hard as I do. He told Tinny to go to the house and he would help me fix my dress. She left us standing in the barn.

Bart looked at me, lifted my curls and wiped my face with his handkerchief. I could smell him and he smelled real good. I reached up to kiss him on the cheek and he kissed me on the mouth. Then he told me to take off my dress and he would try to fix it. I did it because he was my new father. Then he took my petticoat off too, and told me to take off my drawers. I told him I was not to take my drawers off for anybody, because mama wouldn't like it. He told me he was my new daddy and every daddy has the right to examine his daughter, so it was quite all right.

I did not like the way he looked at me. He made me

feel uncomfortable. Then he told me what he was going to do and that I should not tell anyone because it would be our secret. I trusted him cause he is a grown-up. When he finished playing with me, as he called it, he again told me what we had done was to be our secret, and you are not supposed to tell secrets.

Of course, now that I had read that entry in Ginny's diary, I realized what her life had been like at the hands of Bart, how he had betrayed her innocence and used her all of these years. I wondered when he crossed over from play touching to penetration. And yes, I read further and found many other such writings about their long affair. I was dumbfounded and perplexed at what I had read, and I was angry. I sat there crying for a long time with strong feelings that I could kill him, but I had to control myself. This was not the time to talk. What purpose would it serve? Bart was not doing well and was possibly near death. Ginny was slowly recovering from a broken jaw. It was quite clear to me now why she had been a behavior problem as a little girl and young woman. I could understand why she had never wanted to be married or to have children. She had lived a life of deception.

I placed the diary in one of the window seats and would have the seat nailed shut. Again I had reason to hate this room and was even more determined to do something about it. I decided to make it more functional and less feminine. I put a writing table on one wall and covered another with bookcases that I filled with books. On the East side, there were large high windows which could be opened so the sun would stream in most of the morning, and any breeze blowing through gave a fresh feeling to the room. The dressing area where the clothes had once hung became a little sitting room with more shelves. By the time I finished with the changes it looked more like a library than a bedroom.

I never again spoke to Ginny or Bart about that hateful day I found them together, or of my having found Ginny's diary. There developed between us an uneasy peace. Bart was too weak to care and had lost his desire for life. He ate very little and seldom spoke. Ginny, being unable to talk for a number of weeks, spent most of the time alone in her bedroom or reading in the garden. For a change, she enjoyed the quiet peacefulness the garden offered.

To my knowledge Bart and Ginny were never alone in each other's company again. I felt in my heart they were sorry for what they had done. They thought they could make it easier on me by not being in the same room together. I really didn't care anymore. Life became just a routine for me. I was tired and still felt totally betrayed. I'm afraid forgiveness was not in my heart for either of them during that time.

The days were long for me and if it had not been for Jim, my dear old friend, I think I would have lost my mind. He brought news of the outside world to us, and delivered what letters I received from Martha and Tinny. Tinny's letters kept us laughing with the delightful tales of the antics of her four small children. What news there was of plantation business, Harley informed Bart in a separate enclosed letter. Martha was growing weaker and was now unable to write, but she always sent us her love and many times asked us to return home soon.

Jim spent several afternoons a week calling on us, just talking of his adventures after we had been separated. He thought I had drowned after finding the body of my mother and not finding me. He said he buried her on a hill in the high desert where a lone tree grew. When he didn't find my body he figured it had washed downstream, and he finally gave up all hope of ever seeing me again. He too had made his way to Carson City. He made some more inquiries still hopeful of finding me. He said he did hear there was a young woman answering my description working at Ruby's, but he didn't go out to the house. At the time he was low on funds and couldn't afford a woman. Besides the more he thought about it he realized I might not want to see him if I was working in a place like Ruby's. It would have been an embarrassment to me. He decided to let the past be the past, and never thought of trying to contact me after that.

Jim eventually moved on, but not west to California as he had originally planned. His dream had died when he lost his ma and pa, Big Black, my parents and me. After drifting around the country for several years, he ended up in New Orleans. Once there he hooked up with "Old Billy" Hanks at the Red Garter Saloon. When Billy died in a shooting incident, Jim took over the saloon. Now he was the owner. Yes it was a rowdy place, but it was a living. He had never married so the life suited him well.

Bart and Ginny listened to all of his stories - Jim spoke in a quaint mixture of English and Cajun. They asked him questions about life on the trail, what it was like crossing the country in a covered wagon, what kind of people my parents had been and all the details of the flood that destroyed the wagon train and took so many lives. They wanted to know everything about my past. They'd ask Jim a question and then watch for my reactions to his stories.

I was grateful to Jim for finding Ma's poor little body and burying her on that hill. I was shocked to think he had believed I was one of Ruby's girls. Didn't he know me better than that? Ma had raised me to be a good girl, and believe me I knew the difference.

One afternoon when we were sitting alone on the patio

enjoying the splashing of the water fountain, he began to tell me how he had first met Ginny. In the beginning he had no idea she was my daughter, but there was something about her that was strangely familiar.

He said he had chosen to get on with his life and totally forget where he had come from. He didn't want to remember all the people who had been part of his earlier life because it hurt too much. He was able to do this until about a year ago when Ginny started coming into his place. He had no idea who she was, but he could tell she was from a wealthy family by the way she was dressed. She had this weakness for strong liquor, which she tried to quench in his saloon. At first Ginny was more of a lady, but the more she drank, the more foul-mouthed and loose-tongued she became.

Here is the story he related to me:

One afternoon Ginny came into the saloon mad as a hornet and drank the afternoon away, refusing to go home. In a sour mood she refused to pay for her drinks, like she was some kind of queen bee or something. Since she was a good customer and usually paid her bill, the barkeep kept filling her glass, hoping she would leave or pass out. If she passed out he could always put her in the back room until she sobered up. Well, she didn't pass out and she refused to leave. As she continued drinking like a sailor, she began to insult the other customers. That's when the barkeep called Jim up front. Ginny was a sight to behold. Her hair was falling down into her face, although it had been piled on top of her head when she arrived. She had been wearing a smart little hat, which he noticed had fallen to the floor and was smashed. Her dress was dirty and stained from spilling liquor on herself and falling down on the floor repeatedly. Her eyes were red-rimmed, her words slurred, in fact, she was just plain drunk. That was when he began talking to her in a fatherly way. The barkeep said she had been there most of the day. It occurred to Jim that she probably was in need of food, and a strong pot of coffee wouldn't do her any harm either.

Jim talked her into going with him into his back room where he put on the strongest New Orleans coffee he could brew. Then he had the barkeep get him a meal. Ginny drank and ate with relish, but still asked for another shot of whiskey. He refused of course! Around midnight when she was almost sober he asked her some more questions. He wanted to take her home, but she refused to tell him where she lived. Finally, he coaxed her into lying fully dressed on the small daybed he kept in his office. Once down, she promptly fell asleep. He covered her and left the room closing the door behind him.

Returning early the next morning he found her still asleep on the daybed. When she awakened and had recovered some of her composure, she asked for some warm water to wash her hands and face. Once she had a bit of pastry and strong coffee inside her, they had a long talk. During the conversation she mentioned that her mother's name was Lilly. Hearing this he became more interested and said he had once known a girl named Lilly, but that her mother was probably not the same Lilly he had known, because the last time he heard of her she was working in a whorehouse in Carson City, Nevada - a place called Ruby's Social Club.

I guess Ginny began thinking about what he was saying, because as he talked she recognized some of the stories she had heard from me about my Ma and Pa and the wagon train. As she listened Ginny became convinced they were speaking of the same person, her mother and Jim's friend. She was cold sober by then, and upset with what she had heard. She proceeded to tell Jim things about me. How I had always tried to make a lady out of her and how her twin sister, Tinny, was perfect and the favorite of the family. Then she added how disappointed I would be if I knew her precious daughter was nothing but a drunk and far from suitable for a fine finishing school for young ladies. She was anything but a lady, and then she really spilled her guts.

She told Jim she was no good, because she was sleeping with her mother's husband, her stepfather. Then she cried heartbreaking tears and told him she was in love. Bart had always been her secret lover from the time her breasts started to bud. She insisted the two of them were meant to be together and said she had claimed Bart for her own as a child and had resented me for being his wife.

Jim continued that by the time he found out that I was indeed Ginny's mother he had already told her about me and Ruby's. That was all Ginny needed to excuse her own behavior. After that morning, she continued to frequent the saloon, and her drinking got worse. She came in more often and would take up with any man who'd buy her a drink. All the while she blamed me for what she was doing. Jim tried to reason with her by explaining how alone in the world I had been and how desperate I must have felt.

I don't have any idea where Bart was during these hours she was at the saloon. I knew he was away during the day, but what about in the evenings when they met and spent time together? On the evenings she didn't come home, where was he? I had my own suspicions, but didn't want to believe that he had another mistress hidden away somewhere.

Hearing Jim's story I began to think I had made a major mistake by not telling Bart and my daughters the truth about living in Ruby's house and working there as a cook. If I had told them what I actually did there, maybe we would not have come to this tragic time in our lives.

About the time Jim finished, both Ginny and Bart came out to sit with us on the patio. They had overheard what Jim was telling me. Bart simply hung his head and made no comments. I was so angry I could have slapped him senseless, but then when I realized what an old wasted man he had become I felt sorry for him. There was no more love in my heart. In fact, as I looked at him I felt sick, but at least I understood a lot more about our relationship. Ginny was also a pitiful sight. She kept trying to tell me what she called the truth about their love for each other. I didn't want to listen to her, but I let her have her say - none of which made any sense to me. I was still too angry and hurt to understand or forgive.

Bart tried to defend himself by saying he did not know she was going to the saloon every day. He knew she liked her liquor, but had no idea how often and how much she was drinking. As I thought back to when she was a child, we had accused her of getting into the liquor cabinet, but she would never admit it. She even tried to make us feel guilty for accusing her of stealing any liquor. She always told us one of the servants had taken it, and that we should find the guilty person instead of blaming her. She was such a convincing liar we believed her. Ginny had always had a silver tongue in her head, but now she sat silent, just looking at me with sad eyes.

After that day I had no desire to speak to either one of them again. I was content to be in a quiet house. If it had not been for Jim, I would have been lost. He gave me encouragement and tried to make up for, as he said, "spilling the beans" to Ginny about me.

In the next a few weeks I did explain to Bart and Ginny the situation that had led me to Ruby's and what I had done there. Even if they did not believe me it was good to let them know the truth about those years. I found it pleasing to once again recall all the good times I had enjoyed in Ruby's house so many years ago. Jim was delighted to hear about Big Black. He was glad to know that special dog had survived the flood. We laughed a lot at my tales of Big Black, and how the dog had chosen Ruby over me. I also told them about all the girls who worked at Ruby's. It was a good feeling to be open about the past, and in due time the full story about Derrick came tumbling out. I told it all! Ginny had a real interest in hearing about her natural father even though he was a no good gambler. She wanted to know all about her and Tinny's birth in the barn and the wonderful family who took care of us. She vowed to look them up someday. What took me by surprise was that she was interested in the fact that her father might still be alive and possibly living in New Orleans, but she never mentioned wanting to contact him. I suspected he could be found if we hired a detective, but for me that was out of the question.

I told them I had often thought of trying to find Ruby, but felt it would cause an unpleasant situation for the family. Jim told me a woman answering her description had frequented his place, and not long ago he heard she had married a banker and moved to Colorado. Hearing this I knew I had waited too long, and probably would never see her again. I couldn't help wondering about Ruby's second marriage, and what had happened to her first husband.

We were still in the New Orleans house late in the spring, when we received word that Martha had passed away in her sleep. Although we wanted to go, we did not return to Virginia for the funeral. I explained in a telegram to Harley and Tinny that Bart was too ill to travel. I was thankful that Tinny, Harley and the grandchildren had been with her all these months, but I was sick at heart for not seeing her before she died. I was thankful she did not have to know the truth about Ginny and Bart. She meant so much to me. She had changed my life and I was grateful to her. It was because of her that I had found a home and family to belong to.

I was confident Harley and Tinny had taken good care of

Martha and the plantation. Harley was an excellent overseer. When I pictured the old house I knew it rang with the laughter of children all day long. Looking back, I remember our arrival at Kingsley mansion. How wonderful those early years had been for us. I knew it was the pleasant memories that had kept me going while I was caring for Bart and Ginny. I tried to remember all the good things that had happened in my life.

Bart never regained his strength. He slowly weakened and I sat at his bedside night and day listening to his labored breathing. By the time the end came and Bart died, I had resolved my anger toward him and Ginny.

At first Ginny grieved for Bart and went into mourning, but before long her grief turned to anger. She hated Bart for taking her childhood innocence away and deceiving me, though later she told me it was partly her fault because she had wanted him as much as he had wanted her. She felt they were both to blame.

After Bart died, Ginny was extremely restless and wanted to go home to the plantation. She asked me if we could return, and promised she would not aggravate her sister or me again. I had to admit that she seemed to be a changed person, but I couldn't help wondering if the old Ginny would reappear. My question was, "Can a leopard change its spots?"

Twenty-two

Completion

At this time in my life New Orleans was certainly not the place I wanted to be. I knew I had to leave and take Ginny with me. We had to somehow forget the past and begin again. Just living these last few months had taken more strength out of me than I thought. What was I to do without Bart? How would I manage to live in a world without him? Oh yes, part of me hated him and yet memories of the good times flooded my mind. I wondered had we met, as he had suggested, when I was a cook at Ruby's would he have seen me? I doubt it. I was too plain, too shy, and too much of a girl to suit his needs. I was really not his kind of woman then and the truth is I never was. Martha had observed he had married me out of convenience and Ginny claimed he had loved her more than me. All these thoughts filled my mind until I could not think of anything else. I couldn't even eat. I knew I was slowly driving myself crazy. Ginny was grieving, suffering from guilt and at the same time pining away for Bart.

Knowing I had nothing left to stay for, I made plans to leave. Someday I might have to return, but if I did I vowed not to come back to the house in the French Quarter. It occurred to me that all the business holdings would have to be cared for by someone. For the time being I simply turned our affairs over to a partner of Bart's. In the future when there was business to be handled in New Orleans I would send Harley. He was learning more about the Kingsley holdings and certainly had proven himself trustworthy. I was convinced he would be a perfect choice.

Selling the house was less complicated than I had assumed because there were always people interested in a quaint place in the quarter. I let a number of people know I was ready to sell and that was all it took. Within a few weeks the house was sold along with most of the household possessions. Our trunks of clothes were all that remained and they were few. At that point I had forgotten about Ginny's diary and had never read further than on the day I found it. I had tossed it into a window seat and when the room was being changed from a bedroom to a study it was nailed shut. The diary as well as this chapter in my life had truly ended, it was over.

I had enjoyed buying the house with Tinny, and now I remembered the enthusiasm and energy with which she toured the city. Her sweetness as we spent those months together would remain with me forever. Yes, I had to admit there were good memories as well as the bad ones associated with the house. When I thought about returning to the plantation it was Tinny's face that I imagined seeing, and that gave me hope for the future.

When I thought about it I found it strange that I had no real friends in New Orleans. I had not taken the time to form any friendships. I had always been a visitor and had been shut out by the locals. I realized I had been so absorbed with my own family that I had neglected the social part of my life in this city. The servants and maids we employed had been the only people I was around, except when we dined out or went to the opera house. The society women of New Orleans had not embraced me or my family as I had once hoped they would.

Bart always enjoyed showing me off. As I clung to his arm he escorted me with pride to restaurants and the theater. He was a perfect gentleman at all times. Derrick had been so very different from Bart. He took me to the fancy homes and gambling saloons when it suited him, but he left me on my own a lot of the time. I was so pre-occupied with shopping and touring the city I had not taken the time to get to know anyone well. Now I was in need of friends and found myself lacking. The time had come to go home.

When the time came for Ginny and me to leave the French Quarter it would be with mixed feelings. But the good memories could never replace the painful ones. Stopping to gather my thoughts I knew how I really felt. I was beside myself with grief. I could have cried my eyes out but what good would that do? I was already tired to the bone and deeply chilled, as though my heart had frozen over never to thaw out again. I knew no one else but me could change the way I felt.

Ginny was more like a stranger. She avoided me whenever possible and appeared sullen and quiet. Certainly she was not like the old Ginny. Never in my whole life had I felt so lonely. I wanted someone to talk to, to confide in as I had done with Ruby and Martha. Though Jim was still around, it was not the same as having a true female friend. I wanted to talk about my life, my loves, my disappointments and even my heartaches.

Knowing Martha would not be at the plantation when we arrived bothered me. I knew I would miss her and felt guilty for having not been there when she passed away. I had wanted to be near her at that time, and to be holding her hand when she took her last breath, but that was not to be. I was cheated of that experience and I resented it. This was a feeling I would never be able to get over or forget. I kept wishing that things had been different, but the past can't be changed no matter how hard we wish it. That part of my life was gone forever.

The more I thought about all this the clearer it became that I wanted to leave New Orleans and never return.I had asked Jim to drive us to the station because I wanted to spend some time with an old friend. I had imagined him waving good-bye to us as we settled into our seats, but this did not happen and it turned out a blessing. Jim insisted on not only driving us to the train station, but also traveling with us all the way to Virginia! He was sure Ginny was incapable of caring for herself, much less me. I was too exhausted to argue with him, and I leaned heavily on Jim and Ginny as we boarded the train. I had not realized how very tired I was from lack of sleep, or how weak I had become from having eaten little since Bart's death. I wondered if I was really sick or if living had just become too much of a burden. I had noticed in the mirror that I was quite pale around the mouth and I had been experiencing an occasional sharp pain in my chest for some time, but I had passed it off as nothing to be concerned about. Now I decided that whatever the cause, I was not going to let it worry me or burden others with my ailments.

On the morning we left I had our black kitchen cook come with one of the other servants. There were jobs that I wanted no part of, like window washing, carpet beating and endless dusting. I really didn't care how it was done, just as long as it was done. The cook brought her granddaughter with her to help with work in the kitchen and to close up the house until the new owners arrived. That meant cleaning and draping every piece of furniture. I remember seeing the child and marveled how she had grown since the last time I had seen her. She seemed to be an intelligent and pretty little thing. Saying goodbye to the cook, her granddaughter and the other servant, I closed the front door behind me, and as I did my mind relived the time I had thrown Ginny out. She had changed so much since that night, from a smart-mouth, tart speaking young girl to a silent speechless woman. This too broke my heart.

As we rode away from the house Ginny sat with her head downcast concealed in a dark green hooded cape. She didn't even want to take a last glimpse. She wouldn't speak to me but sat like a shadow beside me. Jim was hunched over driving the buggy as if he had all the time in the world. This irritated me and I wanted to crack the whip over the horses. I was sure the sooner we left this place the better.

On the way to the station I remembered the excitement and wonder I had felt the first time I saw New Orleans. At this time of day the city looked desolate. The wind swirled around in the streets making small dust devils as it moved past.There were few people to be seen. It was as though the city had turned its back on us and cared little whether we stayed or left. We would never be missed. The street on which we drove reminded me of a Bible passage Ma had shared with me when I was a child. The story was about Jesus telling his disciples that if a city doesn't treat you well, you should shake the dust of that city off your feet and never return.

At the station Jim saw to the delivery of the buggy back to its owner, and that our trunks were loaded in the baggage car. When he joined us on the train he was jolly and smiling. I suppose he was trying to cheer me up. No sooner had the train pulled out than Jim was on his feet making arrangements for me to have a pillow and light blanket. Because I was so weak he asked Ginny to go to the dining car and get me some tea and crackers. Ginny rose obediently and turned to leave. She had removed her dark cape showing a lovely high collared blouse with long sleeves. It was a shade of blue trimmed with white piping. Her bright blue eyes closely resembled the color of the blouse. The long skirt was a dark navy blue. Looking at Ginny as she left my side and walked away down the aisle, she looked like the school teacher I had wanted her to be. Even her dark curly hair was pulled back and piled on top of her head.

Jim was watching her too, and I am sure he was about to make a comment but thought better of it. He had taken a liking to Ginny no matter what her life had been like in the past. By this time he had heard it all. I think he thought he was too old for her, but he could not hide the longing I saw in his eyes. He was sweet on Ginny and it was obvious, but she never seemed to notice him. He was crude in some ways but as gentle as a lamb when it came to me or my kin. As I watched him I hoped someday Ginny might become aware of his desire for her. She could do much worse. Jim was a good man.

It was a hard trip for me. I slept a good deal of the time and was only awake when Ginny or Jim insisted I drink a cup of tea or eat something. I had seen a doctor once during the time I was caring for Ginny and Bart. He had told me my heart had an irregular beat, but I refused to be concerned and dismissed it. I had always been healthy and strong. No, I was just tired and going home would be the cure I needed.

When we arrived in Virginia we were met at the station by one of the servants, with an apology from Harley and Tinny. Jim helped unload our trunks then joined us in the carriage. We started up the road leading to the mansion. Large old trees graced both sides of the road and arched together over the top. It gave me a feeling of entering paradise. Spring flowers were in full bloom and the grass was a lush green. The grass had been sickled and smelled sweet. It was good to be home where I belonged. I thought that here on the plantation I would be able to gain my strength back.

When we stopped near the stairs leading to the front porch we were met by the family and a few of the servants. Waiting on the stairs stood Tinny and Harley. Harley looked as robust and handsome as the first day I had seen him. He was full of apologies for not meeting us at the station. It was something to do with the horses. I'm not sure what because I was not interested and too tired to care. Tinny stood smiling from ear to ear, overjoyed that we had arrived.

Hanging behind their mother and father were those darling twin boys. The toe-headed youngsters stood behind Tinny with their faces buried in her flowing skirt. They peeked out at us and then dove back behind their mother again. I could see they were quite a pair, just barely over two years of age, and I was sure they would be a handful.

Melinda Ann stood with big blue eyes that sparkled with energy and an eagerness to please. Her long black hair was pulled back and tied with a bright red ribbon. Looking closely at her I at once saw the resemblance she had to her mother and Aunt Ginny. Ginny must have seen the way they favored too. I could see she was a bit astonished but also pleased. Looking at Melinda Ann I wondered if she would be willful like Ginny or gentle like her mother had been. I prayed I would live long enough to see her grown. Melinda Ann didn't make a move toward us but reached over and grabbed her twin brother's small hands and stood watching.

Ginny got out of the buggy with Jim's help and then they turned and helped me down. I stood staring up at the big house feeling a peace I had not known in years. Then I finally became aware of Charles, a handsome lad of almost seven. He reminded me of Derrick in looks, the way he stood and held his head. I could see he had a pleasant manner. He stood alone looking capable and independent watching our arrival. Even at this young age he had an air about him that he could take on the world. When his eyes caught mine he came running with arms out-stretched. It was as if I was his and his alone. He hugged me so hard I thought I would surely collapse.

At that moment I gave a big sigh of relief and my body relaxed, but before I went to my knees Jim and Harley stood on either side and lead me up the stairs into the massive foyer. Seeing the curving staircase I almost broke down. I knew my strength had gone and that I could not climb those stairs, but with one swift movement Jim had picked me up and was proceeding up the stairs. Tinny, Ginny and Melinda Ann hurried ahead and pointed the way to my bedroom which had been totally changed. The room was beautifully transformed from the one I had known. The flowered wallpaper, colorful drapes and elegant French furniture was not as I had remembered, and that was pleasing to me. I remained in the room for days and meals were brought to me, but I looked forward to once again being able to walk down that curving staircase unaided.

In a few months I did regain some of my strength and began to sit up in bed or in a chair in the bedroom. I never walked down the stairs again. Jim or one of the men servants carried me wherever I wanted to go. My favorite places were the front porch or on the green lawn under one of the many large old trees.

My grandchildren were all a delight to me. They kept me entertained and my mind from dwelling too much on the past. Charles was full of questions. We would sit on a pallet of blankets with pillows. He mostly stood however, and paced about endlessly as he listened to my stories. Especially when he and Melinda Ann were with me I told about their great-grandparents and our trip west. Also about how I was a cook in Ruby's house when I was a young girl. I never mentioned the kind of house it was because I was sure they would hear about that later. I explained how I had met their Grandfather Derrick in a saloon in Colorado, how he had promised me everything a woman could want, but then had walked away and left me with their mother and Aunt Ginny to raise. And then I added the story about my first meeting with their step-father Bart on the jailhouse roof. He had been like a prince charming to me. They loved that story the best and had me repeat it many times.

I included all the stories I had learned from Martha about how the Kingsleys had made a place for themselves here in Virginia. I related all I knew about their ancestors whose portraits hung on the staircase wall. These were men and women who had helped shape the state of Virginia and some were well known. My favorite female ancestor of the lot was Callie Mae Franklin Kingsley. She was known through out Virginia as an excellent horse woman, and was as tough as any man when it came to breaking and riding horses. She was as genteel as any southern woman of her day, and rode sidesaddle only when convention demanded.

Out of all the stories I told them, their favorites were about my experiences when I was traveling from the East to Utah and then on to Nevada. They loved hearing about the covered wagon, Jim and his dog Big Black, and my adventures on the trail. Like all children I am sure they fancied themselves doing the same thing. They liked hearing about the Indians we saw along the trail and the stories about the war that had raged between the states. Jim often joined me in the story telling. When I gave out he would jump right in and continue the tale. He was quite an actor and as he told the story he would stand up and play out the various characters.

Charles was the most interested in his great-grandfather

Benton. He liked to whittle just like my Pa and had told me that some day he would try his hand at furniture making too. He boasted that he had already built a birdhouse and whittled a reed flute. He was very confident in his own abilities. Like my Pa, Charles had the dreams of youth and sometimes he would tell me stories and let his imagination run wild.

I knew by listening to him he had the same adventuresome spirit as Pa, and I was sure he would someday take off, leaving the plantation and his family. That would be a time of heartbreak for my daughter Tinny. Several uneventful months passed until one morning when we awakened to find a young girl sitting on the veranda. She carried a small homemade cloth bag and wore a modest cotton dress, white stockings, high-top button shoes, and a straw hat. She had been dropped off early in the morning before anyone was out of bed. One of the servants found her and when he saw a note pinned to her dress he brought her upstairs to my bedroom. He knocked on my door and when I answered he thrust the child into the doorway. She removed her hat and when I got a real good look I recognized her immediately. It was Birdie, the New Orleans cook's granddaughter. The startling thing was her resemblance to Bart. I hoped I was wrong but it was unmistakable. She just had to be Bart's daughter!

I think I had known it all along from the first time I laid eyes on her in New Orleans, but I just did not want to deal with the thought of that possibility. It would have been much too upsetting. It was not obvious that she was of mixed blood. She was beautiful to look upon, but at this moment she was shaking and I could tell very shy. I saw the note and wanted to read it but didn't want to frighten her. She stood staring at me wide-eyed with big tears rolling down her cheeks and a lock of black hair falling over her forehead. I motioned for her to come to me, and when she reached the edge of the bed I opened my arms to her. She seemed afraid at first but then dropped her bag and fell into my open arms. When she had calmed down and snuggled under one of my arms I carefully unpinned the note and read it to myself.

It read, *"Dear Mrs. Kingsley – For sometime now I has been tryin' to tell you this here child is your granddaughter, but when I seen all the troubles you was havin' with your late husband and Miss Ginny I could not bring myself to tell you. My daughter died last week of the fever. God rest her soul. She was Birdie's ma. You didn't know it, but Mr. Bart visited my daughter and even gave her a little house to live in. Thems loved each other and they had this here child, but I can't take care of her no more. I'm too old and have no money. I was goin' to tell you about her, but decided not to until my daughter died. Now I just have to tell you and hope you will take good care of Birdie. You are a good woman and always been fair with me, so now I is goin' to be fair with you. Birdie is a good little girl and wants you to learn her how to read and write. She can work hard too. Please take good care of her and forgive her ma and Mr. Bart for what they has done to you. I done the same thing when I was young. My daughter was half black and half white. This baby girl here is white and should be raised with her kin. She can pass off as your child and she looks just like Mr. Bart. Thank you for doin' this for me and my departed daughter. I is grateful to you forever. Your cook and servant. Lottie*

I sat in the bed stunned with one arm wrapped around Birdie and holding the note in my hand. It was not her fault she had been born, but what was I to do with her? Her tears fell on my cheek and her sobs sounded in my ears. I felt sorry for her and at that moment I loved her. It didn't matter who her father was, she was now in my care and I would take care of her as long as I lived.

As the rest of the family became aware of what was taking place in my bedroom, they gathered around watching. I held Birdie in one arm and handed the note to Tinny. She read it to herself and then passed it on to Harley and Ginny. Harley drew in a sharp breath and whistled. Ginny ran from the room crying. Melinda Ann looked at me and then at her mother and asked, "What is her name and is she going to live here with us?" I told her, Birdie was the child's name and that yes, she would be living with us, then I added, "She is your cousin and both of her parents are dead." At that Melinda Ann put her arm around Birdie and said, "Birdie you are about my age and if you are going to be part of this family you might as well live in my room with me. I have lots of space and many toys to share with you. You'll like it here." So arm in arm out of the bedroom door they went, and now we have another child to care for.

Birdie did learn how to read and write with help from everyone, especially Melinda Ann. As soon as Melinda Ann was completely sure that Birdie was to be living with us she took full charge, just as she had done with her twin brothers. It became easier on Tinny because both of the two girls had a little brother to take care of. The four of them were scarcely ever seen apart. It turned out to be a great help to Tinny because she had no governess and very few household servants.

The fact that Birdie was Bart's daughter was the hardest on Ginny. She had always believed that she alone was his true love. It had never occurred to her that Bart had had other women. She had loved only him and really none other. Ginny was shocked when she read the note and was devastated to find out that Bart had had a mistress all along, and especially that he had fathered a child by her. It was some time before she recovered, but recover she did. She even grew to like Birdie. I

think she somehow wanted to believe that Birdie was her child.
She and Birdie often went horse back riding. If asked by questioning neighbors, she as well as the rest of us replied that Birdie
was a cousin. She had been put in our care because her parents
were both dead, and at least that part was true. Again the
Kingsleys had taken a bold step. We had faced a crisis and the
family was the better for it. Birdie was kin and that was that.

I had had suspicions of Bart's indiscretions, but then I was
always so blind when it came to him. I guess I really didn't
want to know the truth and had to admit that I didn't do very
well in judging men. I had been too young to care about the
men who had come to Ruby's except for Joel, and he was just a
young girl's dream that could never have lasted. Derrick had
promised me everything I wanted; marriage, babies and a place
to call home, but he turned out to be a terrible disappointment. Bart had been my rescuer, my knight in shining armor,
and the love of my life. It had never entered my mind that he
would seduce my own daughter and then father a child by
someone else that I would have to raise, but now I was doing
just that!

Time at the mansion in Virginia passed and when my illness became worse, I was forced to stay in bed most of the
time. Ginny was a great help. It was she who sat with me when
I was feeling the worst. She applied cold cloths to my forehead
when my head was aching. She fluffed my pillows and changed
the bedding when needed. It was her face that I saw upon
waking and again before falling back to sleep. She hovered over
me and not once did I smell any liquor on her breath. If she
ever did drink again I wasn't aware of it. It was as though the
tragedies in her life had left her stone cold sober. She moved
silently around my room, or sat in a small rocking chair reading. I know she spent some time in the family library, and
rarely went to town. When she was not sitting with me she

took walks in the garden or down by the river. It seemed she was deep in thought most of the time, perhaps doing some soul-searching. She certainly had suffered enough pain and guilt in her young life. I felt sorry for Ginny but I knew she was a survivor.

• • •

In a week it will be Thanksgiving in the year of our Lord 1910. I am looking forward to the celebration and being surrounded by all the family. It seems strange to me because I am not getting any better.My doctor has ordered complete bed rest, no more sitting on my pallet or in my chair in the bedroom. This is such a disappointment since I have looked forward to being at the dining room table for a delicious turkey meal with all the trimmings. It was just a dream anyway since I have lost my appetite and the chest pains have increased. I have a very strong feeling that I may not live to see Thanksgiving.

I awoke early this morning to a beautiful sun rise. It was such a glorious day I ignored the doctor's orders and asked to be taken out to the yard. As always Jim carried me down the stairs and put me in the shade beneath this old weeping willow tree. I feel at peace under its swaying branches, and when the family comes out I will say my farewells to each of them. My time is near and I just don't want to die in that bed upstairs. I want to smell the flowers and feel the ground beneath me. I want to feel the breeze bending my large straw hat and pushing the folds of my yellow dress against my body. The dress is soft and without a corset I am quite comfortable. I insisted that I be properly dressed for this day and not remain in my night clothes. I want my family to remember me dressed in the color of sunshine and sunflowers.

As Jim carried me down the stairs he commented on the beautiful day and how I had always been a bright light in his life, how he had loved me as a young girl and vowed to care for my kin as he had always done. He was indeed, a gentle giant. When he put me down under the trees he knelt beside me, took off his hat, placed it over his heart and said, "Good-bye Lilly." Then he put the hat aside and with tears in his eyes he grabbed both of my hands and held them to each side of his face.He kissed each of my palms, closed my fingers and put my hands gently into my lap. He rose to his towering height, backed away, and squatted down several feet from the pallet. I knew my faithful friend would remain with me until I took my last breath.

Birdie had followed when Jim carried me out to sit on the lawn. It was her turn to sit and read to me. She too has been a comfort these last few months. She has often sat and read aloud from one of her favorite books. She has asked me many questions about her past. She wanted to know why her grandmother, the woman who brought her here to live, was a black woman and she herself was white. I tried to answer her questions as best I could. I explained that her father had been Bart Kingsley, my husband, and it was only natural that when her mother died her grandmother would bring her here to me. I assured her that we would love her no matter who her parents were. I just hope Birdie has enough of Bart in her to find a place in the Kingsley family when she is older. As long as she lives here in the mansion with the family I know she will be all right, but I can't help but worry about her future. She is sitting quietly on one corner of my pallet taking in everything that is happening, silent as she watches.

I can see the servants coming. Some are old and bent but

others are young. The older ones have been with the Kingsleys longer than I can remember. My grandchildren are following in a sorrowful little procession. It seems Tinny has told them how weak I have become and that I want to speak to each of them before I die. I am fond of all these people. The children are very dear to me but it has been Charles that I have favored since I first laid eyes on him. I have great hopes he will become an accomplished gentleman.

Melinda Ann is a very responsible young girl and I know she will be a beauty. She is high-spirited like her Aunt Ginny, but the one thing I know for sure about her is the strong love she has for all her brothers and Birdie. The twins are still too young to tell much about. They are healthy and with their big sister and Birdie watching over them, they will be fine.

How does one say a final good-bye to beloved little children? I told them I was going to Heaven to be with God and asked them to remember me. Melinda Ann, Charles and Birdie knew what I was talking about and began to cry. Charles took my hand and said, "Grandma, when you see God tell him hello for me. I'm gonna' miss you Grandma." Then he leaned over, kissed me on the forehead, bowed and walked off. It was so touching I wanted to cry but knew I had to be strong.

Melinda Ann knelt beside me and looking into my eyes kissed me straight on the mouth. Turning, she grabbed her twin brothers, gave them each a hug and pushed them into my lap. They looked bewildered but snuggled close and would have stayed there longer had she not gently lifted them off. She set them on their feet and when they ran she was off chasing after them. I hope the older children will remember the stories I have shared and pass them on for the generations to come.

Harley is the next one to come. Looking at that handsome rugged face of his I see tears flowing down his cheeks and he is speechless so I must comfort him. I pat his hand and tell him he is a good man and that I know he will take good care of his family. And from this moment on, he and Tinny are in charge of the Kingsley plantation and all the rest of the holdings in the East and in Europe. I feel an awareness that I am dying and realize I can welcome the event. I have had a good life, full of adventure with many unexpected turns. My first dream was to travel west and find happiness in California. I have discovered, however, that happiness is not tied to any particular place, but it is being close to the people I love and with those who love me, wherever they are.

As I look at my lovely twin daughters I wish them long, fruitful lives with peace between them forever. For them all I ever wanted was a good man to love them and a happy home. Ginny stands looking down at me with those big blue determined eyes as if she wants to pick me up, shake me and make me well again. Tinny is kneeling down beside me. She takes my hand and cries. I pat her hand with mine and bring it to my lips kissing it lovingly. Then I motion for Ginny to join us on the pallet and fluffy pillows. She eases down beside me, puts her arms around my neck and speaks to me.

"Mama, are you going to die before morning?" I reach over and take her hand, still holding on to Tinny with the other. The three of us sit quietly, with a pleasant southern breeze whispering through the trees and blowing through their lovely hair. I become aware that Birdie is also crying softly into her book that she still holds in her hands. I feel that some how she will miss me more than anyone else.

As we hold hands many thoughts pass through my mind and I know my time is running out. I look into each of my daughter's tear-streaked faces and say my last words, Ginny and Tinny, "I love you both very much and as I hold you one last time, I remember when you were just children and we three sat on the jailhouse roof. Ginny, you asked me the same question then. Do you remember? Well, I was determined then that we would die, but I know now for me this is good-bye. It is morning already."

The End